T0365694

The Outlier

The Gutter

The Outlier

Cory Anthony Madonna

THE OUTLIER

Copyright © 2018 Cory Anthony Madonna.

*All rights reserved. No part of this book may be used or reproduced by
any means, graphic, electronic, or mechanical, including photocopying,
recording, taping or by any information storage retrieval system
without the written permission of the author except in the case of
brief quotations embodied in critical articles and reviews.*

*This is a work of fiction. All of the characters, names, incidents,
organizations, and dialogue in this novel are either the products
of the author's imagination or are used fictitiously.*

iUniverse books may be ordered through booksellers or by contacting:

iUniverse
1663 Liberty Drive
Bloomington, IN 47403
www.iuniverse.com
1-800-Authors (1-800-288-4677)

*Because of the dynamic nature of the Internet, any web addresses or
links contained in this book may have changed since publication and
may no longer be valid. The views expressed in this work are solely those
of the author and do not necessarily reflect the views of the publisher,
and the publisher hereby disclaims any responsibility for them.*

*Any people depicted in stock imagery provided by Getty Images are
models, and such images are being used for illustrative purposes only.
Certain stock imagery © Getty Images.*

ISBN: 978-1-5320-5711-3 (sc)
ISBN: 978-1-5320-5712-0 (e)

Library of Congress Control Number: 2018910956

Print information available on the last page.

iUniverse rev. date: 10/18/2018

Prologue

It was night but not so dark. A layer of clouds seemingly ready to burst with rain coated the sky, but nothing fell. The lack of rain produced a strange, sublime effect of a sky lit with lightning but only thunder present. The clouds covered the stars but not the moon, which was barely visible but still managed to shine a faint light on the man's body sprawled against a tree covered in blood. Lance Richardson lay with a bullet in his shoulder and bone piercing out of his knee. His eyesight was beginning to blur, but in his pain he was still able to make out his attacker.

The man standing over Lance was a large man in the black outfit one imagines would be worn in a special forces op, with long sleeves, a bulletproof vest, and long pants tucked into combat boots. The man seemed white or perhaps Latino, about six feet tall and slightly muscular. It was difficult to tell in the dark. The man's only distinguishing feature was a set of piercing brown eyes, which were engulfed in rage. It was a man that Lance could've fought any other day. But now, lying in his own blood, unable to get up, he might as well have been a deer downed before the final shot to its heart. The man had his gun pointed at Lance. He raised the barrel toward Lance's head as he inched closer. Lance was losing blood fast, and his vision was starting to fade in and out between black and a blurry image of the attacker. With nothing left in this world, Lance, as a last act of defiance, tried to hold his senses as long as possible to maybe get a clue about the attacker before he died. He hoped to at least not die in a state of ignorance, but he only heard his attacker utter in rage one final insult.

"You are nothing!"

Complete darkness ensued.

Lance woke up in a cold sweat, gasping for air as if he had been drowning. He quickly ran his fingers across his body as, disoriented, he looked around his apartment, outside of Alexandria, Virginia. It was not a new experience. After the dread subsided, a new emotion took hold of him, the false hope that always awaits one after a dream, the hope that since what had transpired was not real, one could be more careful with one's decisions, more aware of one's day as it was about to happen. Lance quickly placed his hand over the other side of the bed, feeling the emptiness, again feeling the reality of the horrors experienced one year ago. He finally returned to the empty sadness he lived in now, but he had no more energy for crying.

He got up from the bed and walked toward the dresser where he kept a picture of his wife and daughter. Lance's face grew solemn. Glancing between his ringed hand and the picture, he uttered in a quiet whisper, holding back tears, "Sorry I failed you."

Driving outside the city of Alexandria, CIA agent Danny Smith was heading to an undisclosed location. On the surface, Danny looked like a man who had his emotions together, with his cleanly shaven face and suit tailored to perfection. But Danny was consumed by stress. His clean composition was simply an attempt to give him some control over his life in what the world had become. Danny was headed into the city with one goal: to recruit Lance Richardson for this job.

As Danny continued his drive to the city, he got a call. Dan gasped, knowing what information he normally got on such calls. However, he quickly got over his immediate reaction and picked up the phone.

The voice on the other side of the phone said, "Dan, it's Jacob. Why are you heading to Alexandria? You've been ordered to take leave."

"The Lemurians have been killing people every day, and you expect me to just take the day off?" yelled Dan.

"Listen, Dan, the past year has not been easy on any of us, but that is why I ordered you to take leave. You are no use tired and stressed. I know it's hard, but

1

I sent you home because you hadn't slept in three days. You were more of a hindrance than a help," Jacob said sympathetically and sternly.

"So my crime was doing whatever it takes to stop these attacks."

"I know it's not easy, but you know that it takes more than effort to win a war. It takes strategy and time."

"How did you even know where I was, Jacob?" Dan snapped.

"You know that since the first attacks, we've had to take a more liberal interpretation of civil liberties to keep the country safe. Do you think I don't have ways of tracking my agents?" Jacob replied with a hint of guilt.

"You fuckin' buggin' me?"

"No, but I have people driving by your house, checking on your status, but that's not important. You better have a good reason for disobeying orders. What business do you have in Alexandria?" Jacob asked.

"I'll be honest, Jacob. I'm gonna talk to Lance," Danny replied.

"Do you think he's in danger?" Jacob asked with concern.

"No, well, at least no more than any of us. I'm going to try to get him back into the CIA."

"Danny, Lance has been a wreck since the Berlin attacks. After losing Rachel and Tara …"

"Why don't you let me have a look?" Dan asked.

"You should know better than anybody after seeing him in the hospital. The last thing he needs is for you to get him involved in this war."

"Hey, you said it yourself: it takes more than

determination to win a war. Having Lance back after everything would be a sign of hope to everyone back at Langley. Lance is more than just my friend. He taught me everything I know about the game. Whatever he is going through right now, I know that if he thinks he can make a difference, he will come," Dan replied strongly.

"I'm not going to force you to stop—you are one of my best agents, despite being a headache sometimes—but I think it's a lost cause, Dan," Jacob said with sympathetic regret.

"I will try to prove you wrong," Dan said with similar regret.

Dan put down his phone and continued driving toward Alexandria. He was getting closer and would have to deal with traffic soon. The traffic outside of larger cities had gotten much worse since the beginning of the Lemurian attacks. Danny opened his window and put an emergency siren on top of the car, similar to the sirens undercover police officers used.

With the siren working, Danny pulled onto the shoulder of the highway and started to move ahead of the line of cars to the checkpoint. Dan drove close enough for the soldiers at the checkpoint to notice him, and then he pulled off to the side of the checkpoint and got out of the car.

A soldier walked toward him. "What's wrong?" the officer asked. "The police would have called ahead of time if they needed to go through the checkpoint."

"Do you really want to question me, soldier?" Dan replied sternly, with little emotion. He showed the soldier his CIA identification.

The soldier gasped and then said in a panic, "I thought the Lemurians weren't attacking cities. Why the hell is the CIA here?"

"Relax, soldier," Dan said reassuringly. "I'm just here to see an old friend. We're not expecting a Lemurian attack. Just let me in, and you can get back to your work."

The soldier looked a little relieved, but a sense of worry was still clearly on his face. "All right, go ahead."

Dan started to walk back toward his car, but before he reached it, the soldier yelled, "Sir!"

"What is it, soldier?" Dan asked respectfully.

The soldier replied, trying to hold back concern, "What you just told me was the truth, right? I know sometimes they don't reveal information, because of the stress. They think having us in a panic might make the civilians nervous."

Dan looked the man in the eye and said, "I am telling you the truth."

The man seemed to be reassured and walked away from Dan.

Dan got back into his car and continued toward the city. The moment with the soldier reminded him of what was at stake. These were brave men, mentally scarred by the desperate times they lived in.

Dan was getting into the city, and he finally saw the sights that sickened him, sights that had become all too common throughout the war—tents, hundreds of them, and homeless people, thousands hobbling on the sidewalks. The tent cities reminded him of the Hoovervilles of the thirties.

Danny sped up toward Lance's apartment. It only

took him about twenty minutes to get to Lance's building, not bad given the mass of beggars banging on his window, trying to wash his windshield. The apartment building was not in a slum. Lance had a good deal of money left after leaving the CIA and could afford to live somewhere hospitable, although with the increased number of refugees, it was easy to forget that. The building was nice but nothing extravagant from the outside. The red brick with cookie-cutter windows gave it a rather plain feel that one could say was homely.

After parking in the lot, Danny pulled out the note with Lance's apartment number. Although he had gone over in his head nearly every way this meeting could play out, he was still struggling over what to say. The speech he'd planned now seemed too hurtful. He didn't want to guilt Lance back into the CIA; Lance didn't deserve that. *Just try to convince him that he would improve the situation,* Danny said in his head. No matter what problems Lance faced, he would still want to do anything necessary to prevent more loss of human life.

Dan approached the door of the apartment complex. He kept the nervousness from his face, but his heart was beating a bit fast. He was trying to run through the situation again when a homeless woman jumped in front of him, pleading, "Sir, sir, do you have anything? No amount is too small." She wasn't old; she looked to be in her late twenties, early thirties. She was wearing several layers, probably because she had nowhere else to put her things. Dan knew that she was just another victim of this war.

Dan kept walking, not acknowledging the woman.

She pleaded more desperately, "A town near me was attacked by the Lemurians. I left with my family in the middle of the night. Please, sir, we have no family here. Anything would help."

Dan continued walking briskly. He gave no words to the woman. As he entered the building, the woman, with a clear sadness, walked away. Dan hated the guilt he felt for not aiding the woman, but in these times, if he gave one person something, more would come.

Danny Smith got on board the elevator, which still looked good with marble floors and walls. He got off on Lance's floor and continued to his destination. He was about to knock on the door when, to his surprise, it started to open. A familiar voice on the other side of the door said with a mild happiness, "Hello, Dan."

2

ance let Dan into his apartment. Despite Lance's troubles, the apartment was quite clean. There was nothing out of place on the floor or counters.

"Were you expecting the place to be littered with pizza boxes and whiskey bottles?" Lance asked, apparently having noticed Dan's wandering eye.

"Nah," Dan responded, "you're a vodka guy."

Lance chuckled a bit as he put his hand on Dan's shoulder. "I'm happy to see you."

Lance was truly happy; it showed in his voice. He looked the same as the last time Dan saw him, slightly taller than Dan's own six feet two inches, with well-kept brown hair, even the glass eye had did not even look out of place. He was clearly in good shape, still muscular, and despite his time in the CIA, he did not have a gray hair on him. That could be because Lance was lucky enough to retire before he turned forty. Despite his welcoming appearance, there was an unmistakable sadness to him. Dan could tell something was off just from the tone of his voice, like he was putting on a front.

"Me too, Lance," Dan responded after a noticeable pause.

"Speaking of vodka, how about a drink?"

"No thanks, I'm on duty."

"Never stopped you before," Lance said with a sly grin as he made his way to the kitchen.

"Just following your example," Dan replied as he took a seat on the red leather couch. "You always had a bottle of something in your desk, whether it was Standard or Blyss or St. Pete's Gold, and always insisted I have more than a snort."

"Yeah, I was teaching you to hold your liquor. An agency man has to be able to hold his own with the most stalwart drinkers, and if you can down a tumbler of Moldova vodka, you can down anything," Lance said as he poured out two glasses of something 100, no ice as always. "Need to seem sober when you're drunk and drunk when you're sober."

Lance walked over and handed Dan the drink. "To old times."

"And better ones to come," Dan said before clinking glasses.

Lance took a nice gulp of his vodka, and Dan took a small sip. The 100 was a sign of strength.

"How are you?" Dan asked after a moment's silence.

"I'm the best I can be considering." Lance tensed up.

"Yeah, it's all right," Dan interjected.

"I've been watching a lot of movies, working out a lot, trying to keep myself busy. Even tried online gaming," Lance said, quickly changing the subject.

"The servers still up, you know with everything happening?"

"Yeah, you know how things are in tough times—people need entertainment more than ever. Did you know that many consider the Great Depression a golden age for movies?"

"Really? Wouldn't have guessed," Dan said.

"Yeah, *The Wizard of Oz*, *Gone with the Wind*, *Robin Hood* with Errol Flynn—all made during the Depression."

"Well, I guess it's not so surprising. When the world goes to shit, people need anything to keep their minds off their situation," Dan replied, taking another sip of the 100, trying to not wince from its bite.

Lance got a serious look on his face. Changing his calm demeanor, he said with genuine worry, "I would like to think you're visiting just for conversation, but we both know that's not the case."

Dan froze up. He'd planned on eventually bringing up the true purpose of his visit, but Lance cutting to the chase so soon surprised him. He put his glass down and looked at Lance the way a son would his father.

"Lance, I just thought maybe it would be good to talk to someone outside the situation room for a change. It might give me a new perspective."

"Fine," Lance said. "How much progress are you and Jacob making?"

"Honestly, we are in a holding pattern. We have no leads, and they have made no demands."

"Are we at least closer to finding out who these people are? Only thing I know about them is from the video they released three months back declaring themselves the Lemurians and that the world is corrupt."

"For a while we thought they could be a front group

for al-Hirrshi and other radical Islamists. We know now they are something different."

"Why do you think it's not Hirrshi?"

"A lot of the people we've captured are from places that are not Islamic—like remote parts of Russia, the Congo, and even Cambodia," Dan said.

"So? I've seen white boys from California join some of those nutjobs. I'm not saying you're wrong, but I assume you needed more evidence than that to immediately dismiss the Islamists."

"We did," Dan simply answered, "but a lot of this is classified."

"Dan, I'm not CIA anymore, but I know the rules. I won't let anything out—I swear."

"Lance, things are so intense right now that I can't risk breaking protocol."

"You can tell me anything. I won't leak it."

Dan gave Lance a long, blank stare. Although he wanted to fill Lance in, he knew giving too much would leave him less bait to throw out later.

Lance sat back and took another gulp of his drink. "Just answer me this: Why do you think they call themselves the Lemurians? I looked it up. Lemuria was supposedly a lost continent similar to Atlantis. Why would they choose that name?"

"We honestly don't know. Some new age people have used Lemuria as something to worship in the past, and hieroglyphs, like the one that was shown at the end at some of there messages and tattooed on certain soldiers tend to be popular in some pagan circles. Some people think the Lemurians are just a doomsday cult, a group of fanatics who want to take the world with them."

"I don't think that's the case. They have a plan; I know that," Lance said quickly.

"I wasn't a believer in the cult theory myself, but why are you so sure?" Dan asked.

"You weren't there in Berlin, Dan. You read the reports, but you didn't see them in action. In Berlin I saw their best men. They are smarter and more organized than they like us to think. We like to write off our enemies as madmen, but as much as I hate to admit it, whoever is leading them is very intelligent. The cyberattack on the satellites could just be the beginning."

Lance paused. "No, they used that day to show us what they are capable of, and now all they need is to keep us in fear. They are doing as little as necessary to keep us afraid, but if we back them into a corner, I promise you they will have more."

"Lance, that is why we could use you. This is your element."

Lance grew more serious. "Dan, after everything that has happened, I could use some good news. Are we making any progress?"

"We have one prisoner that could be of use, the leader of a Lemurian cell. We think he might crack and give us some intel about their operations."

Suddenly Lance burst out, "One good suspect! It's been over a year. They have been conducting mass shootings and bombings every day, and you're telling me that is the best lead you got."

"You want honesty? I'll give it to you. We aren't

making a lot of progress, and I didn't come over just to catch up with you. I want you to come back and help me. You were the best at interrogation, and this guy might be our best chance at finding out who their leadership is," Dan said passionately.

"I want to, Dan. It would feel good to help stop these fuckers, but it took me months to maintain even a shred of dignity after I lost Rachel and Tara. If I get close to one of those people, the same people who killed my family, I don't know what I'll do. Sorry."

The toll of Dan's failures took over. He yelled, "What is your plan, Lance? Stay here, live off your pension, and just pass the time until you die alone?" Dan was immediately horrified by what he'd just said to a man he considered a hero. He calmed down and said, "Lance, I'm—"

"No, you're right," Lance admitted begrudgingly. "I have no idea what I'm doing with my life right now. I just tend to live day to day, but if I stay out of it, at least I know I'm not harming you guys. I wish I could still be the man who interrogated terrorists and made them crack. I managed to pull myself together to talk to you, Dan, but trust me when I tell you that I am still not right."

"I understand, but I need to know that I did everything I could to stop them. I can barely sleep, Lance. Every time I close my eyes, I see the people that the Lemurians have killed. It might have been selfish of me, but finding you and asking for your help was the only thing I could think of doing to give me any hope."

Lance looked at Dan with concern and walked up to him. Lance seemed to realize the anguish Dan was feeling and said, "All right, I'll give it a go, Dan, but no promises."

Dan started to get up from his seat. He put his hand on the back of Lance's neck and said, "Thank you, Lance."

The agents walked out of the apartment down to Dan's car in a mutually comfortable silence. As Dan started the car, Lance sighed.

Dan turned to him. "Are you okay?"

"Yeah," Lance said after a pause. "I just can't believe I'm going to do this."

3

Berlin, Ohio, two years ago

As Lance turned into their driveway after the hour-long drive home, he smiled to himself. It was a simple house but enough for him and his family to start their life. After years of service to his country, he finally was close to having time for himself.

Rachel turned to Lance and happily questioned, "Why the smirk?"

"I think she's asleep," Lance said as he gestured his head to the back of the car where Tara lay asleep. He then looked to Rachel and said happily, "I'll take her in. She's had a long day."

As they entered the house, Rachel said, "Now that she's asleep, what did you really think of the recital, Lance? Be honest."

Lance said with sarcastic happiness, "Honestly the best ballet recital that I have ever been to."

"Oh, come on, it wasn't that bad," Rachel jested.

"No, I was serious—Tara did well."

"All right," Rachel said. "It's time to get her to bed."

She took Tara from Lance, carried her into her bedroom, and placed her on the bed. "Should I wake her up?"

"No, let her sleep with her ballet outfit on. It's summer; she doesn't need to get ready in the morning."

Rachel walked over to Lance, and he put his arm around her. He kissed her gently on the cheek and looked approvingly over their sleeping daughter.

"I look forward to having more days like this," Lance said as he and Rachel went to their room.

Rachel looked at Lance with apprehension. "Are you sure things will be all right, Lance, with Langley?"

"You know Danny; he's a great guy, a good friend of mine. He is more than willing to take the job. Along with Jacob and Andrew, the company is in great shape."

Still, despite the words of reassurance, Rachel looked depressed. Lance stroked her hair and calmly said, "You have the right to be scared, Rachel. You know more than most that the world is sometimes a scary place, but after everything we've done, we're entitled to our own lives. I've spent the last twenty years helping this country. I've had countless sleepless nights, times I've been afraid that at any moment someone could hurt me or my loved ones in retaliation for the things I've done. Rachel, for God's sake, I had to teach my daughter what to do if someone ever holds a knife to her throat. I have done a lot for this country, and now is as peaceful a time as I've ever seen. This is my best chance to leave."

Rachel heard the stress in Lance's voice. When he finished, there was a look of guilt in her eyes. She felt bad for bringing depression into a day that had been happy before. "I'm sorry, Lance. I know how much you've sacrificed—the holidays and anniversaries celebrated over the phone, the weddings and funerals you should have been at, not seeing Tara until she was six months old. You deserve to do what you want now. It's just that I have seen you save lives, stop attacks. I know there are people alive today because of what we did together back at the CIA. I feel that even if there is one death you could've prevented and didn't, you would never forgive yourself."

Lance drew closer to Rachel. "I have thought about what you're saying, Rachel. I mean, it would be impossible for me to not have had those thoughts myself, but you don't have a perfect world when you make those decisions. I don't know what will happen if I leave the CIA, but I trust the men I'm leaving behind …"

Lance paused for a bit. He then raised his hand and moved her red hair away from her eyes. He said softly, looking directly into his wife's eyes, "Rachel, I don't know for sure if something bad will happen if I leave, but with Tara getting older, I will lose my chance to be the father she deserves if I don't leave now. That is why I've made this decision."

Rachel gave Lance a look of understanding. Lance looked back at Rachel. They both knew their disagreement would not intrude on the feelings they had for each other. They kissed and embraced, eventually making love on the bed. The rough spot in their relationship was forgotten, and it seemed that life would improve, for the moment.

Present day

The ride to the safe house was a long one, made longer by the lingering silence between Dan and Lance. Having exhausted the small talk at Lance's apartment, Dan was apprehensive about asking too many questions, afraid the wrong one would revoke Lance's participation. Granted, Lance was already in the car, but with Lance's history, he could easily commandeer the vehicle. Dan could tell Lance was deep in thought about something. His eyes were fixed on road, and he'd hardly moved since he'd buckled his seat belt. His breathing had picked up, though. His breaths had become deeper and more frequent since they'd pulled off of the highway. He was nervous. He was going to deal with someone from the Lemurians, an enigma. Dan had told him that the Lemurians were not making any demands. They never made any statements of motive to this madness. They just said that the world was corrupt. In addition to his anxiety, the CIA agent in him held a sense of curiosity about how this organization was formed and who led it—the same curiosity a hunter had over an elusive prey.

Finally they reached their destination, pulling into a lot adjacent to what seemed like a small office building—an oblong rectangle two stories in height, the kind that would house either a small business or a couple of lawyers. It was unassuming but practical for a safe house, especially one that was used to conduct interrogations and monitor operations.

Dan got out first. He stood outside the vehicle for what seemed like minutes before Lance finally got out. "How is the current operation structured?" Lance asked.

"I'm part of a strike force led by Lanser. We have about a hundred of our best men and women working across all seventeen intelligence agencies. Our allies have conducted similar operations. We are talking directly to similar-size strike forces in the Fives Eyes and beyond."

"Beyond?"

"It is now the Nine Eyes practically. France, Germany, Mexico, and Japan have been promoted as allies. We've started talking more in hopes of capturing the Lemurian leadership."

"What are the rest of the Company doing? Shouldn't they be devoting more bodies to this?" asked Lance.

"The rest of us have been sent to help the FBI in counteracting Lemurian attacks throughout the country and unraveling how the Lemurians are getting the resources for their attacks. Protecting civilians is the first priority at the moment."

Lance paused for a moment before giving an

affirmative nod. "What are the current estimates of the casualties?"

"Domestically or worldwide?" Dan asked.

"Both would be good," said Lance.

"In America, people are leaving the smaller towns, so it is hard to get an exact number, but about ten thousand to twenty thousand through the course of this year. Worldwide, we think it is about one hundred thousand. Things are particularly bad in Russia and central Asia."

"Has the Company done anything to stop the bleeding?"

"A bit. We helped crack some codes they were using to plan attacks, but we are still in the dark about their leadership."

"Okay," Lance said with a hint of resignation.

There was further silence between the two men for a while. Lance was still nervous. Would he be able to contribute something of value? He didn't think about it for long before his mind was drawn away by the sign that said "Langley" in the window.

"A bit on the head, don't you think?" Lance asked with a little sarcasm.

"What? It's a lovely name that brings to mind the thought of home and a simpler time. Besides, the people would never expect a CIA house here. That's against our charter," Dan said as he punched in the code for the door.

"Never stopped us before," Lance said with the same dry sarcasm.

The building's interior was as unassuming as its exterior. The narrow doorway led into a small waiting room with a receptionist desk on the right, only without a receptionist. The walls were eggshell white, and the floor was covered with gray carpeting that had gone out of fashion at the end of the 1990s. Lance and Dan made their way past the desk and down the short hallway, which broke off into a T shape with each branch leading to an office space and elevator at the end.

"Going up?" asked Lance.

"The building is only two stories."

"That doesn't answer the question."

"Very good," Dan said with a smile.

As they entered the elevator, Dan inserted a little key into the spot next to the fire alarm button, the keyhole everyone assumed was just there to shut off the alarm when the firefighters arrived. This particular keyhole, however, brought the elevator down below ground level to an underground basement area where the Company had established an interrogation room.

As the elevator started to pull into the basement, Dan said, "All right, we're here. You ready?"

"Yeah," Lance said.

They rode the rest of the way in an awkward silence. There was nothing that either of the men could think to say. As the elevator doors opened, the two were greeted by the friendly face of Andrew Kekso, an African American man standing over six feet tall. He was somewhat muscular, to the point where it was noticeable from a distance, and had a shaved head.

Lance stepped ahead of Dan, the first time he had done so that night. "It's good to see you again, Andrew," he said, extending his hand.

Andrew smiled. "I am glad to see you, Lance."

Lance clasped Andrew's hand and drew him closer. "Dan tells me that Lanser is in charge of the strike force."

"Yeah," Andrew said as he started walking away from the elevator.

Despite Lance's fears, there was something refreshing about being back in this kind of building. It didn't take long for the awkwardness to fade and for him to walk the path he had walked before with a relish of being with people that he respected. This moment reminded him of better times.

Andrew stopped with Lance and Dan behind him. Andrew said, "All right, Lance, Jacob will want to talk to you before anything happens."

"Thanks, Andrew," Lance said quickly. "Can you or Dan tell me more about this prisoner? I understand he hasn't given you anything."

"Not much. His name is Gabriel Landshire, Caucasian, American, aged fifty-four, originally from Wyoming. He attended the University of California, Santa Cruz, before trying to start up an electronics company that went belly-up after three years. We identified him from a drug possession charge in Seattle a few years ago. The cops believed he was homeless at the time. After that he went dark."

"Do you think his company had anything to do with funding the Lemurians?" Lance asked.

"Not likely. It was twenty years ago and never went anywhere."

"I got to say, Dan, based on how everybody was talking about the American traitor, I thought he was ex-CIA or something, not just some random guy," Lance said with a hint of humor.

"You know people—it always seems worse when the terrorist is one of their own," Dan replied.

"Actually, in retrospect, it kind of makes sense that he was homeless. Homeless people don't leave much of a record. If the Lemurians provided him with food and shelter, it could give him a motive for joining them. A loser who finally was given a chance—fits the pattern of a lot of terrorists," Lance said.

"His past doesn't make him seem like much, but do not underestimate him. He was the leader of a group of Lemurians, and when we got him, we just barely stopped his cell from launching RPGs into a shopping center. Almost killed dozens of people," Dan said sternly.

"Don't worry, Dan," Lance said. "After what I experienced, I will never underestimate these people."

A voice came from the back of the room. "It's good to hear that, if you are going to be back here."

Lance looked toward the back of the room and was honestly surprised to see a certain someone was present— Jacob Lanser, the leader of the Trantor task force back in Bucharest during the early 1990s. Jacob, despite being an older man in his late fifties, still had a fairly strong presence. He was clearly in shape and stood at an intimidating six feet three. His graying hair was the most clear sign of aging. His face had a sense of determination, but he seemed to force a smile as he approached Lance.

"It is a surprise to see you here, Lance," Jacob said with clearly mixed emotions.

"I know," Lance said. "Last time you saw me, I

probably didn't seem like the kind of person you'd want on this job."

"I remember," Jacob said in a serious tone. "Are you sure you're up to this?"

"From what Dan tells me, you really have nothing to lose by letting me talk to this guy," Lance replied.

"I wouldn't be so sure about that," Jacob said sternly. "Landshire may be a piece of shit, but he is one of the best leads we have. I wouldn't blame you for wanting to hurt him, but we need him in decent shape."

"I would never endanger a lead, Jacob. I have interrogated some of the worst psychopathic and egotistical fucks on the planet and have never abused my authority."

"None of those men were involved in the deaths of your family. It is always different when the killers attack your own."

Lance pulled back and said somewhat sternly, "Look, if my word means nothing to you, I understand, but I'm not a hothead looking to prove something. I want to catch these bastards and bring down their whole organization, not just one member. So with your permission, may I have a go at extracting any info that can help take the Lemurians down?"

"All right," Jacob said softly. "Dan, take him to the prisoner."

Jacob turned around and began toward the interrogation room where they had Landshire waiting. Andrew followed, but before Lance could take a step, Dan firmly gripped his shoulder.

"Lance, are you sure you can handle this?" Dan asked.

"I'm sure, Dan," Lance replied solemnly.

Lance started to walk toward the cell but then looked back at Dan. "Can you hold something for me?" Lance asked with a stern face. "I don't want this to be in there when I am with him."

"Sure. What do you want me to hold for you?" Dan asked.

Lance tossed a small gold band into his hands. "My wedding ring."

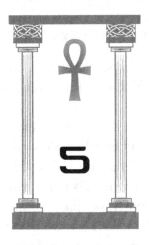

Lance didn't know what to expect when he went into the cell. The room was small and empty except for a rectangular table with two chairs at each end with Landshire sitting in one. Landshire was staring at the right-hand wall. The man looked quite old and, despite being formerly homeless, seemed clean. He did not seem like a soldier. He was a small man, close to sixty, and not in great shape. He looked frail, with wrinkled hands and face and gray hair. The only thing that marked him for a soldier was the look of intensity on his face.

"Mr. Landshire, is it?" said Lance, breaking the silence.

"Yes," the man responded quickly.

"This is my first time meeting a Lemurian. I have heard a lot about your organization, most of it bad," Lance said harshly as he took the seat across from Landshire. Although the table was wide, he could probably still grab Landshire from across it.

The man continued to sit in silence. Lance had experienced this all before, though. He looked into Landshire's eyes and saw some fear break through the man's intensity. It was like he was doing all he could to control himself. Lance knew the prisoner could be provoked.

"It seems to me that they used you, Gabriel—took a homeless man and bought your loyalty with food and shelter, am I right?" Lance asked condescendingly.

"Even if you're correct, is that a reason why I should help you, this country, or this government?" Landshire replied angrily. "Is it not better to have insincere charity than the sincere apathy that the American people have given me?"

"I know some things about you, Landshire. You messed up your company, failed to plan correctly, and ended up homeless because of it. How is it the country's or government's fault? And how does that give you the right to try to take the lives of dozens of people that never did anything to you?" Lance finished angrily.

"Every war has collateral damage," Landshire said with little emotion.

Lance sensed that getting him angry was only going to make him retreat into silence and short answers. Whoever the Lemurians were, they'd been able to get some genuine loyalty out of this man. Lance calmed down and asked with genuine curiosity, "Gabriel, why that name? Why the 'Lemurians'?"

The man seemed generally befuddled by this question. Indeed, the most unassuming questions could yield the greatest impact.

"Is that important?"

"Just curiosity," Lance said confidently. "I've been hearing a lot about your organization over the past year.

Most terrorist organizations' names make sense. It's mostly just the word for *God* or *sword* in Arabic or some other language or something like that … Now Lemuria, why call yourself after a mythical continent?"

"I don't know exactly," Landshire said. "I wasn't in contact with the leadership. I'd like to think they chose the name of a lost country to signify the hope of a nation for the nationless."

Lance had gotten something. "So you never had contact with the head of the Lemurians? So who contacted you?" he asked inquisitively.

Landshire, realizing the mistake, began to worry. His face showed it. "No, I didn't mean that."

"You think I'm going to believe that, Gabriel?" Lance asked. "How were you contacted to be a Lemurian?"

"I've said enough," Landshire snapped with a hint of anger. "I will not talk to you anymore." He turned away from Lance.

"Do you think they're coming for you? Do you think they're going to get you out of here? For your sake, I hope so, because it's the only way you're not going to spend the rest of your life in solitary—that is, unless you give me something."

"No! I will not betray my people," Landshire snapped.

"You told me insincere charity is better than nothing. Well, then let me help you. Give me something I can use to trace back to the Lemurian leadership, and you might be put in witness protection or at least be given a sentence where you can see the outside of a prison before you leave this earth," Lance said harshly but confidently.

"I don't want to help this nation," Landshire yelled

defiantly. "Fifteen years I sat on the streets of this country, men, women, children looking down at me like I was some sewer rat. I sat in despair thinking that all I would ever end up being was a John Doe in the morgue one day, until a group of people offered me a chance to have a life again, a mission, a goal. No prison you can put me in would be worse than what my life was before I was a Lemurian."

Lance was honestly taken aback by Landshire's genuine sense of commitment to his cause. It was a somewhat humanizing moment for the man. Lance knew all too well what someone would do for purpose.

Lance sat in silence for a moment before asking in a calm, sympathetic tone, "What did they say to you? You don't have to tell me about your handlers. I'm just curious what message they told you when you joined them."

"Just that there were people around the world just like me, abandoned by a society that failed them, and that the government was beyond hope. They told me I could become part of a new order that would put the people's interests above corporate interests once and for all. They didn't give me details about how they were going do that, but it seemed like a noble goal to dedicate my life to."

"I'd like to think it took more than that to make you willing to kill," Lance said.

"They showed me proof of our government's wrongdoing around the world—wars, killings, secret deals to deny people sovereignty, and illegitimate regimes allowed to prosper thanks to secret agreements among the global elites. This convinced me that their cause, their work, was right," Landshire said.

"I'm sure the fact they gave you a place to live and some money helped your decision," Lance said.

"Of course, but I am sure the CIA pays you as well. It is only normal for any person to be affected by money, and it's laughable if you think some guilt about money is what's going to get to me," Landshire said. "Am I not living the American ideal, doing whatever it takes to make it in this world?" he added sarcastically.

He was starting to get more talkative, for better or worse. It might be time to provoke Gabriel a bit further.

"I'm sorry, but you've been had, Gabriel. I bet whatever they showed you was just some Noam Chomsky bullshit. 'Boo-hoo, some politician was corrupt, so I can kill innocent people,'" Lance mocked.

"I'm not giving you anything else," Landshire said in a calm but stern manner. "We're done."

Lance was not happy with the amount of progress he was making with Landshire. It seemed the man's loyalty to this cause was absolute. But Lance had done this enough to know how to maybe use that loyalty against him.

"Have you ever thought about what would have happened if you'd said no to them, Gabriel? They never would have let you live after revealing themselves. They would have filled you up with drugs and dumped your body in an alley hoping we would just think you were another bum that OD'd," Lance stormed.

"You created the society where that plan would be possible, one where people live without meaning," Landshire replied.

"You know your bosses are cowards," Lance said, almost in a mocking fashion.

"What?" Landshire asked with a hint of confusion and anger.

"They send you, some homeless, one-and-done business failure to take out their enemies while they hide. You're left facing the full force of law enforcement and the military with your dick in your hands and sucking the barrel of a gun. Your superiors are so damned desperate for bodies they can't send someone who has actually shot someone to do this. I mean, hell, a Boy Scout getting his rifle-shooting badge probably has more experience with firearms than you."

"Everything the CIA has done, you have the nerve to criticize us," Landshire said.

"I'm here," Lance taunted.

"And you are failing. What does that have to do with anything?" Landshire's blank look was slowly giving way to anger.

"Really? You've spent our entire time talking about how corrupt this country is, but we've spent the last year putting innocent people into cities away from your organization's attacks, saving thousands of lives and leaving you no targets. We have utilized air superiority and surveillance to shell wimps like you that the Lemurians call soldiers, and we've sent actual trained troops like me to mop up the rest. We send trained professionals to the front lines, and your precious Lemurians recruit some sucker who would easily be the first to die in their attacks to do their shit work, while they lean back and enjoy a drink. Stupid fucking cowards!" Lance said in a long droll.

"Raul is not a coward!" yelled Landshire.

Lance paused for a second, registering his victory. "Who is Raul? Your boss?" he said inquisitively.

Landshire went numb. Lance knew he'd gotten some information out that he wasn't supposed to. There was a look of dread on Landshire's face and an emptiness in his eyes. He knew that he had lost. He remained quiet.

"It's over, Gabriel. Maybe if you'd kept quiet, we would have believed you know nothing and they just left you to rot. But now we know you know something concrete, and if you don't give us something, you never see the sun again."

Lance stood up and walked over to Landshire, towering over the beaten man. "I mean solitary confinement, drugging, sleep deprivation. By slipping up here, you've given us permission to do whatever is necessary to get information from you."

"I won't tell you anything else," Landshire said with a clear undertone of fear.

Sensing weakness, Lance lowered himself to Landshire's eye level and returned to a sympathetic tone. "Just give me anything, Gabriel. Just one name, one place is all. Once you do that, nothing will happen to you. Those things I offered—a shorter sentence, witness protection, a new life—are still on the table."

Landshire sighed with a clear look of defeat.

"Just tell me about him. Who is Raul? Just that, and I'll leave."

The room was quiet for what seemed like a lifetime. It was make or break now. If Landshire didn't talk here, he most likely never would.

"His name is Raul Candellario. He is the leader of

the Lemurians in North America." Landshire spoke with a distinct quiver in his voice, as if he was about to break down in tears. "Last time I heard, he was based near Copper Canyon in Mexico. I honestly don't know much more about him. We never met in person."

"The leader of the Lemurians in North America," Lance said. "Who is his superior, the top leader of your organization?"

"I don't know who the overall leader is. I have never met him or heard his name," Landshire said.

"Is there anything else you can give me, Gabriel, anything else that could help? Maybe I can send you to a non-supermax prison before the trial, if you offer up something good."

"He goes by a code name, our leader—the Historian," Landshire replied.

"The Historian, okay," Lance said. "You have been a big help, Gabriel. I think we are done here."

With that, Lance started to walk away from the man and toward the door of the interrogation room, but Gabriel Landshire spoke again. "You called my people cowards, and maybe some are. After all, I failed them." Landshire had escaped his look of defeat and was now in a state of severe anger. "You're not the only one looking for names. I find it funny you didn't know any of the names of our leadership. That is enough to know that you're not winning this war. I'm glad to see they're still getting the best of you."

Lance had been holding his hatred in check until that point, but those words reminded him what kind of man Landshire was and what he was willing to do. Lance's hand started to make a fist, and he stepped toward the man. However, his rationality got the best of him, and he walked out of the room, albeit with a slam of the door.

As he walked down the hallway to get back into the command center, Danny Smith met up with him. "That was amazing," Dan said. "You got the name of a Lemurian leader. That's something we've been fighting for since the first attacks."

"He didn't give much information on this Candellario, but it's a start," Lance said.

"Finding his name might be more important than you realize. Jacob was listening to your interview, and they were able to find out that this Raul Candellario might be someone a little more prominent than we expected."

"Really?" Lance said.

"Yeah, there's a human rights activist from Central America with that name. He was previously a lieutenant in the Guatemalan army. Right now he's the leading suspect."

"Let's not jump to conclusions," Lance said. "There's probably more than one person in the world named Raul Candellario, or it could be a pseudonym. Let's not convict the guy before we have the evidence."

"Yeah, but it does seem like the best fit. He has the military experience," Dan said.

"It certainly won't hurt to check any lead. Let's get to the command center," Lance said as he made his way to the door with Dan.

"Still hard to believe this man Landshire was willing to do all this for the Lemurians after just being some homeless guy," Dan said.

"I'm not surprised at all," Lance said. "Think about what they gave him—food, shelter, a reason to live. I've seen people kill for a lot less."

Dan took the words in with understanding and replied solemnly, "Yeah, I guess you're right."

The two men then walked into the command center, where Jacob was waiting with a confident grin and his hand outstretched. "Good work, Lance."

"Do you guys think the human rights advocate Dan was telling me about is the man we're looking for?" Lance asked.

"Yeah, there's a lot of fishy stuff about him. Since about three years ago, he has gone completely dark. He has not produced any medical, tax, or banking records since he disappeared."

"Do we have any pictures of him?" Lance asked. "I'm curious who exactly we're looking for."

"There's a picture of the man we believe to be the correct Raul Candellario pulled up on the computer over there if you want to take a look," Jacob said.

"Sure," Lance said, walking over to the computer screen.

When he saw the image of the man, he fell to his knees. It was an image that haunted him, an image of a man with piercing brown eyes. He whispered silently to himself, "No, no, please, God, no."

Dan, seeing Lance fall to the floor and begin to shake, hurried toward his friend. As he helped pull Lance up, he asked what was wrong.

"Dan, tell Jacob we don't need to keep researching whether this is the correct man. I know he is."

"How?" Dan asked.

"I've seen him myself, on that horrible day in Berlin," Lance answered, the stress clear in his voice. He had to fight back against collapsing.

He turned away from the monitor to look Danny directly in the eye. "He was the one who killed them. He was the one who killed my family."

6

Berlin, Ohio, one year ago

Lance and his family were on the way home from spending the Fourth of July with Rachel's parents. Tara was very tired from the day but still showed a visible happiness on her face. Rachel turned to look at Tara in the back seat, and then she and Lance shared a brief mutual smile. Lance tilted his head in a quick nod to Tara, as a sign to bring Tara into their moment of personal happiness.

"Did you have fun today?" Lance asked Tara.

"Yeah, yeah," the young girl said.

Lance said excitedly, "And your summer is only going to get better. In a few day we're going to Hawaii. How do you feel about that?"

"I can't wait," Tara replied with a more tired tone.

Tara soon drifted off to sleep, and Lance looked back at Rachel. "What about you, Mom?" he asked happily.

"I'm looking forward to it too, Lance," Rachel said in a reassuring tone. "It's good that we can treat Tara to these things at her age."

"Thank the pension the CIA gives me and a few successful stock choices," Lance replied.

"You can thank me for that last one," she said with a giggle.

"Thank you, dear." Lance planted a kiss on her cheek. "Next summer it'll be Europe with stops in Barcelona, Paris, Vienna, and everywhere in between," Lance said with a smirk. He then noticed a noise in the distance. "Do you hear something, Rach?"

"It's probably just some fireworks. It is the Fourth of July, after all," Rachel said.

"That's true, but then again, your parents live in the middle of nowhere. Why do they want to live out here again?"

"They're not city people, Lance. They like it out here where it's quiet."

"Yeah, but—"

At that moment, their car flipped over. Lance was possessed with fear and a morbid curiosity about what had happened. The last thing he heard was the sound of an explosion. He'd seen nothing in the road before the attack.

Lance was drifting in and out of consciousness. His sight was blurry, but he could still see. He made the terrifying look to the passenger seat. Rachel was dead, shards of glass through her neck. Her eyes were clearly lifeless, and there was no sign of breathing. Lance sat back, having to look away from his deceased wife, and started to shed some tears. Then he heard crying from the back seat. Tara screamed, "Mommy! Daddy!"

Lance stopped crying, instantly reacting to his

daughter's cries. Tara was upside down, still strapped in with the seat belt, her arm visibly broken.

Lance unlocked his seat belt and fell to the ceiling of the turned-over car. He tried to lie on his side to limit the amount of pain he felt. In his panic he still knew that he had to get Tara out of the car. He looked up at her and said quietly but seriously, "Tara, be very quiet. I know it hurts, but we can't let anyone know where we are."

Nervously, Tara asked, "Are the people you told me about coming?"

As Lance reached in the back seat to get his daughter, he replied, "Yes."

Tara grew more cautious. It looked like she was about to yell out in fear, but Lance covered her mouth and said, "Tara, you have to listen to every word I say."

Tara simply nodded, and Lance said, "Good."

The two of them exited the wreckage of the car, Lance taking the lead. "Stay down," he said in the most intense manner a father could use with his child without yelling.

Lance stood up and looked at the surrounding area; he saw no signs of their attackers. He got down on his knee to talk to Tara. He breathed heavily a few times. He had to consume every bit of rage and fear. He knew this threat was not over yet. In this moment his only goal was to save his daughter.

"We are going to go down into the woods. The people who want to find us might be down the road."

Tara fell to the ground. She screamed, "Daddy, I can't go! I'm hurt!"

Lance was worried seeing his daughter in such pain,

but he had to get her out of any immediate danger. He responded quickly, "All right, I will carry you."

He picked up his daughter and started to walk into the forest near the road. As he was holding her, Tara said, "Dad, we have to go back to Mom."

A new sense of horror entered Lance's mind. He only now realized that Tara did not know about her mom's death. After a quick debate with himself internally, he decided it was necessary to tell her now. Tara was young, but Lance knew he couldn't lie to her about something of this magnitude successfully, especially with his own mental state in doubt.

"Tara, Mom died in the crash."

The young girl started to cry. Lance wanted to think of something that would calm her down. It was a cold thing to do to quiet her so close to her mother's death, but the danger was still close. It was necessary to scare the young girl.

Lance went with honesty, blurting out in a sincere whisper, "Tara, you have to cry later. We are still in trouble. Your mom would want you to listen to me now."

After this harsh truth, Tara quieted, fear visible on her face. Lance continued pushing into the forest while holding Tara. He did not hear any sounds of gunfire. Maybe the danger had passed. Suddenly Lance fell to his knee, still holding Tara. He was in immense pain. He looked down at his feet and saw bone piercing out of his skin right above his left foot, an injury he must have received from the car crash. The adrenaline must have been able to keep his pain in check. It was only now that he started to feel the pain. In addition to the pain, he started to hear sounds: footsteps, coming closer.

Lance was feeling hopeless, but he noticed some lights coming through the trees. They might be from a building, Lance tried to get up, but for Tara to have any chance to survive, she had to move quickly. Lance put her down. The young girl was still visibly shaking, continuing to huff and breathe heavily. He tried to move closer to Tara, but the pain in his leg stopped him. The wound sent agony throughout his entire body. Lance had to somehow prepare his daughter to leave him. He felt that was her only shot now.

"Tara, I know you're scared and sad about Mom, but you have to listen to me. You have to listen to what I'm going to say. You understand?"

"Yes," the young girl muttered.

"Okay, I need you to leave me here. Take my cell phone and run. Hide until you are sure no one is around you, then call the police. They'll know where to find you. You get them to take you to Grandma's, all right?"

"No, I don't want to go," Tara said desperately, tears in her eyes.

"I love you, Tara. Please run for me and Mom. We need you to make it. Please run, Tara," Lance said in emotional desperation, his own eyes filling with tears.

With clear panic in her eyes and her tears beginning to fall, the young girl started to run away.

The pain in Lance's leg was immense, causing him to drop down on the ground even further. He was feeling strange mixed emotions in what he thought might be his final moments. Lance thought that Tara had a chance to live because of him, but the joy of that thought was tempered by the knowledge that this was probably the last time he would see his daughter. The only thing he could think of to try to help his daughter one last time was to make some noise to draw some attention away from her. Lance crawled toward a large rock, took a smaller rock in his hands, and started banging it on the large rock, hoping to draw the attention of any nearby assailants toward him.

Lance waited for a few minutes. It looked like the fighting might be over, but then came the sight he'd known in his gut was coming. Out of the brush came a well-armed military man wearing body armor and camouflage. On the side of his uniform was a symbol Lance did not recognize. It was not the insignia of any country or terrorist group he knew of. The man looked at Lance lying on the ground, and with an uncaring look on his face, he raised his pistol and shot Lance in the shoulder.

Lance put his back up to the large rock, wincing from the pain. The man continued to walk toward him with the gun in hand. The man facing Lance was at least six feet tall and muscular. He had slightly brown skin, the kind of ethnicity that was hard to identify at first sight. Lance thought he was going to die, but before he let the assailant finish the job, he wanted one last act of rebellion.

Lance yelled, "You failed! I got my daughter out of here."

The man paused and then replied in an almost emotionless, businesslike manner, "If you are talking about the young girl that tried to escape, she has already been taken care of."

Lance didn't know for sure whether what this man was saying was true, but his gut told him it was. He'd failed. One of this man's cohorts had found Tara. Feeling defeated, Lance did not know what to do. He'd sacrificed his own chance of survival to save his daughter, and now it seemed he had failed. The only thought that filled his mind was getting an answer in his final moments, to know who did this.

"Please," Lance cried in desperation, with some of his last strength, "before you kill me, tell me who sent you. Who did this? What was this revenge for? What did I do to deserve this?"

The assassin's emotionless demeanor was replaced by what seemed to be a genuine sense of confusion. "What do you mean?" the man asked.

"After everything I've done, who finally got their revenge? The Russians, cartels, al-Hirrshi himself? Who paid you to do this? Who? I have the right to know," Lance yelled in anger.

The man's eyes suddenly shifted from confusion to heated look of rage. He raised his gun in line with Lance's head, angrily proclaiming, "Listen—I want this to be the last thing you hear: You are nothing! Whatever you were before this day does not matter. You and the others we killed are statistics, nothing more. You, that girl, the woman in the car are just numbers that will alarm people watching the news tomorrow. I don't know who you were or what you've done, and I don't care to know. You mean nothing to us."

And with those words, the man pulled the trigger.

"Huh!" Lance shouted with a gasp as he returned from one of his nightmares. He awoke in the bunk room at the safe house, once again reminded what state he was in. It didn't take long for him to recover his senses anymore. He was able to get up and go to the bathroom almost immediately upon awakening to wash his face. The whole affair happened so often that it had lost much of its shock, though none of its sting. After drying his face, he checked his watch and saw he had been asleep for only two hours.

"Are you feeling better?" asked Danny, whose shadow Lance had noticed since drying his face. How long had he been standing there?

"About the same as I normally do when I wake up," Lance said. He turned serious and asked, "Where are we with Candellario?"

"We expect he's held up at Copper Canyon in Mexico. It used to be a tourist attraction, but since the attacks started, most towns near it are deserted. It seems like a perfect place for him to hide out."

"Sounds like as good a place as any for him to hide," Lance said,

"Lance, you did a helluva good job here yesterday. You've given us the best lead we've had in months," Dan said reassuringly. "You have done a valuable service for your country. If you want, I can have a ride back to Alexandria organized for you within minutes."

"Dan, thanks for the offer, but I'd like to keep helping you guys. If Jacob allows it, I would like to be a permanent part of this task force."

The room became quiet. This was the response Danny had subconsciously hoped for, but it opened a Pandora's box. Lance had shown incredible skill and control in yesterday's interrogation, but being in the field was a whole other matter. Who knew how much his year-long bender had blunted his senses. Additionally, getting clearance for something like this wasn't normally a said-and-done kind of thing, although, in times like these, maybe an exception could be made, especially considering the nugget Lance had just mined.

"Lance, are you sure? You did good this time, but you told me yourself that you're not 100 percent right."

"Getting the job done back there was the most good I've done and the best I've felt since I lost them. Landshire was right about one thing: we're not doing as well as we could be, and I honestly think that I can be of more help, Dan. With what I got from Landshire and with you vouching for me, I'm sure I can stay on."

"Do you want this only because Candellario is the person responsible for Tara's and Rachel's deaths?"

"No," Lance snapped. "I want this man brought to

justice for what he did, but I want to stop these people over anything else."

"Lance, an interrogation is one thing, but having you out in the field armed is completely different."

"Can you help me, Dan? As a friend, help me convince Jacob to let me stay on, maybe just as an advisor for the mission. I don't even have to carry a weapon. I just want to be there when we snag him."

"I'll do what I can with Jacob, but I don't think you should be at the front lines."

"That's fair," Lance said with a begrudging acceptance.

Dan started to head out the door of the barracks with Lance following. Before opening the door, Dan turned back around and told Lance, "I will talk to Jacob. If you really want to help with this mission, get some rest, Lance."

Lance headed back toward the barracks and lay down. "I'll try my best," he said, once more begrudgingly.

As Lance tried to settle himself back into bed, Dan stopped again at the door and came back. He quietly placed Lance's wedding ring on the little table adjacent to Lance's bed. "Lance, I know it hasn't been easy for you, but I can honestly say that I'm glad you're back."

"Me too," Lance said with a light happiness as he headed back to sleep.

8

ance was sitting in a military plane on the way to Copper Canyon, Mexico. The plane was a large cargo cruiser holding a team that would aid the Mexican military in the killing or capture of Candellario. Danny had been able to convince Jacob of Lance's importance as an advisor by reminding him of Lance's experience with the Berlin attacks and promising that he would stay with Lance every step of the way. Lance was happy to be on this mission, on the hunt, but despite telling Danny his involvement wasn't about Rachel and Tara, he couldn't ignore that he was going after the man that had taken his family away. This was just another sacrifice he had to make for this war.

Danny walked near Lance's seat, interrupting Lance's thoughts. "Lance, you're needed in the briefing room on the back of the plane."

"Okay." Lance got up, and as he walked with Dan to the main room, he asked, "Who are the main players for this briefing?"

"Andrew is in charge of our strike force here, but the Mexican Army sent a major, Federico Cortez, to be their main representative to the mission and the commander of the forces on the ground."

"That sounds about right. This mission is being conducted in Mexican territory. Anyone else?"

"I think the NSA sent a liaison, but Andrew and Cortez are the main players. You will be our expert on the Berlin attacks."

"Is that an honorific title, or do you expect me to actually do something?"

"Jacob would like you to say a few words on the importance of this mission, give the men a personal take on the story."

"Dan, I don't talk about that, for obvious reasons," Lance said with a sense of concern.

Dan moved closer to Lance, looked him in the eyes, and said sternly, "Lance, I know you are going through a lot, but you told me you wanted to be on this mission, and bringing up your experience in the attacks and the interrogation was the best thing I could think of to get you on."

"I know, Danny. You kept your part of the bargain; this is my part. I'm just venting while I have the chance."

"I understand, Lance, but don't forget it," Dan replied sternly. "Come on."

Lance was able to conceal his fear as they walked into the briefing room. Many military men in uniform sat around the room, with Andrew Kekso sitting in front of a screen. The unnerving feeling inside Lance got worse as he saw a photo of Raul Candellario on the screen behind Andrew. Even seeing a picture of his family's murderer made him feel sick to his stomach, but he kept going.

Andrew saw him enter the briefing room and said in a stern but welcoming tone, "Welcome, Agent Richardson."

The other men in the room, both American and Mexican agents, looked at Lance attentively. Lance looked back and said, "Greetings. I am Lance Richardson, a twenty-year veteran of the both the US army and the CIA and a survivor of the Berlin attacks. I am here to advise you on this mission."

One man raised his hand eagerly, the Mexican agent Cortez. "I respect you doing this, Mr. Richardson. We understand that you have personally seen Raul Candellario. What can you share about him and what you experienced in Berlin?"

"I was just about to get into that," Lance said, disliking being interrupted. He continued, "We suspect that Candellario and whoever is guarding him have better technology than what's used in the average Lemurian attack. The first thing Candellario did that night in Berlin was slaughter every police officer in the Berlin station before moving on to the nearest 911 phone operators and then killing over two hundred civilians in thirty minutes. They clearly planned the attack well in advance. They had a clear escape plan that even today we have not figured out. Their equipment was of the highest quality in terms of weaponry, body armor, and obviously communication. One surviving policeman, who was out of the station at the time, heard from radio chatter that smoke bombs were used, and autopsies of the victims revealed the use of armor-piercing rounds. Now that we know Candellario is the leader of the Lemurian forces in North America, his presence at the attack site makes it safe to assume that he was involved in the planning of these attacks and that he has a similarly well-equipped outfit surrounding him."

"Why do you think they have not constantly used the military style teams they had at Berlin?" one soldier asked. "It would only hurt them to stick to the most basic weapons if they have more than that to use."

"In my opinion it's a strategic tactic. We only used the A-bomb at the end of the war. Like anyone else, they don't want to reveal their secrets too early in the conflict," Lance replied.

Danny turned to the soldier who had asked the question. "How 'bout the opposite question, solider? Why did the Lemurians reveal their capabilities in the first place? If they are saving more for later, why give us the warning to be prepared?"

"Fear!" Lance answered. "It seems their satellite attack was necessary to help them move throughout the country, but I believe the use of professionals in the first attacks was meant as a sign to the people in this room that they are serious. Killings alone are enough to scare the civilian populace. It doesn't matter if the deaths are from a drone or an IED; it has the same effect. Their use of that technology, along with the satellite hacking, was a show of force to the governments of the world that they can fight us and that they think they can win."

Several men audibly gasped at this grim statement. Cortez asked, "What is the best lead on where the Lemurians got some of these capabilities?"

Lance continued, "We suspect these advanced Lemurian troops have stolen Russian technology. The Russian border is the worst right now, with Lemurians actively fighting a guerrilla war in southern Russia and along the former Soviet republics. Although the number of Lemurian insurgents have been have been obscured due to Islamists insurgents taking advantage of the chaos, we know that somehow they either stole a lot weaponry or have the capability to mass-produce it.

"Is there any knowledge of where the Lemurians have gotten access to capital?" one soldier asked.

"Based on Lemurian communications we have intercepted, we suspect some early capital was from drug running near Malaysia," Lance answered.

Andrew then chimed in, "Let's let Lance talk about the main reason we're here today. Lance, give the men more information on Raul Candellario."

"He is a veteran of the Guatemalan army, won some medals of distinction for actions against the drug cartels. Oddly enough, after that, he quit the army and became an activist for the poor in Guatemala, speaking out about how the government failed to help people in the rural regions, causing them to join the drug cartels in the first place."

"Why do you think he ended up high in the Lemurian leadership?" Cortez asked.

"Military experience probably, and personally I think his good intentions were perverted by whoever recruited him. Since we have knowledge from the captive Landshire that he is one of the leaders, it is likely that he joined early on. His recruitment could be the secret to finding out the core of the Lemurian organization and its goals."

One woman got up and asked pretty abruptly, "What do you know so far about Candellario's movements in the past few years?" It was Eliza Churchill, a ranking NSA agent Lance recognized. She was talented but stern. Maybe her abruptness was because she was starting to get bored.

"Why the tone, Eliza?" Lance asked.

"We have the best hacking abilities in the world. I feel we should be able to have a larger profile on this man than what you're telling us. We should be taking this opportunity to truly study a Lemurian leader."

"What do you want me to tell you, Eliza, his grades in high school, the names of his parents? Guatemala is not a hostile country where we keep tabs on every member of their army, and Candellario wasn't even on any watch list until five days ago when Landshire gave him up. We asked the Guatemala army for any leads, but they weren't able to trace any of his friends or family to the Lemurians. They have even detained some of his former contacts from his army days for questioning. We are doing all we can to get more info on him."

"You mentioned he started to make fewer public appearances recently, around three years ago. Are we assuming that is when he started his work with the Lemurians?" Eliza asked.

"Correct," Lance answered.

"You're asking me to lead some men into this canyon to get this man," Cortez chimed in. "What do you know about how you think he will fight?"

"During the Berlin attack he was on the offensive, so it's not the same scenario, but from his vicious attack on the police department, he seems to target the leaders of an operation first. He knows how to limit a response.

For any strike force, I suggest that all the orders for the front lines be sent out by transmission. We should not give Candellario the chance to strike at our leadership," Lance said.

Another soldier asked Lance, "What is our plan for the attack of the canyon and the capture of Candellario? If we launch an all-out assault, he could kill himself or destroy as much information as he can."

"That is a valid point," Lance said. "We sent some stealth drones above the canyon to do spying. We still think that whatever the Lemurians have can't detect them. Our estimate is that they have about a hundred men in the canyon. As for how we are going to get Candellario, I will let Federico answer the question."

The Mexican agent stood up and said, "Five days ago after Lanser called Mexican intelligence about Candellario, we increased our efforts to find any links to him in Northern Mexico. We did extensive wiretapping to see if we could find anything suspicious. We were able to detect increased activity outside Copper Canyon. We started raiding cars at random, and we found the jackpot.

"We captured several Lemurians from the Congo who, in twelve hours' time, are scheduled to meet with Candellario himself, according to the information we picked up. We are going to send a group of agents led by Mr. Kekso to pose as this group. Once they are near Candellario, they will subdue him and signal the invasion. They will hold Candellario until we can send our strike force to secure him and take the base. The agents posing as the Lemurians from the Congo will have nine hours to subdue Candellario before we invade the base."

"That sounds like a solid plan," Danny said. He then turned to Andrew with worry. "Andrew, are you up for this? There seems to be a strong chance you won't make it out of this."

"It's a risk every agent takes," replied Andrew.

With apprehension Eliza Churchill of the NSA then asked, "Won't Candellario know what his soldiers look like? What if they have a code or something as a check?"

"We learned a lot from our raid on the Lemurian soldiers," Federico said. "It seems they have vague orders to cause damage but not much else and there was no sign of a them having a code. The African insurgents had orders to cause at least fifty casualties any way they knew how. They already carried out a shooting, but we were luckily able to stop them from poisoning a water supply. The last orders we retrieved from them were to head to Copper Canyon to meet Candellario. The letter did not mention he was the leader of the Lemurians in North America, but with Landshire's intelligence and what we've found, he seems to be a powerful man in the organization."

"It is good to know that our intelligence is being backed up, I am worried but the lack of the confirmation of a code, but I"ll take the risk" Andrew said.

"Indeed," Eliza said, "but I have one more question before we close this briefing. Agent Richardson, is there anything else that was mentioned of the Historian?"

"Not much else," Lance said. "There was a brief mention of him in the data from the recently captured Lemurians. They asked in a message to an unknown

Lemurian if Candellario was the Historian, to which the unknown Lemurian said no."

"Still, it is good to hear that name mentioned. It gives us evidence that the information you got from Landshire was accurate," Dan said.

"Agreed," Lance said.

Andrew then stood in front of the people at the briefing and said, "I think we all have enough information. It is time to finish the final touches to this operation. Time to finally strike back."

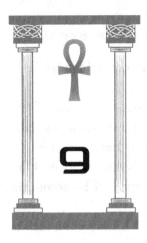

A ndrew and a few other soldiers were planning on taking a truck into Copper Canyon to infiltrate the Lemurians. Lance looked at that convoy with apprehension and a hint of jealousy. In that canyon was the man who had killed his family. Lance was so close to being able to get Candellario, yet he would not be part of the team to capture him. Lance knew, though, that he needed to lend support anywhere he could.

Dan walked up to Lance and said, "Some of us are going to wish Andrew's team luck. Do you want to come with us?"

"Sure" Lance said.

As they walked toward Andrew's convoy, Lance asked Dan, "How are we going to track Andrew in the caves?"

"We inserted a tracker under his skin, so we'll have an idea of where he is," Dan said.

"What is the best thing I can do for the mission?" Lance asked.

"Federico and I are going to monitor the tracker on Andrew to see his progress. With the briefing over, you can come and continue your role as an advisor."

"All right," Lance said begrudgingly but without complaint.

They walked outside a series of tents near the truck. With Andrew were two agents Lance did not recognize.

Andrew greeted Lance and said, "Nice to see you're here, Lance. This is Agent Michael Freeman and Agent Gloria Cutter. They will be accompanying me on this mission."

"I wish you all sincere good luck today," Lance said humbly.

Agent Freeman said, "You're Richardson, right? The guy who got the info from Landshire?"

"Yeah."

"Thank you for that," the man said happily.

"You're welcome," Lance said with a hint happiness.

Andrew reinserted himself above his two subordinates, saying, "All right, it is time to head out."

"Good luck to all of you," Danny said sincerely.

"Same here," Lance added.

"Time to go," Andrew said, and with that, he and the two agents started off in the truck toward Copper Canyon.

ndrew was nervous, but he showed no emotion. He was the most experienced agent in the group. Though he still felt some nerves, he felt that any sign of it would weaken the resolve of the other two agents.

After a while Agent Cutter asked, "Do you think we're close to the Lemurian base?"

"If the intel is accurate, we should be. The canyon is only a few klicks ahead," Andrew replied.

After a few more moments Andrew saw a man wearing body armor and holding a gun near a clearing of rocks. Andrew figured he was a Lemurian and started to slow down the truck.

The armed soldier stood out in the center of the dirt road into the canyon with a gun pointed at the truck. He gestured to Andrew and the agents to get out of the truck.

Andrew hesitantly said to the two other agents, "All right, we need to get out. We did not come this far to bow out now."

Andrew stopped the truck and got out with his arms up. The other two agents followed. The man continued to point the gun at the three of them. Andrew heard a creak behind him and looked back.

It was an ambush. Soldiers decked in even better armor came out of hidden holes, surrounding them in a strategy similar to what the Vietcong had used. Before Andrew and the other agents could say a word, they were surrounded by five soldiers.

Fear started to consume Andrew, and he began to sweat. Agent Cutter suddenly fell to the ground, followed by Agent Freeman. Then Andrew felt a sharp pain in his neck, and he fell as well. On the ground, Andrew felt his neck and found a dart, some form of tranquilizer. He retained some sense of calm as he was blacking out, realizing that the Lemurians probably did not want him dead. However, the last sight he saw before he faded out caused the calm to evaporate.

Andrew looked toward the original soldier he'd seen holding the gun, and from behind him came a brown-eyed man he easily recognized—Candellario. The Lemurian leader walked up to the soldier who had led their capture and said, "Good work. Take them to the base."

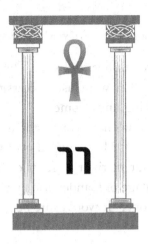

ndrew was starting to regain his vision and consciousness. He saw some figures, but they were still not clear to him. After blinking a few times, he recognized the figures to be soldiers in body armor. He tried speaking but was still too weak from the tranquilizer.

Andrew suddenly heard a yell from close by. "Bastards!" It was Agent Freeman. It seemed he was regaining full control of his body more quickly than Andrew.

Andrew could see rock walls and assumed they were in a cave. Now that he'd regained consciousness, he wanted to say something, anything to show that he was not going to take whatever the Lemurians had in store for him lying down.

Andrew noticed he and the other agents had been stripped to their underwear, causing him further distress. Emotions consumed Andrew, chief among them a desire to know what had happened while he was knocked out, but the emotions were eventually overcome by nerves.

Candellario himself walked in front of the soldiers and, addressing Agent Freeman's yell, said in a jovial manner, "Relax, soldier. You didn't think we got this far by not taking precautions, did you? The drugs we used are not harmful. They were just a necessity to make sure you brought nothing unwelcome."

Some of Andrew's hope was restored. It seemed their cover was still intact. He struggled over what he should say. He had his target right in front of him. Maybe he could take advantage of Candellario's jovial attitude. He said in a joking tone, "It would sure be great to have our clothes back."

"Your clothes are in the cavern behind me. You are free to get them as soon as the drugs wear off."

"Okay," Andrew said.

"Balogun, when the drugs wear off and you're dressed, come see me. I want to debrief you on the attacks we carried out," Candellario said, sounding like a senior officer in the military.

Andrew was silent but then remembered the name Simon Balogun was his cover. "Of course, sir," he blurted out quickly.

With that last order, Candellario left the area where Andrew and the two agents lay, some Lemurian guards still near them.

Andrew turned to Gloria and Michael and asked, "How are you doing?"

"Holding up," replied Agent Cutter.

"Good, even though I wish I did not have headache," Michael said.

"That is a side effect it will over as soon as the drugs wear off," one of the Lemurian guards said in a calm manner.

Andrew was happy about the clothes being ready, but

he was unnerved by how easily the Lemurian was able to hear them. It would be tough to get information to his agents with the Lemurians around.

Andrew thought of asking the Lemurians something useful. He had to contain a small amount of panic as he wondered how much time they had to complete the mission. He asked in a friendly tone, "How long have we been out?"

"Eight hours," replied the same Lemurian guard.

Andrew was worried. They only had one hour to get to Raul Candellario and launch the signal.

Andrew tried to move his body and was able to finally get up. "Where is Candellario? I want to start the briefing."

The Lemurian pointed down the cave. "Raul should be down through there. You should see your clothes on the way. I assume you'll want to have this meeting in more than just your underwear," he added jokingly.

Andrew got up and started walking to the back of the cave. He was caught off guard by the Lemurian's sense of humor. The fact that these killers were able to get on so easily sickened him.

Andrew then saw Raul Candellario in the back of the cave examining a shotgun. Candellario looked up at him, still holding the gun. "Hello. Here for the briefing?"

Andrew's feelings of inner disgust only grew more intense looking at this man. While not the top leader of the Lemurians, he was responsible for every attack that had happened in America. Andrew remembered the reports of some of Candellario's more sadistic attacks, which had included burning people alive, and that was not even counting the killing of his close friend's family. He had to keep this all in to preserve the mission. He mustered a simple "Yes, I would like to start."

"All right, Balogun, tell me about your missions out in the field. How many casualties have you and your team caused on your mission?" Candellario asked in a formal manner with little emotion.

"We caused twenty casualties in a small town in North Texas, but it seems that the national guard was able to stop us from poisoning a local water supply. We heard no reports of our effort working," Andrew replied, following what he'd learned from his briefing.

"All right, it is enough," Raul Candellario said. "You can spend the night here at the base, get hot food, and have a good night's sleep. We will give you some new targets in the morning."

Andrew was kind of taken aback by the machinery of the Lemurian operation and how simple its goals seemed. Candellario seemed to want so little from his soldiers. Andrew had a realization that since Candellario thought he was just another one of his soldiers, this might be the best chance to get information.

"Sir, is there any chance that we get to meet the Historian soon?"

Raul Candellario stopped moving away from Andrew and looked back. "That time will come soon, soldier, but we still have to make some preparation for the next stage," he said in a harsh tone. "I'm sure you would agree that after everything, you don't blame him for being cautious," Candellario added sympathetically.

"Fair point," Andrew said. He thought about what

information he could get from Candellario. It seemed the Lemurian leader was not going to reveal any more on the Historian to a lower-level soldier.

"What is the next step of the plan? My soldiers and I have being going off all over America risking our lives. We believe in the mission, but they are curious," Andrew said.

Raul Candellario came forward and put his hand on Andrew's shoulder. He said in a happy lilt, "Conquest, my friend. Soon we create Lemuria—a place where we run things directly."

At hearing the happiness in the Lemurian commander's voice, it took every fiber of Andrew's being to hold in his disgust. He swore to himself that this man would never have his nation, but for now he had to consume every ounce of hatred for the sake of the mission. Still, he could only force himself to say one word to keep up appearances. "Great."

Danny and Federico were seated in front of a console that showed Andrew's location in the caverns. Lance was behind them, pacing.

"We have half an hour until we strike the canyon," Danny said.

"Give it some time" Federico said. "Candellario and the Lemurians haven't disabled the tracking device. Andrew might be trying to stay in cover for as long as possible to get more information."

"Maybe," Dan said.

"I don't like this feeling. We need to strike," Lance

snapped. "Federico, is there anything I can do to help?" he asked, regaining his composure.

"I already ordered the men to prep for the strike. Just be around, Lance. You did your job on the plane. We aren't part of the same organization, but we respect you for fighting after your loss and getting us the information to lead us here," Federico said.

Lance felt like he was being humored. This role of an advisor was something Dan and Jacob had done to appease him. He seemed to be here as a symbol or a figurehead, something to inspire the people who could still fight. Lance felt he should be doing more, but he also knew his limitations. He knew he might not be in a state to have a weapon, especially with Candellario near him.

He said to Federico, "I'm going to talk to the soldiers, check on their morale."

He started off to see the soldiers, feeling that he could at least raise the morale of others. Walking slowly to the camp, he kept thinking of Candellario, the man who had killed Rachel and Tara, the man who had shot him in the head, causing him to lose his right eye. Every moment he could feel the emptiness in his head, an eternal reminder of what had happened. Candellario wasn't even the real leader, just a stooge the Historian used to carry out orders. Lance did not even have the solace of knowing the name of the man who had ordered the attack.

The soldiers in the camp looked at Lance with respect as he approached. He considered himself a modest man, but he wasn't going to lie to himself: it felt good to be respected. Feeling useless near his family's killer, he would take any boost of confidence he could get. The soldiers started moving, grabbing their guns and walking away from the camp. Lance asked one of the soldiers running by him, "What are you doing?"

"Getting ready, sir. We're getting into formation. It's almost time to invade the canyon."

Seeing the soldiers spring into action while knowing that he was expected to stay reignited Lance's frustration and the feeling that he needed to act. Without thinking further, Lance saw an abandoned handgun on a crate near one of the soldiers and took it.

Andrew's time was running out. It was mere minutes until the attack by Cortez's men. Candellario was walking away with his back to Andrew. This would be Andrew's best chance to knock out Candellario and operate the beacon to call the strike force.

Andrew looked down the cave. For the briefing Candellario had taken him to a secluded part of the complex of caves, which seemed like a grave oversight on Candellario's part. He probably thought it would serve him best if he needed to kill Andrew for some reason, since he wouldn't have to deal with any interference from the rest of Andrew's team, but that decision was going to pay off for Andrew now.

Andrew saw a rock on the ground, lifted it, and hit Candellario on the back of the head, causing him to fall down. Andrew examined Candellario. He was breathing but at a much more depressed rate. To Andrew's surprise, he seemed to have easily knocked out the Lemurian. It was time to activate the beacon and alert the strike force.

Andrew took out a knife he had on his person, cut

into his leg, took out the beacon, and activated it. The pain of cutting into his own leg made him crouch down near the wall of the cave.

Candellario was suddenly standing in front of him, aiming a handgun at him. "Impressive, hiding a tracker underneath your skin. I did not expect an American agent to be willing to go so far to hide something."

Andrew felt confused and scared at seeing a man he knew was willing to do despicable acts pointing a gun at him. "How are you standing? You were knocked out."

"If you are so surprised at someone having the ability to slow their heart rate and breathing, then perhaps I was impressed with your skill too soon, Balogun, or whatever your name is," Candellario said in a confident taunt.

Andrew was still bleeding after the process of getting the transmitter out from under his skin. He was kneeling on the cave floor in visible pain. Andrew, in his anger, said, "You failed, Raul. They know where you are. In a few short minutes we are going to completely control this base. You have failed."

"I have prepared for this possibility. I will be able to stall for enough time to destroy all information in this base. By the time any more of your friends enter these caves, I will be gone, and this base will be useless," the Lemurian snarled.

"I am prepared to die," Andrew said. "This was a mission I knew I might not come back from."

"Maybe you are prepared to die," Candellario said, "but your superiors will prefer to save you. They will do anything to keep you alive."

He then yelled to the back of the cave, "Men, assemble!"

Andrew saw a sight that sickened him to the pit of his stomach. Out came Agents Freeman and Cutter in handcuffs with tape muffling their voices.

"How?" Andrew asked Candellario in a panic, without much thought.

"I give you credit for successfully ambushing me. You showed me that I need to be more careful, but you could not have thought you were the only person who had safeguards in place. I told my men to take your two friends hostage here if I didn't make it back in ten minutes."

"If they could speak, they would tell you the same thing I told you. We are willing to die to die to stop you!" Andrew yelled.

"Well, one of them will have that chance," Candellario replied coldly.

Candellario raised his handgun toward Agents Cutter and Freeman. They were both clearly screaming beneath the gags. He shot Cutter in the head, causing her to fall quickly to her death. Agent Freeman started tearing up and continued to make muffled yells through the gag.

Candellario continued in a serious, cold manner, "All right, the troops could be here any second."

He pointed to a random soldier. "You, take the body and put it near the entrance the army are mostly likely to enter through. I want them to see it," he added coldly.

Candellario then pointed to Andrew and said, "Take whoever this man is to the other hostages."

"Other hostages?" Andrew asked nervously.

"Yes, we have captured about a hundred locals and have them in a cavern below, something to use in case I ever needed a bargaining chip," Candellario said.

Andrew wanted to say something in response to Candellario's brutality, but he was growing fatigued. Seeing one of his agents die had taken a lot out of him. He felt that he needed to say something, though, anything. He could not be led away in silence. "What are you going to do with Freeman?" he asked in desperation.

"I am going to free him as proof that there could be a chance for your survival if they listen to me," Candellario said.

"What do you mean?" Andrew asked quickly.

"I'm going to talk to your friends," Candellario said.

He then looked at Andrew with anger and snapped, "You will not get the better of us today." With that Candellario started to walk away.

Raul Candellario was walking down one of the cave passageways underneath Copper Canyon. Despite his defiant stare, he was nervous and started to sweat. "Antonio, come here."

A Lemurian soldier came close to him and said, "What is it, General?"

"Get men at every entryway, and send ten people to the server in the large cavern with the files and start destroying every piece of information we have. Burn any paperwork. Then wait for further orders," Candellario said.

"What are you going to do, sir?" the Lemurian soldier asked.

"I am going to negotiate," Candellario said.

Lance was sneaking behind the soldiers. He was thinking of breaking rank and attempting to go in the canyon to find Candellario himself. He was conflicted. He couldn't stand around being useless when his family's killer was so close to him, but at the same time Danny had helped him get closer to Candellario and it would be wrong to break Danny's trust. But could he forgive himself for ignoring his shot at revenge? Lance thought of the state of his daughter's body when the rescue workers found her, a bullet wound through her head disfiguring her face. Lance had cried himself to sleep many nights thinking of the fear Tara must have felt in her final moments, and the man who had done that to her was close.

Lance's contemplation was finally broken when an unwelcome voice came from a loudspeaker. "Soldiers, this is Raul Candellario. I have captured the team you sent in. Your mission has failed. The leader of your spies is being held with a group of over a hundred civilian hostages. If you want any information from this base or the release of the hostages, come to the large cave in the northwest section of the canyon, and we can negotiate a deal. You have thirty minutes to send a negotiating party, or else I will kill every hostage." The message ended.

Lance was filled with emotion but couldn't say anything. The feelings of fear, anger, and self-loathing started to consume him. Somehow the bastard had done it. He'd found a way to stand off against an army.

Danny Smith came over. "Are you coming to meet with Candellario?"

Lance stood in silence. In a way he wanted this, the chance to confront the man and even the chance to kill him, but now he was unsure. Lance replied with a simple "I don't know."

12

Lance was walking behind Danny and Federico Cortez. They were heading to the caves to meet with Candellario. He felt it might not be best to dwell on his emotions, better to bury himself in the job and treat this like any other moment. He thought about why Candellario would even offer a chance of negotiation. Lance remembered the pictures of Tara's body and the last time he'd seen her alive. With reports of similar attacks pouring in throughout the country, there were many more like her. Lance knew this man was willing to do anything to win. The butcher was close, and all must be done to end his evil.

"Dan, can I talk to you for a second?"

"Sure," Dan replied, dropping back to walk next to Lance.

"I don't think it's a good idea to do this. We should tell Federico to launch the attack now. We should save any hostages we can, but getting the information in those caves comes first. When Candellario comes out, we capture him and start the invasion."

"Andrew is in there."

70

"Andrew knew what he was getting into," Lance said quickly. "I know him well enough to know that he would not want a terrorist like Candellario to be allowed to roam free in order to save him."

"That might be true, but there's no reason we shouldn't try. Look at your success with Landshire. Maybe Candellario will be willing to give the Historian up in exchange for immunity. We owe it to Andrew and all those people in the caves to at least try to save their lives."

"Dan, you know how much I hate that man, and even I will give him a chance to surrender if it will save lives, but I don't have hopes that he'll do that. You saw how committed to the Lemurians Landshire was, and he was only a minor soldier. Do you think the head of the Lemurians in North America will give up?"

"I wouldn't be so dismissive. A lot of times the higher-ups are more cowardly. Have you ever studied Hamas? The lower-level guys are willing to blow themselves up, while some of the higher-ups sit in mansions drinking, resting, and having sex with underage women."

"I saw him in the line of duty. That is more than anyone else here," Lance let out in frustration. "I have a strong feeling that Candellario is committed to his cause. Right now he is living in a cave and for the past year has probably spent his time in hiding across America planning," Lance said with a clear sense of pessimism.

"Tell this to Federico. The hostages are Mexican citizens. He probably will have more skin in this game. Even if I wanted to launch the attack now, I don't think he would let me."

"All right."

Lance sped up into a short jog to catch up to Federico Cortez and a few other Mexican soldiers with him. Lance could tell from how he was walking that he was scared. This was probably one of the biggest operations the Mexican Army has conducted since the war broke out, and he was in charge of it. Lance wasn't unaware of the burden he would be placing on Federico. Federico would be condemning his own countrymen to death if he listened to Lance, but Candellario had to be stopped at all costs. One tragedy was better than a thousand more.

"Federico!" Lance yelled.

Federico turned around to reveal a stern face that was focused on the task at hand. "What is it, Richardson?"

"We shouldn't talk to him. He's not going to give us anything you want. As the only person that has had any contact with Candellario, I think this is purely a scam to buy time to destroy as much information as he can."

"Richardson, with at least a hundred civilians in there, I have to try. We are fighting today to save lives, and you want me to not even attempt to save them?" Federico responded.

"Do you honestly think there is any chance we can save the hostages and get the information we need to stop him?" Lance asked in a sympathetic but worried tone.

"I've been thinking … We hate the guy, but he must know that we probably won't trust him. He must know that he has to give us something for us to even consider negotiating," Federico said.

"Dan thinks Candellario might offer to give up the Historian if we give him immunity," Lance said.

"Do you agree with him?" Federico asked.

"Not really. Dan himself isn't completely sure if that is what Candellario wants; it's just something Dan thinks he could want," Lance replied.

"Does Dan think we should talk to Candellario, or does he agree with you?" asked Federico.

"He thinks we should see what Candellario is offering before we start an attack," Lance said.

"I can't just let a hundred Mexican civilians die without at least trying to save their lives," Federico told Lance sympathetically.

"More than that could die if we let this chance to raid the base go to waste. Thousands have died in America and Mexico because of the Lemurians. I think that deep down you know this is the best chance to stop the Lemurians in their tracks right here."

Federico sighed. "You're not going to change my mind, and I'm not going to change yours, but as long as this operation relies on the Mexican Army, you know that my ruling will stand. You can either leave now, or you can come with me to the talks."

"I'll come. I disagree, but I will do whatever it takes to aid this mission," Lance said respectfully.

"I am glad to hear it," Federico said as he turned away to start heading toward the caves.

Lance stood still for a bit to wait for Dan. He didn't want to do this, but he hadn't been lying to Federico. He knew Federico's motivations were not born out of malice, and as much he hated to admit it, he wondered if he would feel the same as Federico if it was anyone except Candellario.

Dan could tell simply by the look on Lance's face that he hadn't been successful. Dan gave Lance a sympathetic look and walked with him toward the caves. Without words, a consensus formed to continue to follow Federico to the meeting point.

13

Lance continued walking close to Dan, Federico, and a few other Mexican soldiers as they headed to the clearing. They were close enough to see the outline of some men who looked like soldiers about one hundred yards away. The men were standing in a line formation with one man in the center whom Lance could recognize even from a distance.

Candellario's eyes were the same as on that ill-fated day, but he was older than Lance remembered. Perhaps not bleeding to death gave him a clearer view of the man. Candellario looked to be in his fifties. He had some gray in his hair and some lines on his face. Lance was starting to feel sick to his stomach. Merely being in the presence of that man drove him to the brink of illness. His hand began twitching. His anger was starting to trickle out of his mind and into his body. He made the conscious decision to try to keep his face stoic. He did not want to give Candellario the satisfaction of seeing him in this state. He also did not want Dan to see him this way either, being devastated by someone's mere presence.

They continued walking closer until they were about

fifteen yards away from Candellario and the Lemurian soldiers, at which point Candellario yelled, "Stop!"

Federico, concealing his own anger, said sternly, "We know why we are here. Let's not get into pleasantries. Why are you bothering with this negotiation? What do you want to come out of it?"

"I am going to offer you all the chance to be heroes," Candellario replied.

"What do you mean?" Dan asked.

"I will free all the hostages, and I will give you the location of some lower-level bases that we have conducted attacks from," Candellario said.

"Whatever is in those caves is more important," Lance snapped loudly. "That's the only reason you would be willing to give up what you are offering."

"Why even come here, if you are not going to listen to what I have to say?" Candellario responded with a smug sense of superiority.

"We are here because of the innocent people you have imprisoned, not because we have any sense of respect for you," Lance hissed back with clear hatred.

"He brings up a good point," Federico said in a businesslike tone. "How do we know the hostages are okay?"

Candellario signaled one of his soldiers with a tilt of his head, and the soldier handed him a tablet. Candellario pulled up a video feed on the tablet that showed people huddling together. He then took a piece of paper out of his pocket and said, "Here is a list of every hostage I was able to identify. I don't have access to your intelligence, but I am confident that it will show that all of them are missing with no bodies found. That should be proof enough."

Federico walked forward and grabbed the list from Candellario. He turned to one of the Mexican soldiers near him and said, "Go back to the camp and run the names through the computer. Let's see if this is true."

"Feel free," Candellario taunted.

The soldier took the list. "I'll radio you once I see if his intel is accurate," he told Federico. He then started walking back to the camp.

Lance's nerves were still on edge from being near Candellario. He thought of Andrew, if only to get the image of Tara's body out of his head. "What about our people, the agents you captured?"

"The woman is dead. I still have the agent that was using the name Simon Balogun," Candellario said in his businesslike manner.

"That still leaves one agent unaccounted for," Lance said angrily.

Candellario waved his arm to signal two soldiers, who brought Agent Freeman forward with a bag over his head. Lance could tell Freeman had been gagged by the audible but muffled screams.

"Release him!" Lance yelled uncontrollably.

The Lemurian soldiers threw Freeman on the ground before Lance and the others and walked away. Lance rushed over, took the bag off Freeman's head, and ungagged him. Agent Freeman started to breathe more heavily, finally being free of the gag. Lance helped him up, slinging the agent's arm over his shoulders to help him walk.

Lance was sick of being here, having to deal with Candellario, seeing the smugness of the man even after everything he had done. Helping Freeman was an opportunity for Lance to get out of there before he did something he'd regret. Lance yelled to Danny and Federico, "I'm going to help him back to camp. I'll debrief him there."

"Roger," Federico said.

As Lance and Agent Freeman walked back to the camp, Freeman said in a voice of extreme exhaustion, "They … killed … Cutter."

"I know," Lance said. "We will find her body and send it to her family."

Lance kept walking toward the camp with Agent Freeman. He was getting tired, but he saw a tent in the distance where they could rest. Freeman was starting to pant. Lance thought it would be a good thing to get him talking. Although his body seemed bruise, he didn't look like he'd been tortured. Lance figured he could use some conversation to keep his mind off what he'd experienced. "Would you like some water, when we get back to the camp?"

"Yeah," he said. He seemed to be in shock still. He was still panting and wasn't looking Lance in the eye.

"Do you want to talk about what happened in there?" Lance asked.

"We have to attack," Freeman said forcefully. "We have to attack them now!" he yelled, ignoring Lance's inquiry.

Lance agreed with the agent, but he wondered what Freeman had seen in there to make him so sure, to make him yell out uncontrollably. Despite Lance's own desire to attack, he was aware that Freeman might want to do so as revenge for them beating him and killing Cutter. Lance certainly was no stranger to that feeling, especially when it came to Candellario, but even he felt a need to confirm whether the agent's desire to attack came from accurate intel.

"How do you know?" he asked.

"They had the bag over my head, but I smelled smoke. The Lemurians are probably burning as much as they can," Freeman said.

It wasn't absolute proof, but Freeman's assumption that the smoke meant the Lemurians were destroying files made sense.". Lance said, "Freeman, I agree with you. I want to attack as well. I just need to convince the others. Is there anything else you can tell me?"

"I just know!" the agent yelled as Lance led him to a tent in the camp. "He was completely loyal to the mission. When we were undercover, there were no signs that he was second-guessing himself or that he would hurt the Lemurians to save himself. We should have been in charge of this mission. We conceded too much to the Mexicans."

"I agree with you, but you can't blame the Mexican government for being paranoid after the satellite hacks. Frankly, they are being more open than we would be," Lance replied quickly.

Lance was somewhat unnerved about quickly agreeing with Agent Freeman. He wasn't lying to Freeman, but it wasn't in his authority to launch an attack on the caves even if he wanted to. False hope was something the agent didn't need after the ordeal he'd just gone through.

Following up, to be sympathetic, Lance said, "I agree with you, Michael, but I'm going to need more evidence than that for me to convince Federico to put the lives of Mexican civilians at risk."

"There is nothing more," Freeman said with a hint of regret, Lance hated looking at the agent. He had a look of defeat in his eyes, a look Lance might have had when he was on the ground before Candellario that horrible day outside of Berlin.

Lance's mind was cleared of everything but his hatred of that one man. The knowledge that he was closer to Candellario than he'd ever thought possible but couldn't attack consumed him until he had no words to describe his thoughts.

Lance stood there in silence looking at Agent Freeman, starting to sweat, until he had a moment of clarity. Lance felt a new confidence. He now knew what he had to do to stop Candellario. If Federico wasn't going to attack, if he was going to fall for Candellario's trick, then Lance had to do whatever it took to make sure that the Lemurian base was invaded. Lance was more focused than he had been since he'd started this operation, maybe more focused than at any time since the Berlin attacks.

In the tent with Agent Freeman, Lance started to arm himself, putting on a SWAT-like military uniform and grabbing a rifle, several handguns, and finally several grenades.

Seeing Lance grab all these weapons, Agent Freeman got visibly distressed. "What are you doing?" the agent asked.

With his head turned away from the agent toward

the door of the tent, Lance said sternly but confidently, "Agent, I think it would be good for you to not know anything else. I'm just going to make sure that Candellario pays for what he has done."

Agent Freeman looked at Lance with clear understanding, and after a lengthy pause, he looked away, as if he knew what Lance was about to do but wasn't going to try to stop it.

Lance walked out of the tent quietly. He was clearly armed, but most of the soldiers around the camp were armed as well, so his gear shouldn't raise suspicion. Despite this, he moved slowly in order not to tempt fate. Lance scanned the area for a potential blind spot. When he found one, he escaped from the camp. He took off at a jog, careful to avoid being too loud, but as he moved away from the camp, he ran faster.

Lance's mind was still in a trancelike state focused on his task: stopping Candellario at all costs. Lance was going to find an unmanned space and launch a grenade. He knew whatever deal Federico made with Candellario would end at the first sign of trouble. The soldiers would hear the grenade go off and attack the base. They probably would eventually realize that Lance had forced the attack, but by that time they would have found something in the base to vindicate him, and if not, Lance was willing to take responsibility for what he planned to do.

Lance thought of Danny and stopped for a moment. What if he started the attack right when Danny was near a Lemurian soldier, maybe putting him into the conflict unprepared? But the contemplation did not last. Lance was willing to risk the lives of the civilians; it would be wrong to stop only because someone he knew personally would be in danger too. After that last doubt, Lance was once again consumed with a strong sense of determination and even pride. He was going to stop Candellario today.

With that, Lance took two grenades and launched them into the field. Once they exploded, Lance knew that his mission was finished, but he wondered if his desperate gambit had worked. Had the soldiers heard the grenades? Had he been careful enough in leaving the camp, or had someone seen him leave with the weapons and reported there was a possibility of him doing something like this? But he then saw a welcome sight: military helicopters going toward the caves. His mission was a success. Lance had only one more thing to do before the night was over. He cocked his rifle and headed toward the caves.

14

ance could hear gunshots in the dark, and he figured the fighting had started elsewhere. He knew this could very well be his last day as a free man, but before this was over, he was going to kill Raul Candellario. He continued on the path toward the caves for a while. He heard more gunshots in the distance, in another part of the canyon. Through all his focus, Lance had some fear that at any moment a sniper would kill him. He was not ashamed of this fear. There was a danger to thinking you were unstoppable. After a few minutes that felt like hours to Lance, he saw an entrance to the caves.

Lance heard yelling in Spanish. He wasn't sure whether it was Lemurians or some of Cortez's men. Lance was frustrated. Not knowing a second language was always something Lance had considered a personal flaw in his career as a CIA agent. He figured the only thing he could do was go up to the entrance for a closer look. Lance could not see any soldiers and was worried that some Lemurians had spotted him and were hiding around him, ready to make their move. Lance then heard a different noise, one of a vehicle. The vehicle looked like a small truck a company would use for shipping, but there were no logos on it. Maybe the Lemurians were planning a retreat, trying to take supplies out of the caves before Federico's team found them.

Lance quickly hid behind a large rock. Three soldiers walked out of the entrance. They were armed and in body armor, but the armor was different from what Federico's forces wore, so Lance assumed they were Lemurians. They started talking again in Spanish. Two of the soldiers walked in front of the truck while one of them stayed behind at the entrance. They were yelling to each other in a panic, making Lance think he was right about them retreating. One of the Lemurians got into the truck and started to drive away. The remaining two Lemurians took up post at the entrance. Maybe they were planning to guard more transports escaping through this route. Lance did not recognize most of what they were saying, but he did pick up a mention of Candellario, which piqued his interest. There was no doubt in his mind.

Lance took out a knife and slowly crept toward the men. There were several rock formations between him and the entrance where the two Lemurians were stationed. Lance inched forward in a crouch, using the rocks as cover, until he got close to the Lemurians. Lance had an idea. He found a pebble and threw it at the corner of a rock formation off to the side of the entrance.

The Lemurians heard the noise, and one of them gestured to the other that he was going to check it out. Lance could tell from his position what path the Lemurian soldier would take to approach the rock formation. Lance crouched down and moved toward where he'd thrown the pebble. When the Lemurian got there, Lance jumped him from behind and grabbed him in a sleeper hold. The man started to struggle, but Lance was strong enough to stop him from making too much noise and was able to finish the sleeper hold.

Lance was happy he'd been able to avoid killing the man. He had killed before, but he was proud of avoiding it when he could. The other Lemurian guard was starting to panic. He knew it shouldn't be taking so long to check on the noise. He raised his gun and moved toward Lance's position. Lance had a feeling he wasn't going to be as lucky in avoiding conflict with this man. If Lance fired his gun, the noise could signal reinforcements, so he grabbed his knife instead. As he leaned against the rock wall, he heard the Lemurians' footsteps approaching from around the corner, and he prepared his knife.

The man came around the corner, and Lance threw his knife into the man's neck. The man started to gag immediately. He dropped his gun and grabbed his neck. Blood was pouring around the knife in his neck. Lance knew the man only had a few minutes left to live before he would bleed out. He snapped the man's neck with his hands to finish the job quickly. It was finished. Lance now had his chance to go into the caves and hopefully finish off Candellario.

On his way to the entrance, Lance thought about how the man he'd just killed had made an amateur mistake. He'd gone around the corner quickly without considering the danger. That was something anyone with basic training should have avoided. Lance had many words to describe the Lemurians, but despite his hatred, *incompetent* had never been one of them, although it didn't take an extremely trained man to mow down civilians.

As he approached the entrance, he heard gunshots and the moaning of death. Lance figured Federico's men were closing in, pushing the Lemurians farther into the caves. Lance ran into the entrance. He didn't see any Lemurians, but he stayed cautious. Lance was through the main entryway and had still not seen any Lemurians, but the sounds of gunshots grew louder. Lance was now in a long cave with openings on all sides. It looked like a hall with many pathways branching off. Lance saw some shadows moving quickly across the cave wall. From their outlines he could tell that two men were running quickly toward the main cave, where Lance was. Lance ducked down one of the pathways into an adjacent cave and once again hid, pressed against the cave wall. Two Lemurians ran into the main cave. They seemed panicked and were talking in Spanish. Lance heard the name Raul. He was near.

Lance thought of using this opportunity to kill the two men and move down the caves. He sensed they were amateurs like the ones he'd deposed of outside the caves, but if he made a ruckus, he could warn other Lemurians and maybe even Candellario himself. Lance moved farther along the wall of the adjacent cave to avoid being seen. He then lay down on the ground, further reducing his chances of being spotted.

Lance then saw what he was looking for. Five Lemurians were marching in a diamond formation behind the two men he'd seen earlier. He sensed that they must be mobilizing themselves this way because they were guarding something, or someone, important.

Three more Lemurian soldiers came around the bend of the cave, with two of them guarding an inescapable presence, Raul Candellario. Lance's vision was obscured somewhat. He couldn't see Candellario's exact facial expression, but he could see enough to recognize the man. Here was his chance to get his revenge, to bring Candellario to justice, but Lance was worried. Did the fact that Candellario was here mean that he'd killed Danny and Federico when the fighting started? The thought of his best friend being killed by the same man who had taken his family sickened Lance, but that thought had to wait. It was time to finish the mission.

The Lemurians were getting closer to his location. It was almost time for him to make his move. Lance grabbed one of his grenades and threw it into the central cave at the Lemurians, surprising them. He immediately ran into the central cave and jumped behind some rocks sticking out of the wall. Some of the Lemurians saw Lance running toward them and started to aim their guns at him, but then the grenade went off.

The two Lemurians closest to the grenade had their legs blown off and died instantly. One more was on the ground yelling in agony. Lance couldn't tell where the other Lemurians were, because the grenade had launched a huge smoke cloud up in the air. But it was clear that he'd successfully panicked them. Gunshots fired. On reflex, Lance launched a second grenade through the smoke, hoping to clear out a few more of them. The explosion went off, but this time there were no screams. The

Lemurians must have pushed farther into the cave than Lance thought. Lance started to get up, but bullets shot through the dust in the air, so he took cover again. The dust started to settle, and the outlines of the Lemurians became visible. He shot one through the head, killing him. Even after losing his eye, Lance still had good aim.

Lance returned to cover. He engaged two more Lemurians in a shoot-out till he eventually killed both of them. He moved forward into the cave. Another Lemurian came from behind the bend, and Lance quickly shot him down. Lance pressed his body up against the cave wall. The wall wrapped around into the entrance of a new cave, and he quickly looked around the corner.

Several soldiers stood in formation aiming guns. Before Lance pulled his head back, he saw Raul Candellario's stern face, which showed little emotion except sheer determination. Candellario, without any hint of worry, took a page from Lance's playbook and threw a grenade at him.

Lance jumped back as fast as he could, ducking behind another rock structure. The grenades went off. They were loud and set off a ringing in Lance's ears, but he was able to avoid injury. Bullets rushed past him. Lance's ears were still ringing, but he felt it was time to fight back.

Lance started to return fire. He looked over the rock he was using for cover. He saw some of the Lemurian grunts fighting him, but there was no sign of Candellario. Lance wondered if Candellario had used the time the grenades had bought him to escape farther into the caves. Lance kept firing at the men. He continued to pick them off, but he could not deny he was getting tired. He hadn't slept in over thirty-six hours, and the constant adrenaline that had been pumping through his body since the start of the assault was wearing off. Lance was able to shoot one more Lemurian coming close to him. His gun was then out of ammo, and he started to reload.

Almost immediately, Candellario appeared around the bend in a sprint and leveled an assault rifle at Lance's head. Lance was in a panic. The only thing he could do before Candellario fired was grab his knife. He threw it at Candellario as a last gambit to stop him from getting the killing shot.

Candellario saw the knife coming and jumped out of the way. The jump caused him to lose his grip on the rifle, which clattered to the ground. Nimbly, he grabbed a handgun at his side while still midair. When he landed the jump, he shot Lance with the handgun.

The bullet grazed Lance's shoulder. He felt some pain but nothing major. Lance was able to pull his sidearm while Candellario caught his balance. Lance fired and hit Candellario in the chest, causing him to fall to the ground. Lance knew Candellario wasn't dead yet, not with that body armor on, but the shot gave Lance a chance to finish him off. Lance jumped out from behind his cover and took off toward Candellario. He was going to shoot Candellario in the head, to end him once and for all.

Lance felt a sense of glee as he ran toward the wounded Candellario. He'd never felt happy killing someone before, but it was impossible to deny that he truly was going to enjoy seeing this man die. In that moment, the twenty-year CIA veteran was replaced with a mourning father and husband who had his chance at revenge.

As Lance got close to Candellario, almost close enough to get the perfect shot, Raul Candellario snapped to life. He grabbed the assault rifle he'd dropped beside him earlier and in a quick move sent out a spray of bullets. He didn't have time to aim, but the move worked well enough for a bullet to hit Lance's shoulder blade, causing him to fall. Now Lance was on the ground, and Candellario was preparing for his finishing shot, aiming his assault rifle at Lance's head.

Lance couldn't let it end like this. He may have failed in killing Candellario, but he was not going to let the man who had taken his family finish him off. He used his cunning, honed from his years of experience, to produce one final trick.

Lance screamed, *"Wait!"*

Candellario did lower his gun, but not because of Lance's shout alone. Lance, bloody on the cave floor, was clutching a grenade, ready to pull out the pin. The two men were close enough that if Lance pulled the pin, they would both die.

For a moment there was silence. Knowing that any move could be their last, both men were frozen. There was finally a break in the fighting.

Lance didn't know what to do. He'd managed to stall Candellario, but now he didn't know his next move. Candellario was less injured. Lance's only hope was to stall until reinforcements could arrive. He had to convince Candellario it was suicidal to try to kill him with his hand on the grenade.

They were still frozen in total silence except for breathing. Lance feared that the longer the silence continued, the more confident Candellario would be that he could kill Lance before he could activate the grenade. Lance was trapped on the ground in front of Candellario again, but this time he had something to give Candellario pause. He thought of what he could say to Candellario while he had this chance to confront him, and his anger for the person in front of him consumed him once more.

"*Do you remember me?*" Lance yelled with all the energy his wounded body had.

"Yes, in Berlin and in the conference with Federico Cortez," Candellario said in a reserved manner.

Lance was taken aback by Candellario's nearly emotionless answer. It took him back to that night, to how Candellario had acted before he'd shot him the first time. Lance thought about his next words. He wanted to play up his desperation to convince Candellario that he could do it, that he could kill the both of them.

"I'm here, Raul," Lance taunted. "Am I still just a statistic?"

"We all are statistics to some degree," Candellario said in the same emotionless voice. "It's true you avoided being one of those who died on that day, but at best you will still only end up as one of many names on a monument after this war is over."

Lance didn't think he could actually do it, activate the grenade and kill himself along with Candellario, but hearing those words made him want to do it. He could finish this once and for all. He could see the Lemurians lose, and his smiling face would be the last thing Raul Candellario ever saw in this world.

While in the midst of these thoughts, there was a

CORY ANTHONY MADONNA

new development, something Lance could not ignore—
gunfire in the distance.

Candellario started to look around, nervous. It seemed
he did not know who the men behind him were. Lance
caught a break. Candellario started to move away slowly.
Apparently he was going to take the chance, risk his life
to see if Lance had the guts to do what he'd threatened.

"Don't!" Lance yelled in a loud snarl.

Candellario turned slightly, about to make a break for
it. Lance tugged on the pin, not enough to activate the
grenade but hopefully enough to tell Candellario he was
serious about ending it.

Candellario turned back around, visibly panicked.
Lance's move seemed to have worked. Lance wondered
what he was doing here. If those were Lemurians coming,
he would have little chance against them. They might
even be lucky enough to shoot him before he could pull
the grenade's pin and kill Candellario.

Lance also wondered why his plan was working. Why
was Candellario waiting? The more reasonable thing to
do would be to risk running. Candellario's choices were
to stay here in front of Lance with the grenade, waiting,
or to try to escape. If he stayed and Federico's troops
came, there was a strong chance he would be captured
and interrogated, something that would be a great harm
to the Lemurians.

Lance had a feeling the answer to why Candellario
stayed was simple. Despite Candellario's best attempt
to remain emotionless, Lance could tell that, even after
everything he'd done to cause death and destruction,
Candellario still wanted to live. He still valued his life.

A person valuing his or her own life was something that Lance had never thought he would hold against someone, even someone who was his enemy. Lance was proud of not succumbing to suicide after the loss of this family, proud of the value he'd placed on his life. But the fact that Candellario valued his life made Lance hate him more than ever. Maybe this hypocrisy was because of what Jacob had told him back in Virginia, that it was different when someone killed your own, or maybe it was the rhetoric of the Lemurians getting to him, Candellario calling him and his family statistics back in Berlin. Candellario had said he was gunning down civilians for the sake of a news report, and now here he stood willing to possibly hurt his own cause to save his life. Lance knew it would feel good to kill and defeat Candellario in his final moments.

Raul Candellario grimaced slightly but tried to keep his composure. "I am going to leave," he finally said in a fairly calm voice.

"No. Stay," Lance snarled. "Today, one way or another, you are going to pay for the things you have done."

"Pay for the things I have done," Candellario said with a bit of a condescending tone. "Do you know how many people around the world want the CIA to pay for the things it has done, like the corrupt organizations and leaders it has supported to rid the world of the Soviet Union? And the CIA is at least known to be controversial. What about the people you Americans call heroes?"

Candellario's voice grew stronger. "Abraham Lincoln ordered cities in the South to be burned down during the Civil War, and the firebombings of Tokyo and Dresden killed more people than anything the Lemurians have done, and that war is considered your country's crowning moment."

Lance heard Candellario's points. Despite his deep hatred, he knew that Candellario probably didn't see himself as evil, that he had to have some internal logic to his actions, but Lance rejected his logic. "I'm not going to deny those things were done, even to you. But all those things you mentioned were done to fight greater evils— Nazism, imperialism, Communism, slavery. When you attacked, we were in a golden age. The number of people in poverty was the lowest in world history, and the era of war between nations was at an end. In this time of peace, you Lemurians came and ruined it!" Lance yelled.

"If that's what you thought the world was, you must be either more arrogant or more ignorant than I thought," Candellario snarled.

Lance grew more enraged. He felt more certain than ever that it would be worth dying to kill Candellario.

Candellario seemed to regret angering Lance. He probably noticed the look of pure hatred in Lance's eyes and realized that Lance was willing to die to end him. He exclaimed in near desperation, "The Historian is still out there, our leader, the man who planned the attacks. If you kill me now, he wins. You will die without even knowing the name of the man responsible for the death of your family." Candellario tried to go back to his emotionless facade, but some signs of stress still broke through.

Lance was entranced by thought of the Historian. He wondered what kind of man could have founded the Lemurians and gotten Candellario to follow him. In his moment of hesitation, Candellario ran. Still thinking of the Historian, Lance started to pull on the pin of the grenade, but in the end, he could not do it. Candellario had escaped.

Lance lay down on the cave floor. He was depressed Candellario had gotten away, and he knew there was something in him that had let Candellario escape, something he hated to admit but knew to be true. Even after everything that had happened, he shared something with his worst enemy: he still valued his life.

Lance heard footsteps getting louder and grabbed the grenade again. If they were Lemurians, he would blow them up and have one last act of rebellion in his life, but as the footsteps grew closer, Lance heard his own name—Richardson—spoken in a sympathetic tone.

It was a group of Mexican soldiers. Lance was saved for the moment. As he slipped into unconsciousness from the blood loss, he wondered whether he'd accomplished anything by coming here.

15

A few hours later, Lance woke from his unconsciousness in a medical tent in Federico's encampment. Feeling better, he opened his eyes and saw a blurry figure he couldn't recognize. "Lance," the figure said in a surprised tone.

Lance's eyesight started to improve. Seeing the face of Federico Cortez, Lance wondered what was happening. Maybe Cortez was here to tell him the charges against him.

"Are you all right, Lance?" Cortez asked.

"Yeah," Lance responded, surprised by Cortez's sympathetic tone. Lance was preoccupied with thoughts about going to jail and what would happen to him. "I'm surprised you're not more upset after what I've done."

The grizzled veteran of the Mexican Army sighed. "I was angry with you for not following my orders, but that doesn't seem important now."

Lance was scared, thinking there had been some type of disaster. He still didn't know Dan's fate either. "What happened? Is Dan okay? Did we find any information?"

"We were able to secure some computer files and documents, no thanks to me," Federico said, clear disappointment and anguish in his voice. "You were right, Lance. They were going to destroy everything. If you'd listened to me, everyone who died in the operation would have done so in vain."

"What about Dan and Andrew? Are they okay?" Lance asked with concern.

"They're both okay. The assault didn't start until Candellario went back into the caves, and some of my commandos liberated the cavern Andrew was in before he was shot. Half of the other hostages were not as lucky," Cortez said solemnly.

Lance put his head down, remembering the other hostages and the Machiavellian decision he'd made in going into the caves. He lifted his head to look Cortez in the eyes and asked with sadness in his voice, "How many deaths?"

"We have thirty confirmed. Ten more are still in critical condition in the medical tent, so the number will probably go up," Cortez replied sternly.

Lance didn't say anything. He still believed that logically his decision was for the best, but the casualties tore at him. He sat in front of Federico in silence, just breathing heavily, and then sighed at what had happened.

Federico noticed Lance's sadness and tried to console him. "Lance, we both know that people were going to die today, no matter what. At least the choices you made will help others."

Federico went silent himself for a moment. "I failed, Lance. We were able to capture a few of Candellario's men. They told us Candellario was never going to give us anything and always planned to kill the hostages.

Everyone would have died if you'd listened to me. After my final report, I'm going to resign," he said, holding back tears.

Lance did not like seeing Federico like this. Federico was a good man, despite their disagreements. However, knowing that he'd made the right choice did manage to make Lance feel better.

He looked to the depressed Federico and said, "Securing some captured soldiers, saving the majority of the hostages, and let's not forget saving my ass—you did good, Federico. You are a good man and a good soldier. The fact you feel this way shows you're worthy of your job. If you quit over this while the people above you stay after having failure after failure, it would be a huge loss."

Federico gave Lance a small smile after hearing this. Just then a soldier came through the tent door. He seemed worried and told Federico something in Spanish in a panicked voice.

Federico got up and snapped orders at the man, panic in his voice. The solider then rushed out of the tent.

"What happened?" Lance asked.

"We got some new intel. We need to warn London, fast."

Lance felt a deep anguish. After everything he had gone through in the last twenty-four hours, he dreaded what could possibly come next.

16

Thirty miles outside Manchester, United Kingdom, one day later

Derek Conkland was driving to his home just like any other day; however, he soon would make his mark on history. He was happy. It was not too long ago that he'd been near death, suffering from an advanced form of Lou Gehrig's disease. Many in the community considered his survival a gift from God, but Derek knew differently. What had saved him was not divine intervention but something more earthly. Despite what the world thought, he knew that the cause of the man he considered his personal savior was just, and today was the day he would finally return the favor.

Derek parked his car. He pulled out his phone and placed a call. When the call was answered, Derek said in a subservient yet serious manner, "Historian, I am almost done with the bomb."

A voice altered to be a few tones higher replied, "Good. How long till you get it to Manchester?"

"I plan to get it done by the end of the week," Derek said confidently.

"I have received some information from Candellario. We need to make this go faster."

"Consider it done," Derek said obediently.

"Be careful, Derek," the Historian said, concern visible even through the filter.

"You and the Lemurians were there for me when the rest of the world failed. I know that this attack today will bring us one step closer to a world we can be proud of," Derek said. "Goodbye, Historian. I will report back when I am finished with my mission."

Derek walked down the steps of his basement to his makeshift laboratory filled with vials and flasks that wouldn't look out of place in an old-fashioned horror movie. At the back of the basement, he spun the combination lock for the secret compartment in the ground and opened it. Inside the compartment was a lead safe. With excitement, he slowly unlocked and opened the safe as a well.

He pulled out a suitcase with wires attached. He knew what had to be done. Derek took a deep breath and mentally prepared for his important mission. With the suitcase in hand, he walked out of the house and slowly entered his car.

As Derek drove toward Manchester, he received a call. Once again it was the Historian, hiding behind the filtered voice. "There has been a change in plans."

"What do you mean?" Derek asked.

"You are going to blow up the bomb here in Manchester. Do not go down to London. The UK has received word that we are going to attempt an attack, and it is too risky to travel across the entire country."

"That won't have as much impact as blowing up the capital," Derek said, curious about the change.

"In a few hours we are going to launch the first nuke since Nagasaki in the heart of the Western world. It won't matter much what city. I was thinking about changing the target anyway. After all, it would be a shame to lose London's history in the new world," the Historian said.

"With the change in plans, Do you need me to be there when the bomb goes off? If that is what is needed, I am more than willing," Derek said with conviction and no hint of regret.

"Let us hope it does not come to that. There has always been that chance, but I never intended this to be a suicide mission, Derek."

"I know that's not your style, but the only reason I am still alive is because of your organization. I'm willing to give my life for you. I want you to expand your work."

Derek was starting to get emotional. He had to consciously hold back his emotions to focus on the road. He said, "You need to win the war, sir. You must help others the way you helped me."

"Every generation after this one will realize that this was the turning point of humanity," the Historian said with a strong sense of pride.

"I'll report back if there are any problems," Derek said and hung up.

Derek drove a while longer, until he saw a blockade of police cars off in the distance. Nervous, Derek pulled onto the shoulder to call the Historian. In a nervous haze, sweating and gasping, he dialed the buttons. Derek was more fearful of getting caught than dying.

The Historian answered. "Status, Derek," he said in a businesslike manner.

"There is a police checkpoint in front of me. They're checking cars," Derek said.

"Okay, how far away are you from the city?" the Historian asked with concern.

"About fifteen miles," Derek said in a clipped, professional tone.

"Ha," the Historian chuckled. "They think there's going to be another 9/11, but what we are about to do is so much more. Derek, turn around and go plant the bomb in the woods near where you are. Once you get to a safe distance, remote detonate it. You are close enough to get the job done."

"Okay," Derek said.

As he was about to turn around, he heard a loud shout through a megaphone. "Police! Pull over."

Fear struck Derek's hear. He was caught. He heard the megaphone again. "Police! Get out now, or we will shoot."

"What's going on?" the Historian asked with concern.

"They are near. They're threatening me with guns. Do you think I can talk them down?" Derek asked as he crouched down in his seat.

As the Historian started to answer, an officer started the countdown and yelled a second warning through the megaphone.

"They know something is up. They would not have come armed otherwise," the Historian said.

"I'm going to detonate it now," Derek said, holding back tears.

"You don't have to. If you're caught, I will free you someday," the Historian said in a panic.

"You have given me a chance to change the world. I will die for you and the Lemurian cause."

The police opened fire at the car while Derek was crouched down. The Historian was silent on the phone and then finally said, "You have done a lot for our nation. You deserve to hear my voice."

"No, sir, it is too risky," Derek said.

With the filter off, the Historian's true voice came through. He said in a friendly tone, "Hello, Derek. My name is Victor Webb, and you will be remembered forever for your service to Lemuria."

Derek had tears in his eyes, happy in the fire of bullets, as he said his final words. "Thank you, Victor." He hung up the phone.

The police were closing in, but in his final moments Derek felt a sense of euphoria. The man condemned to die would change the world, and with that thought, he reached out and activated the bomb.

Undisclosed location

As the bomb went off, Victor was sitting in a building receiving news feeds from around the world. People were starting to learn what he'd done today. Sitting in the shadows in his windowless room, he absorbed the information with mixed emotions. He had a sense of pride for getting as far as he had, but there was still a feeling of concern within him. He wasn't sure what it was exactly, maybe some guilt that he hadn't been able to purge from his being or maybe a sense that the mission he was undertaking was even more real now.

The door opened and revealed a muscular Asian man in his late twenties. He had serious eyes and darker skin. "We did it, sir," he said quietly, trying to hold back his happiness for a sense of professionalism.

Victor sat up and said in a happy tone, "Yes, we did, Zhou." The two men started to shake hands and then embraced instead.

"What is next for us?"

"I'm leaning toward making some demands, but I want to talk it over with some of the others."

"Perhaps I can help with those plans," said a new voice.

"Raul," Zhou said, "we haven't heard from you since you escaped Copper Canyon."

The confident Raul Candellario walked into the room toward Victor. When he got close, he fell to his knees and said, with a slight hint of crying, "Forgive me, Victor. I have failed you and Lemuria. The enemy has gotten a lot of information from the base. It will take a while to rebuild what we had in North America."

Victor looked displeased. "Get off you knees," he said, scowling.

Candellario got up, and the Historian looked him in the eyes. "Do not apologize," the Historian said. "You fought the strongest army in the world on their own turf for over a year. I would be an idiot to punish you after everything we've been through together."

The two men embraced. Zhou walked over to a cabinet and picked up a bottle of wine. "For better or worse," he said, "we really are getting into some new territory. I think this calls for a celebration."

"I agree," Victor said.

The three men toasted the things to come.

Langley, Virginia

As Lance and Jacob walked down a corridor in Langley, Lance asked in a businesslike manner, "How are the operations going throughout the country?"

"Great. With the information we gathered we've been able to clear many places the Lemurians were hiding. They're in a death spiral. I think a lot refugees will even be able to head back to their homes soon."

"Best news I've heard in a long time," Lance said confidently.

Lance's happy mood was soon interrupted when Sarah, Jacob's wife and a fellow agent, found them in the corridor. She was a short, somewhat portly redhead, and currently her appearance was dominated by one feature: the look of absolute dread on her face.

"What's wrong, Sarah?" he asked, attempting to sound stern but unable to prevent some worry from breaking through.

"A nuclear bomb went off in the UK, taking out half of Manchester," she said in stern sadness.

The two men were shocked. As horrible as the Lemurians had been, neither had thought they would or could do something like this, but somehow they'd gotten the ability.

Jacob was the first to speak, muttering, "How many casualties?"

Sarah paused. Her eyes were watery, but no tears fell. "About eighty thousand so far. If there is any good news to this crisis, they launched the bomb outside of the city. It appears we forced their hand to launch."

"Today is the most devastating terrorist attack in the history. I don't think there is any good news to celebrate," Lance said.

Jacob was still in a state of shock after absorbing what had happened. "Lance, go and rally the agents in the command center. I want a few moments with Sarah alone."

"All right," Lance said, and he walked away.

Alone with his wife, Jacob started to cry. Upon seeing him cry, Sarah started to shed tears as well. The couple held each other as they cried.

"I failed, Sarah," Jacob said, Sarah's head on his chest. "I had no idea this was coming. I had no idea they could do this."

Sarah pulled away and said sternly, "Don't you blame yourself. The only people responsible for this attack are the Historian and the Lemurians."

"It's my job to stop these people. The American golden age made me arrogant, and I didn't see this coming," Jacob said. "Lance, the man I doubted, was successful in getting the information in those caves because he was willing to do whatever was necessary. He disobeyed orders, and now the army has cleared all the Lemurian bases in half of the country." With anger in his voice, he added, "I need to change my strategy."

"I think we should find out how they got this weapon first. The most likely explanation would be that, they got it from the Ex-Soviet republics" Sarah said.

"Agreed, but to be fair to the Russians, I don't think they would help the Lemurians with this. The fighting has been really bad there, after all. If anything, the Lemurians stole it from them," Jacob said.

Jacob furrowed his brow, thinking about what to say next. "We need to go to work, Sarah. Contact MI6 and do all you can to find the origins of that bomb. I'll go figure out a way to secure the homeland once and for all."

"All right, honey," Sarah said in a comforting manner.

As they started to walk away from each other, Sarah turned back to Jacob and said, "This was not your fault. You won't help anyone by beating yourself up."

Jacob looked at Sarah. He didn't know what to say to comfort his wife. He felt guilt and still felt like a failure, but he knew that finding a replacement for his position would take much-needed time and resources. So he gave her a response that he knew was truthful. "Sarah, I will do whatever I can to stop these monsters."

With that, he walked away, leaving Sarah standing in the hall with a look of worry on her face.

Lance walked toward the main command center of the strike force at Langley. He didn't know what to do. Andrew had just been released from the hospital and had undergone an extensive debriefing following his time as a Lemurian hostage, and Danny had been distant ever since he'd gotten back from Copper Canyon. But Lance, being an optimist, figured that after what had happened in Manchester, everybody would be focused on the task on hand.

Lance walked into the command center, and all the analysts' eyes turned to him. Thanks to his successes in his short time back with the CIA, they were already looking to him for leadership.

Lance knew that this nuclear attack was going to make 9/11 seem like an average shooting. It was only natural to be nervous and disgusted by the sheer loss of life, but Lance, with everything he'd already lost, did not cry. His hatred for the Lemurians was already strong, and he already knew that there were no limits to what they would do.

Lance looked at the agents. Some were still looking at him, some had gone back to work, and some were crying at the situation. Lance wanted this all to stop. He wanted to get the Historian as soon as possible and make him pay for everything. For now, Lance could not let anyone fall into despair. He remembered how useless he'd been after the death of his family, crying and moaning every night. Now he was going to use his mourning to fuel his resolve. He wanted to prevent the others from feeling a sense of defeat.

With determination Lance ran to the front of the room and yelled, "Everybody!"

The analysts looked forward at him.

"We all know what happened today, and I know what you're feeling, but take it from someone who has been there: you cannot let their cruelty get the better of you.

We had a victory a few days ago, and what happened today does not change that. As we speak, the army is rooting out Lemurians across the nation. That does not change despite what they did today," Lance finished loudly, almost like a battle cry. He took a deep breath and resumed his loud rant. "We will find the Historian, and we will kill him."

The analysts cheered, and Lance momentarily felt good, but then he worried about what he'd just said. He'd never before called for a target's death outright.

Lance recollected himself from his rallying cry and said more calmly, "However, we cannot forget what happened today. I think we should have a moment of silence for the victims."

The agents in the room seemed to respect Lance's call. Some bowed their heads; others seemed to be praying. Lance took some time to reflect on himself and how far he was willing to go. He hated the Lemurians, but he didn't want to lose himself. He knew Rachel wouldn't want that.

After leaving the agents in silence for a while, he said, "Okay, back to work. Let's get the job done."

As the agents got back into their work, Lance spotted Sarah at the back at the room and headed over to her. "I hope I didn't overstep my authority," Lance said with concern.

"No worries, Lance," Sarah said with a small smile. Her smile then faded, and she said, "I think someone needed to step up. Jacob is a mess. I'm worried."

"What is going on with him?" Lance asked, concerned,

"I think he's taking the failure too hard. In his state, I think he could make the wrong move. If he proposes something that will endanger the mission, will you talk to him?"

"You're his wife, Sarah. Why do you think he would value my opinion more than yours?"

"He respects the choice you made in Copper Canyon. He thinks you stepped up when he couldn't."

"All right, I'll try to keep him in check if he does anything rash," Lance said confidently.

"Thanks. Andrew is rushing back here from leave, and Jacob wants a meeting in conference room C in fifteen minutes," Sarah said.

"Okay," Lance confirmed. "See you then." He started to walk to the bathroom to comb his hair and freshen up for the meeting, but on the way he saw Danny Smith leaning against the wall and paused.

"Hello, Lance," Dan said in a way that seemed a little off.

"Hello, Dan."

"That was a nice speech," Dan said, sounding disingenuous.

"Thanks," Lance said anyway.

"We will kill him," Dan said in a mocking tone. "Not even bothering with trying to find our targets alive anymore," he added, his tone more anger.

Lance couldn't deny he felt some guilt. He answered honestly, "I was in the heat of the moment."

"I think we should be on the way to the meeting," Dan said in a stern, emotionless voice, clearly trying to change the subject.

Lance walked in front of Dan briskly and said, "Dan, if you have something to say to me, I want you to say it now. With what just happened, we can't have any secrets between us."

"Lance, I know what you did in Copper Canyon was the right move tactically, and I'm not proud to admit it, but right now I don't know what to feel about you. Launching that attack with me and Federico near the Lemurian caves could have been a death sentence for us. We were outnumbered. If we hadn't already started heading back to camp, we would have been slaughtered."

Lance gave Dan a look of deep concern and thought about what to say. "I know," he said finally, trying to show that he felt guilt but didn't regret doing what he had to do.

"You know," Dan snapped. "You were willing to sacrifice me."

Lance could feel the guilt on his face upon hearing Dan speak this truth, but he did not lower his head. He looked Dan directly in the eyes. Gaining intensity, he said, "Do you know who Gloria Behar is?"

"What does that have to do with anything?" Dan snapped,

"Gloria Behar was one of the people I condemned to death when I threw that grenade."

The anger disappeared from Danny's face, replaced by stunned surprise.

"She had two children, not even teenagers, and there were many more like her, Dan. Doctors, grandparents, sons, daughters. All people I condemned to death when I made the tough choice. I was willing to sacrifice people like Gloria to defeat the Lemurians. What kind of man would I be if I wasn't willing to accept the same loss that I made so many others accept because of my decision?"

Danny stood in still silence. He seemed to understand Lance's point, but despite that wasn't quite satisfied yet. He thought about what to say to his friend. "I know you're right. There is nothing logical I can say about why I feel the way I do, but part of me does not want to admit what we might have to do to defeat the Lemurians. Is there anything that is sacred, Lance, if you would make a decision that could kill your best friend?"

"I don't know the answer to that question," Lance said. "But I feel that for now we have to continue forward and deal with those decisions when we get to them."

"That's fair," Dan said in a genuine way.

"I think we should go to the meeting now," Lance said.

"Okay."

The two men walked into the conference room, and Lance looked around the table to see who was attending the meeting. Jacob and Sarah sat at one end of the table, and near them was Eliza Churchill, the NSA liaison. At the other end of the table was Andrew. Lance nodded to Andrew, who reciprocated the gesture. Lance was happy that Andrew seemed to agree with his decision more than Dan did. He didn't need any more drama right now.

The final face at the table was someone he didn't expect to be there—Zach Franco, the president's national security advisor. His presence gave Lance mixed feelings. He was worried about interference from the executive branch, but he could not blame the president for being concerned after the nuke.

Lance was surprised that the Historian had targeted the UK first. Was the Copper Canyon raid so successful that it had forced the Lemurians to change their plans?

Before Lance could stew in his thoughts further, Jacob said, "I think we should start. Do you want to speak first, Zach?"

Zach Franco was an older man, a few years older than Jacob, and bald. He still did not look frail despite his age, with a defined chin and intense blue eyes. He had some weight on him, but not enough that Lance would call him fat.

Franco stood up and said calmly, "We've intercepted a video communication from the Historian. So far we've managed to stop this message from leaking, but we feel that it is only a matter of time before the public at large knows about it."

"With that nuke going off, the Historian might think it's a good time for him to reveal himself—do it in a moment of victory," Andrew said.

"We're not ruling out the possibility that he will reveal himself soon, but his voice was still disguised in the intercepted video, so it seems the message has another purpose."

"Why do we think we can't contain the message?" Dan asked.

"It was delivered to many media sources across the world. We're grateful that so far they aren't pushing the story, but we know that a message from the Historian is a tempting story. It might also get to the point where the Lemurians get impatient enough to release it on the internet," Franco said in his businesslike manner.

"I'm happy about the cooperation, but it seems almost too good to be true that there's not a single media source pushing this story," Lance said skeptically. "It isn't like the media and the CIA have been great friends."

Franco looked Lance in the eyes for the first time in the conversation and said, nerves evident in his voice, "Their silence probably has something to do with how the message was delivered. Sarah will explain more."

Sarah got up and put an image of a dead man on the screen. He had a gunshot wound in his forehead but did not show signs of extensive torture.

Sarah said, "This man is Yuri Slavensk, a notorious sex trafficker that European authorities have been looking for for many years."

"Do we think he was a Lemurian?" Dan asked.

"We do not, but it seems he did have some unfortunate contact with them," Jacob said.

"The Lemurians attached a disc containing a copy of their message to Slavensk's corpse and then sent it to the BBC. And it's not just him," Franco said forcefully. "Every media organization the Lemurians sent the message to received a different known criminal's corpse."

"How many of note?" Lance asked.

"Quite a few, including Hector Padrone, one of the largest drug lords in Latin America," Franco said. "It seems the Lemurians have killed a lot of people we have been looking for—criminals, assassins, and in some cases terrorists. The *Lagos Times* received the body of Omar Al-Salem, an Islamist extremist whose group frequently attacked girls' schools in the countryside."

"I'm not exactly mourning the loss of these men, but I do find it odd how effectively the Lemurians were able to find some of the most wanted people in the world," Jacob said.

"Sometimes in Africa and the Middle East Islamists use the fact they can restore order as a selling point for their harsh tactics to the locals," Lance said. "You know—if you cut off the hands of thieves, there's a good chance people won't steal. When I was in Afghanistan, that was the main argument the locals gave me for why people would tolerate the extremists."

"Do you really think the Lemurians are trying to win over hearts and minds?" Dan asked. "A few days ago I might have agreed with what you're saying, Lance, but killing a few bad guys that the average person has never even heard of isn't going to make up for committing the largest terrorist attack in world history."

"Well, that's a good point," Lance said, "but you're thinking like a normal person. I still think that in the Historian's sick mind he thinks he can appeal to the common man."

"That is a fair point," Franco said.

Sarah started the video, and the projector flashed a familiar symbol on the screen—the Menes hieroglyph with a purple background.

The Symbol was so minimal, by itself nothing threatening. It was merely a long a circle containing a rectangle that looked like a old tape at the top, with one line below that formed a wave like zig zag pattern in the middl, and at the bottom of a circle a shape that looked like a knife in legs. They small symbols were colored in black but the entire coloring behind it was purple. Maybe it was a bid for attention, but Lance had no idea why it was purple. After a few moments of silence, an altered voice came through, the audio muffled slightly.

"Hello, people of the world. I am known as the Historian. I won't reveal my name today, but know that I am the leader of the Lemurians. You are no doubt dealing with what we had to do in Manchester, England, today. The measures I took today are no doubt extreme, and many people will condemn me for my actions and I am willing to take responsibly for them, but I feel that soon history will judge me in the right, because today I bring a truth to the world. The governments of the world today have been lying to you. They wanted you to believe that we were in a golden age and that you were safe from all possible dangers."

The voice grew more intense and angry. "Today in Manchester, I have proven that was a lie. I was able to launch a nuke directly into the heart of the Western world. People of the world, the injustices do not end there. Today I will also prove that your governments have purposely let legitimate dangers stay in place in order to consolidate their power."

The Lemurian symbol disappeared from the screen, and the faces of what must have been hundreds of individuals started to flash on the screen, one after another.

The Historian continued as faces kept flashing, "These men and women before you now were people who caused the world a great deal of harm. They were slavers, drug dealers, warlords, and terrorists. My organization, with inferior resources, was able to eliminate these individuals, something the most powerful intelligence agencies in the world could not do. We have done this not because we are stronger but because we truly want a better world and are willing to do anything to achieve these goals.

"For the governments of the world, I have some demands you will meet if you wish to avoid another Manchester incident. Many nations today want independence, but the great powers of the world refuse to give it to them because of a lust for resources, power, and the pure desire to preserve the status quo. My first act to forge a better world will be the independence of these nations.

"In one month's time I want the nations of Kashmir, Somaliland, Tibet, East Turkestan, Chechnya, Punjab, and Ryukyu to be put on the path to independence. If that does not happen within one month, I will launch nuclear attacks in three more cities. The freedom fighters of the past were willing to make tough choices to fulfill their goals, and I am no exception."

He finished with "Long live Lemuria."

The room sat in silence for a while. Lance was in a state of shock, and Danny was twitching, holding in anger. Franco, who had seen the video before, looked down on the ground and sighed, looking almost as if he felt guilty for showing people the video.

Dan stood up, and with his face growing red, he pounded the table in front of him. "The nerve of that guy! He thinks he can tell the entire world what to do!"

"It is sickening," Eliza said in agreement.

"I agree with Eliza. It really is," Sarah said in a soft tone.

"I think we can all agree on that, but the question is, Where do we go from here?" Franco asked.

"I think we have to be absolutely sure that we clear out every single Lemurian in our homeland," Jacob said. "I hate to say it, but our loyalty is to our country first. We need to make sure a nuclear attack does not happen on American soil."

"What do you think the best course would be to do that?" Franco asked.

"It's only the Midwest that we have not yet completely cleared," Jacob said. "I suggest we send drones to scan for activity, drop leaflets warning that we are going to clear the area, then launch an invasion."

"For the rest of the country we had the exact location of the Lemurian bases, but we don't have that info for the Midwest. If we do it your way, we could kill many civilians," Lance said.

"I agree with Lance," Andrew said. "I have some family in Texas, and they stayed in their homes despite my warnings of Lemurian acitvity. If you go through with that plan, you could be killing many civilians, if we don't have precise information."

Jacob gave Andrew and Lance a sympathetic look. "If this was a week ago, I would agree with you, but look at Manchester. Are you reading the Twitter feeds? Do you realize what's going on there?" Jacob started to choke up. "The people who died first were the lucky ones. There are thousands of people right now who are going to spend their last hours in pain dying of radiation poisoning."

Jacob started to breathe heavily. "The Lemurians got stronger on my watch. I did not see this coming, but I will not let them do what they did to Manchester to our country or our people!" Jacob yelled manically. He started pacing now and had a look of embarrassment on his face, as if he realized he might have gone too far.

"Jacob," Sarah said softly, sympathetic concern in her voice.

"We won't let that happen, Jacob," Lance said. "Franco, are the other CIA cells or the NSA finding anything useful on the bases we captured, anything that could help?"

"They're still sorting out a lot of data. The FBI is conducting interrogations with some Lemurians we've caught. We should have more information soon."

"Good. We have a month. That should be enough time to secure the country," Lance said. He grew quiet and more desperate. He looked around, trying to think of things that could calm Jacob.

"Andrew, when you were undercover with them, did they give you anything?" Lance asked gruffly.

"While, trapped with the other hostages, I heard some Lemurians mention an escape to to Texas," Andrew answered.

"There a few cities in Texas that are at least the same size of Manchester. Taking any one of them out could be his plan," Jacob said.

"The Historian is going to give us some time," Lance said. "He's not going to launch more nukes immediately. I think he wants to be able to say that we failed to liberate these places and thus the additional attacks are our fault."

"Do you think he might be trying to appeal to the developing world, attacking the UK and then us, making a stand against us like the Communists during the Cold War?" Dan asked.

"It's a possibility. There have been Lemurians from those regions. Hey, for all we know, maybe the Historian is from Kashmir and wants independence, and that's the entire reason he is doing this," Lance said. "But I think it is safe to say the Historian is not working with the main separatist groups. I'm guessing giving these countries independence is not his main goal."

"Why do you say that?" Dan asked. "I think we might finally have an idea who the Lemurians are. They could be an alliance of separatist organizations, thinking that they could get more done if united."

"Most of those separatist organizations are regional," Franco said. "They normally at least try to sound sympathetic, saying their people are mistreated. Attacking the UK, a country they don't even want independence from, would ruin any chance of public opinion being on their side."

"Countries they want independence from," Lance said forcefully. "Think about where most of these places are— Russia, China, India. The Lemurian threat has forced intelligence agencies around the world to work together. I think the Historian is trying to cause paranoia and get the agencies of the world off his trail. As we speak, the Russians are probably going to refocus on the Chechens way more than necessary."

"I disagree," Jacob said. "It's what Zach said—most of the separatist groups are known to be regional terrorists. Do you really think that other intelligence agencies are going to be misdirected so easily?" Jacob asked with confusion.

"You underestimate human bias and hatred," Lance said. "The Lemurians are the worst terrorists we've faced, but China and Russia have been dealing with separatist groups for years. Many people in the Chinese intelligence community have lost friends and loved ones to the East Turkmenistan rebels. Do you really think it would be that hard to make negative feelings resurface? All the Lemurians would need to do would be to affect some people in the intelligence organizations of these key countries. If they misdirect the intelligence agencies at all, it would help them."

"We can't get too bogged down about what the Russians or Chinese will do or even why the Historian is doing all this," Jacob snapped. "Our number one concern is that we secure every bit of the mainland. We need to search every home possible and send a thousand drones over the Midwest. Any town that's suspicious, we bomb. We have to destroy any places the Lemurians could possibly reside and prevent a nuke."

"Jacob, that's going to destroy many homes, and you know the drones aren't going to be a hundred percent accurate. There is a good chance we'll kill more civilians than necessary," Dan said.

"I know there will be some casualties, Dan. You think I like that? But as much as I hate to admit it, I believe the Historian when he says he has more nukes. Anything we can do to stop him will save more people in the long run," Jacob said, looking Dan in the eye.

"Lance, you have to have my back on this," Jacob said in an impassioned plea. "I'm doing what you did in the canyon, a choice for the greater good."

Lance sighed. He was sick of being reminded about what he'd had to do, but he looked at Jacob and said, "I was in the middle of a battle when I made that choice. We still think there's time before the Lemurians launch any more bombs."

"The Historian said we have a month," Jacob said.

"Do you want the horror show that is happening in Manchester to happen to our home … to our citizens?"

"No, but people are already protesting the government for the actions we've taken—the roadblocks, the random searches of homes. What you're suggesting would make the people riot and protest. The last thing we need is more instability, which the Lemurians can take advantage of. And another thing, Jacob—I know for a fact there are people who want to stay in their homes. They don't want to retreat. My in-laws, after losing their daughter, still stayed on their farm. They feel they've lost so much else that all they have is their home. How many more people are like that?" Lance said in a compassionate plea.

Tension was building between Lance and Jacob, and Sarah butted in. "Figuring out where the bombs are is not even our job. Franco, what does the FBI think we should be doing about this?"

"The FBI thinks we should expand the blockades around major cities and have surveillance drones survey the skies around the cities too. They also think we should expand phone and email surveillance to see if we can close in on where the nukes are and where the attacks will happen."

"That's more violation of civil liberties than I like, but I can understand with nukes out there," Eliza said.

"Are you saying that I should just ignore the threat, that I should forget there's a chance a nuclear terrorist attack could happen in America?" Jacob asked. "Franco, you and the president came to the CIA to ask for additional help when the Lemurians were carrying out terrorist attacks on an almost daily basis, and it was one of my agents who got the information of where the Lemurians were hiding. Now you and Sarah are suggesting to back off?" he yelled.

Lance stood up quickly and shouted, "Hey, lay off. Everybody in this room is stressed and, to be honest, a little bit scared, but we are not going to get anywhere snapping at each other."

Jacob sat down, guilt on his face, and let out a sigh. "What do you think we should do, Lance?" he asked calmly, gesturing with his hands.

"I agree with the FBI. For now, if the Historian is going to give us some time, we might as well use it against him. We have the Copper Canyon information, and we've destroyed Lemurian safe houses across America and captured some Lemurians. I'm willing to talk to any of them to see if I can get any information out of them like I did with Landshire."

"The FBI is already leading the charge in the interrogations," Franco said. "They report that the lower-level captures have been cooperating, but I appreciate the offer, Lance. I will definitely tell the FBI director to keep that in mine."

"You know what we have to do," Lance said. "We get the information, and we take the fight to them. Franco, I'm guessing you're already getting some brigades ready to attack if we can pinpoint the location of the main Lemurian base. When we find that, we take out the Historian."

"Yes, we have about twenty thousand of our top marines ready for that assault."

"I'd be willing to relive my army days and go on that mission myself," Lance said impassionedly.

"We seem to have a plan for now," Sarah said. "Let's go carry it out."

The group started to move away from the table. Lance hurried out, not quite running but walking briskly. As Lance got into the hallway, Jacob said calmly but sternly, "Hey, Lance."

Lance was annoyed. After everything that had happened today, with Dan and the nuke, he'd had enough and didn't want to deal with any more drama. He tried to preempt Jacob, saying, "I'm going home, Jacob. It's been a long day. I need sleep."

Jacob said abruptly, "I could've used your support in there. You and I both know what needs to done in times of crisis."

Lance walked directly in front of Jacob, looked him in the eye, and said sternly, "I honestly did not think your plan was the best, Jacob. I appreciate everything you have done for me, but as an agent, I have to put the safety of this country ahead of our friendship."

Jacob paused, a look of dread on his face. "You're right," he said with some guilt.

Lance gasped a bit, surprised that Jacob would turn around so quickly.

Jacob sighed. "Lance, what the hell is wrong with me? Have I made any right decisions today? I failed when it mattered. I've been useless."

"You got the team together. You don't have to do this alone, Jacob. We're scared now, but we can come back." Lance looked at Jacob with some compassion. He then smiled and said, "Do you remember what I was like six months ago?"

"I prefer not to," Jacob said with a small smile.

"I think I became at least a little stronger—uh, you know, mentally—when you and Sarah let me stay at your house for the holidays. I mourn Tara and Rachel every day, but I'm here now doing something, and I think part of the reason why is you and Sarah. I'm here for you now, Jacob."

"Thank you, Lance," Jacob said in a soft but sincere voice. It almost sounded as if he was holding back tears.

"You're welcome, Jacob, and I'll be honest—I really liked my Christmas present."

"Yeah, I know you're a big fan of Hitchcock," Jacob said happily.

"One of those days after Christmas, I watched *Rear Window* like seven times," Lance said jovially, gesturing with his hand.

Jacob chucked, and then they fell into silence. Jacob said finally, "Thank you, Lance, for giving me a laugh today."

"You know, I needed that too," Lance said. "So are you going home soon to get some rest?"

"Maybe soon. Andrew is more fresh than me, but I think I'll stick around for a little while longer."

"All right. We'll get through this. This country took on the Nazis and the Soviets. The Historian won't know what hit him," Lance said, getting more confident.

"Yeah, we'll get them," Jacob said, echoing Lance's confidence.

Lance left in a mood he hadn't expected. He was happy just talking to a friend for that moment.

As Lance took the elevator up to his apartment, alone for the moment, he had time to think. He'd thought about bunking at the CIA headquarters but figured it would be good to have some time alone to think. Lance used to like being alone sometimes, before the war started, but recently he'd been alone too much for his liking. However, with the chaos of what had happened today, he was ready for some alone time again.

Lance walked into his apartment and placed his briefcase on the desk. It was late, but he didn't want to go to sleep yet. His conversation with Jacob had cheered him up, but he was still focused on the day.

Lance walked over to his movie collection and picked out one of his favorites—*Duck Soup*, starring Groucho Marx. Lance must have seen that movie over a thousand times, but with all that was going on, he could use something familiar.

He sat down on the couch and started watching the movie, which still made him laugh after all this time. He felt good finally having a chance to relax and enjoy the moment, and then his phone rang.

"Oh shit!" he yelled in a panic, wondering what would cause the CIA to call him at this late hour. But when he picked up the phone, it was a number he didn't recognize. It could just be a wrong number, but Lance felt a strong sense of curiosity. His gut wanted him to answer the call, so he did.

"Hello?"

A filtered voice came through. "Hello, Mr. Richardson."

"Who is this?" Lance asked angrily.

"Just call me Anubis. I am a friend. I want to give you some information," the voice said sternly.

"I want more details than that. Who are you, and how the hell do you know my name?" Lance snapped.

"You will know more about me soon, but for now I can tell you that I'm a hacker and have contacts in the government."

"How do I know you aren't a Lemurian trying to trick me?"

"I can give you something that might be able convince you. The Historian—what if I told you I knew his name?"

Lance was speechless. He stood in silence for a moment.

Anubis added, "I can tell that you might not believe me. When you go back to the CIA, tell them to look up Victor Lazarus Webb. I don't know much else about him that would narrow your search except that he's American."

"Why are you doing this? Why are you calling me now?" Lance asked.

"I'm not the biggest fan of the CIA, but I've seen what has happened in Manchester. My contacts said you were the best man to talk to in order to make that bastard pay."

"Tell me where you are. We can work together," Lance said.

"Check the name, Lance. I'm sure this won't be the last time we speak." And with that, Anubis hung up.

Lance sat down and thought about what to do next.

17

Lance and Danny were walking down a hallway of the CIA office. Lance had just told Danny about the phone call.

"I don't know. That sounds pretty suspicious—some random guy calling and telling you he has the Historian's name," Dan said.

"Yeah, Victor Webb," Lance said.

"Should we tell Jacob or Andrew?"

"I don't know. The guy said he had contacts in the government. Jacob will probably want to tell the entire group, and I don't want us to be to sidetracked from tracking down the Lemurian base. Who knows this might be a Lemurian trying to distract us. I'll tell everyone when we get more information," Lance said.

"What do you think the guy's agenda is?" Dan asked.

"If he is being honest, he could be a hacker, maybe with Anonymous someone who normally doesn't like the government but felt that he had to come forward after the nuke," Lance said.

"Do you think his information is accurate?"

"He gave us a name. I don't think there's any harm in having someone look in to it."

"All right, is there any analyst you want in particular?" Dan asked.

"Try Josh. He was a hacker before joining us. He might be more sympathetic to keeping a secret for a little while," Lance said.

"Okay. What are you going to do now?"

"I'm gonna go to another meeting. I think Director Samson will be there. I'm hoping we have a plan for taking down the Lemurian base."

"All right, keep me posted."

Lance headed down the hall to the conference room with mixed emotions. He had the nervous feeling he always did when dealing with the Lemurians, and the nuke going off in Manchester hadn't exactly helped, but despite everything, he also had a sense of optimism he hadn't felt since he'd begun fighting this conflict. Today he might finally learn where they were based, and there was even a chance he knew the Historian's name.

While walking, Lance saw Andrew and yelled in a friendly tone, "Hey, man!"

"Hey, Lance, how are you doing?" Andrew replied.

"Good. I had some rest. I'm still worried about the world, but I think we're closer than ever to catching the Historian."

"I can't wait to see that bastard dead or behind bars," Andrew said sternly.

"You know what, I just want to find out what he looks like, so I have a face to put with this hatred, you know. Sometimes I feel like I'm hating some kind of evil spirit or force of nature. I hate that, because I feel like that's exactly what the Historian wants."

"I hear ya. I promise you that we are going to get that son of bitch."

"That's good to hear, Andrew."

Talking with Andrew, Lance suddenly had a thought. "Andrew, wait. I never apologized to you for my decision at Copper Canyon. I put you in danger when I made that decision. I'm sorry I had to put you in that situation."

"I knew the risks. You have no need to apologize, Lance," Andrew said.

"Thank you, Andrew. It's good to hear that."

"Hey, I've put plenty of good people at risk myself. I'd be a hypocrite if I was mad at you."

"You doing good—you know, outside of all this? Anything good happening?"

"Outside of this, I guess I'm doing as good as I can be. It's funny, you apologizing to me. I've been thinking about Copper Canyon a lot myself. I wrote a letter to Agent Cutter's parents telling them that she died bravely and the mission she died in was a success. I thought it was the least I could do," Andrew said.

"I see what you mean. Past year and a half has truly been something, huh?"

"After this is all done, I just want to go to Hawaii again, get my board, and go surfing."

"Maybe I'll come with you," Lance said happily.

"I'd like that—you and me out in Hawaii. Maybe we'll have some luck with the ladies."

Andrew realized what he'd just said and looked

awkwardly at Lance. He nervously said, "Lance, I'm sorry. I just blurted it out."

"No, it's fine. I'll have to think about that someday, but I don't think that's in the cards for now. Let's go to the meeting and see how the war is doing."

"All right, let's go," Andrew said, sounding relieved, as if he'd just gotten away with a mistake.

The men went into the briefing room. Zach Franco and CIA director Aaron Samson were both present, along with someone Lance recognized but had never met in person before, Robert Ramirez, the president's chief of staff.

Lance was worried about seeing Robert there. He felt the executive branch was maybe getting more involved than needed. Ramirez was a tall, slender man. He seemed to take great care of his appearance in general, with not a single wrinkle or a seam out of place in his suit and red tie.

Lance took a seat at the far side of the conference table and continued to look at Ramirez. Realizing that he should probably not draw attention to himself, he switched his gaze to the phone on the center of the table to avoid standing out.

Jacob came into the room with a determined look on his face. He did not seem depressed or consumed with passion. He walked briskly to the end of the conference table.

Eliza walked in behind Jacob with a similar intensity in her eyes, sat down to the right of him, and looked at Ramirez.

Jacob then started to talk. "Everybody here knows we have roughly a month to track down the remaining

Lemurian nukes. For the past few days, all of the nation's intelligence agencies have been attempting to find the Lemurian strongholds. I'm happy to announce we are closer than we've ever been to achieving this. I will defer to Director Samson for details on the mission."

"Thank you, Jacob," Samson said. "We've believed that the Lemurians were deeply involved in the Malaysian drug trade. This was confirmed by a successful operation in coordination with the governments of several Southeast Asian nations. There were some key bases along the Thai-Malay border that we successfully raided; however, we do not think the main Lemurian stronghold is there. In one of our successful raids, we found two important leads."

Samson stood up, and some of his aides in the back of the room set up a PowerPoint presentation. Samson took a breath, as if to prepare himself for a long speech.

A topographic picture came up on the screen showing a chain of islands. Lance didn't recognize exactly where the islands were in the world.

In a businesslike manner, Samson said, "Based on the information the CIA and the NSA have received from captured bases, we believe the Lemurians are using one of the islands in Micronesia as a main stronghold. As we speak, we are using drones to scan the area and find the exact target. We are going to make a move on the base as soon as possible. The attack on the island will be a joint strike between American, British, Chinese, and Indonesian armed forces."

Samson looked directly at Lance with a fierce look and said, "Agent Richardson, the joint chiefs are grateful for your outside-the-box thinking at the Copper Canyon assault, and we would like for you to advise on this mission as well."

"I would like you to know that the president agrees with this recommendation as well, Lance," Ramirez said, the first words he'd said in the meeting.

Lance was caught off guard by Ramirez mentioning him. He hadn't been expecting that, let alone being mentioned in a positive way. After pausing for a few seconds, Lance said, "I'll gladly go. I'm in this until the Lemurians are no longer a threat."

"I'm very happy to hear that," Ramirez replied quickly.

"Have we had any luck with the drones scanning for remaining Lemurian bases?" Jacob chimed in.

"Some," Samson said. "But with the Vela satellites down, it will be harder than ever to find loose nuclear material."

"I think this is as good a time as any to ask—are we any closer to finding out how the Lemurians were able to launch the cyberattacks?" Andrew asked.

"Not really," Samson said. "Since Vincent Sykes, the Lemurian spy who launched one of the main attacks, committed suicide after he was successful, we haven't been able to find out much new info."

"We think the Lemurians were not able to get another high level spy in since Our main focus is locating the main base," Eliza snapped, clearly frustrated.

"No, Eliza, this is a failure we have to deal with," Lance said. "I still wonder how the hell you let the military satellites get crippled."

"I've done extensive background checks on everybody in this group. That is why I created the strike force.

We needed to have a clear team, and with the military satellites back up, we can attack." Jacob said.

"I find it hopeful that the Chinese want in on this," Lance said. "It looks like I was wrong in saying they might lose focus after the Historian mentioned he wanted independence for East Turkestan."

"China saw through the ploy," Franco said, "but as we speak, Russia is planning on launching a massive offensive in Chechnya, and Pakistan and India are thinking of launching offensives as well."

"What about the groups themselves—you know, the separatists? Are they accepting the Lemurians' help?" Lance asked.

"No, the vast majority of them, even the Chechens, have condemned the Manchester attack. There has been some isolated chatter talking in favor of the Historian that we're currently monitoring," Franco replied.

"The Historian only needs a few more recruits to expand the operation against the Russians," Lance said.

"That's true, but it is still a hopeful sign that the Historian hasn't gotten wider support," Samson said.

"Agreed," Lance said.

"We have another announcement I think we should mention to everyone," Jacob said. "Sarah and I have been monitoring suspected Lemurian communication, and we believe the Historian will launch one of his nuclear weapons in Houston, Texas."

"Good work, Jacob. How exactly did we narrow it down to there?" Samson asked.

"The analysts were able to decode several files form captured Lemurian safehouses, and the NSA was able to find some Lemurian supporters planning the attack. It is by far our best lead."

"All right, Jacob, send someone down to lead the efforts in Houston to find that nuke. If we secure the nuke, we might be able to confirm that Houston is the target location," Samson said.

"Great! This could be the missing link that helps us find the Lemurian leadership," Lance said.

Although Robert Ramirez hadn't spoken much in the meeting, his brown eyes were clearly attentive. He could pay attention to the entire room in the absence of the speaking. He got up and quickly said, "All right, I think we're done for now everyone. I will report what you told me here to the president and the cabinet."

"Wait," Jacob said loudly, in a pained way, almost like he was debating his next statement. Nonetheless, he continued, "I want to go to Houston myself. I started this strike force. Whether it succeeds or not, I think it is my duty to be in Houston when this operation happens."

"Fine. Go soon," Ramirez said. "We need someone there to coordinate the attack as soon as possible."

"If there is nothing else, I think we should end it here," Samson said.

Lance was caught off guard by Jacob wanting to go to Houston, and he started to breathe a little more heavily. With the meeting ended, people were already starting to leave the room. No one else seemed to care about Jacob's request to go to Houston.

Lance walked up to Jacob, close enough for their conversation to be more private. Jacob was standing there in silence in an almost contemplative state. Lance said quietly, in a sympathetic manner, "Jacob, are you sure you want to do this?" Lance failed to hold back a sigh. He wanted to say more to Jacob, but he couldn't figure out what.

"Yeah," Jacob said. "I've made some mistakes in this job, Lance. Who knows, maybe if I'd gotten you on the team earlier or made different decisions, we could've stopped the nuke in Manchester," he added with a heavy heart.

"Listen, Jacob, we all know what happened in Manchester was a disaster. America isn't the only country in the world, we can still stop the same thing from happening here. I promise you, Jacob, this time we'll capture the Historian, and you will be a hero when this is all over."

Lance and Jacob shook hands and went their separate ways. There was still one thing Lance had to attend to. He headed downstairs to a bunch of the analysts' terminals. Dan saw Lance heading that direction and joined him in the hallway. Lance turned his head a bit and said, "Did you ask him quietly?"

"Yeah, he's in."

"Did he find anything?"

"He'll tell you."

Lance and Dan were close to Josh's cubicle. Lance had talked to Josh only rarely, except for helping him out when he first got hired. Dan probably knew him better from working with him over the past year.

"Josh," Dan said.

The man turned around, and Lance got a closer look at him. He was overweight—not obese, to be fair—and had unkempt brown hair. He was wearing a T-shirt. The informality stood out, but Lance had never cared about a dress code as long as the job was done.

Josh said happily, "Dan."

"Do you have any information on Victor Webb? Is there anything that could tie him to the Lemurians?" Lance interrupted.

"It's good to see you, Lance. After this is done, I'm hoping some positive words from you might get me moved upstairs."

"Find me proof that the supposed hacker is right or wrong, and I will, Josh—I promise. But you might have to dress up a bit," Lance joked. "Any news of the hacker Anubis?"

"Anubis is known in hacking circles. Right now, none of my contacts knows his identity. We don't know much about him except that he hates the Lemurians."

"Who doesn't? Is there any info that is less general?"

"About a month into the war, his website LemurianJudgment.com went live. He keeps it on the dark web. He uses the site to try to recruit hackers to help bring down Lemurian networks. He lists criminals that he suspects are Lemurians."

"Anything else?"

"He seems pretty intense. On the website there are pictures of several corpses that Anubis claims are Lemurian soldiers that tried to assassinate him."

"Can I take a look at this?" Lance asked.

"Yeah, it's right here." Josh gestured to one of his monitors.

Three corpses were pictured on the screen with the

title "Less Lemurian Filth." The sentiment was something Lance could understand, but Anubis didn't seem like a man who would cooperate easily. Still, Lance would seek out any ally necessary to find Webb.

"Good work on Anubis, Josh. Now tell me what you found out on Webb."

"All right, take a look at this. I searched for connections to a Victor Webb for every single captured or known Lemurian. At first the only Victor Webb I could find was the dead grandfather of one, so that didn't look likely. But I expanded my search to see if there were any Victor Webbs connected to the locations the Lemurians came from."

"Find anything?" Lance said anxiously.

"There's a small tribal village in the DRC that two Lemurians came from. Seven years ago an American aid worker named Victor Webb died from falling into a river. No one ever found the body. I think this Webb might have faked his death."

"That's how I would fake my death," Lance said.

"Why do you say that?" Dan asked.

"Falling into a river gives a decent reason why the body would disappear. If he'd said he was murdered, it would have caused some suspicion, and more people would have investigated it."

"So you can understand why I think this is the Historian," Josh said.

"Yeah, it finally seems to be adding up," Lance said.

"Do you think we should tell Jacob?" Dan asked.

"No. There's a nuke that could go off in Houston right now. Jacob needs to be focused on that at this moment.

Besides, Even if Webb's a Lemurian, the Historian might be someone else. The hacker might be trying to throw me off course," Lance said.

"Isn't it worth looking into Webb, if there is any chance he's the Historian?" Josh asked.

"Yes, but the lead can wait. We just have a name and nothing else. If he is the Historian, we still don't know where he is. I promise you that after we take the main Lemurian base and Jacob is done, I'll come forward with this info, and if I die at the base, you and Dan have my permission to tell Samson or Jacob."

"We have to tell some someone, Lance," Dan said.

"Do you not see why we can't expose this?"

"No. Why?"

"There is no way some aid worker could have founded the Lemurians. Whoever the Historian is, he knows what he is doing. He has to be very intelligent or have military experience. If this guy is the founder, there is something else we don't know about him. He could be a former agent and the aid worker was a cover he escaped from."

"So do you think you was former deep cover agent for us. Maybe he could be ex-Mossad or a Russian spy," Josh said.

"We can't be sure."

"You're saying he was one of us?" Dan asked.

"We can't rule it out, and if he started as an agent, it could explain how he has friends helping him out in the government. I think you would agree that it was too optimistic to think that Sykes was the only mole. That's why we need to keep this to ourselves until we have a plan."

"You trust this idea, Dan?" Josh asked.

Dan looked at Lance and said with some resignation, "You were right before at Copper Canyon. I didn't bring you back to not listen to you now."

18

It was four o'clock in the morning, and Lance was starting to get up. Today was the day he was heading to Micronesia.

He walked slowly to the bathroom and washed his face. While he was reaching for his razor, he noticed himself in the mirror. He just stood there looking at his unkempt appearance. Behind him through the doorway was nothing but the dark apartment. Lance reflected on his memories. When he was a newlywed, he still had missions like this. The last thing he always did before he left was kiss Rachel on the way out. Even in this moment, when he might finally be able to stop the Lemurians, these thoughts were still in his head.

Lance thought about the chance to finish this war, to go on with his life. It wasn't something he thought about much, but while he got dressed, he had the opportunity to think of life after the Lemurians. Would he get married again, have kids? Lance partly felt bad even considering it, but he also thought it was something he should think about. He felt that Rachel would want him to be happy, and maybe it was selfish of him, but he did not want to die alone. Aside from a few close friends and some cousins and uncles, he did not have a lot of people in his life.

Lance left his apartment. He was calm, calmer than he'd expected himself to be. After all, there was still a war going on. With this reminder, Lance forced himself to tense up and keep his guard up as he got onto the elevator.

Lance pressed the button for the ground floor, and the elevator started down. Lance continued to be on guard. The building was old, and the elevator had a bell that clanged as the elevator went down. After a few rings of the bell, the elevator stopped on the third floor. Lance was already on edge, and the fact that someone else was up this early in the morning worried him. Lance grabbed his sidearm but did not take the gun out, thinking it could just be a civilian. He didn't completely take his guard down, though.

The elevator opened, and he saw a familiar face. It was Robert Ramirez. Lance took his hand off his sidearm and said in confusion, "Robert."

"Yes, Lance. Move over a bit. We have something we need to talk about," Robert said.

Lance moved over, and Robert came in. "Why are you here, Robert? Coming to talk to me seems like a small job for the president's chief of staff."

"I figured you would be surprised to see someone coming at this time in the morning, and I thought seeing someone you recognized might calm your nerves a bit," Ramirez said.

The elevator reached the ground floor, and the doors opened. "Come on, Lance," Ramirez said. "I have secured your ride to the airport. We can talk on the way."

Ramirez walked confidently out in front of Lance. Lance was still caught off guard from seeing the president's chief of staff. As they walked to the car, Lance felt that he needed to say something, so he said, "You were right about me being worried. When the elevator stopped on the third floor, I thought it might have been an assassin or something."

Ramirez replied confidently, "I tend to be right, Lance."

They were getting close to the car, which was a limo. Robert had what looked like Secret Service agents around the vehicle. Even with the sun not being up, Lance could tell that the limo was in perfect condition with no dents or dirt on it. Lance also noticed there were no homeless around like normal. He couldn't help but think that Ramirez had something to do with that.

One of the Secret Service agents opened the car door. Ramirez got in, and Lance followed. The limo was just as neat on the inside as it was on the outside, with black leather seats and a fully stocked bar on one side.

Ramirez sat in a relaxed manner, like he'd just finished a job. His suit was noticeably starting to wrinkle. Lance made himself comfortable but kept his body slightly tense, not relaxing fully.

"Do you want a drink?" Robert asked in a manner that suggested he was trying to break the ice.

"It's five o'clock in the morning, Robert," Lance responded.

"Trust me, you're in for a rough couple of days. You might want to enjoy the finer things in life while you can."

That was honestly a good point. Lance grabbed some

of the whiskey and poured himself a glass. Who knew if he would have the chance to have a good drink again. "Are you trying to get me drunk, Robert, maybe before you give me some bad news?"

"You seem to be accusing me of something, Lance," Robert said.

"I'm sure you don't get to where you are without telling a few lies," Lance said in a somewhat joking manner.

"Nonsense—people in politics are much more honest and kind than people give them credit for," Ramirez responded in a subtle and confident tone.

Lance sighed. "Why are you here, Robert? Just tell me. I think we've had enough small talk."

"Fine. I know you were contacted by a person who claims to know the Historian's identity."

Lance kept his face emotionless. He could not believe Ramirez knew. He didn't know where he'd messed up in keeping Anubis's call secret.

"Are you tapping my phone? How did you know?"

"How I know is not important. I'm chief of staff for a reason. I make it my business to know everything."

Lance, realizing he was now trapped in a car with this man, snapped, "Oh, it's goddamn important. You got your job as chief of staff because you were one of the president's chief donors. You've never held a gun in your life, and here you are spying on me, judging me."

"Oh please," Robert said with snide disgust. "You expect me to bow down because you joined the army, Lance? I ran a company that every day gave the world technological advances in medicine, energy, and weaponry. I've contributed more to this country than a thousand marines, and besides, your anger is unwarranted. I'm not mad, Lance. If I was in your shoes, I would try to keep it a secret as well."

The fact that Ramirez was supportive of the move calmed Lance down somewhat, but he was still angry. "How did you know, Robert?"

"I'm sure the hacker said she had support in the American government. Well, I am one of those people," Robert said.

"She?"

"Yeah. Back at the Horizon Corporation, I got to know some of the more prominent hackers. I suspect the hacker Anubis's real name is Erin Cahill, and if you ask me, I don't think you should trust her."

"How did you meet this hacker?" Lance asked.

"She does work if you pay her. She never was the idealistic type. In my political campaigns I sometimes recruited various hackers to do some questionable work for me," Ramirez responded coldly.

"All right," Lance said. Any other time he might have put up more of a fight, calling Ramirez out for his possible corruption, but with everything going on today, he thought it wasn't the time for that.

"Why do you think we shouldn't trust her? Do you have evidence she is a Lemurian or that the Historian paid her?" Lance asked.

"I think she's genuine, but her information might not be. The NSA and DIA have shown me proof of Lemurians pretending to be informants in order to lure out hackers that might be a threat to them. I think this Webb is a

Lemurian but not the Historian, someone disposable to throw us off track," Ramirez said soundly.

"That seems circumstantial. We know Webb faked his death. Even if he's not the Historian, he is someone fairly high up. The hacker, if she is this Erin Cahill, told me she would contact me again. I still think we should follow this lead."

"I disagree with you, Lance, but you have done enough to earn some leeway. I only ask of you one thing. The president wants me to deal with hackers directly. If you hear any word from Erin, report back to me and continue to leave Jacob out of the loop. Understand?"

"Yeah," Lance said, though he didn't like what he was hearing. Maybe agreeing to this, doing something that someone like Ramirez would approve of, would end up adding to his regrets. But that was something he could worry about later. For now he still had to complete his mission and find the Historian.

Ramirez looked out the window. They were close to the military airport; the ride was almost over.

Ramirez looked back at Lance and said, "All right, we are close to the airport. Before you go, I have something I need to explain to you outside."

"All right," Lance said respectfully.

The car pulled to a stop at the military airport, near the runway. Even though the sun had started to rise, it was still dark. There were a large number of headlights moving around the airport. A lot of soldiers were running around, but there still seemed to be some order to them. Lance had known it would be a large operation, but the scale of it still surprised him.

Ramirez got out, and Lance followed. Outside of the car, Robert fixed his suit, which was a little disheveled from the car ride. After he'd fixed his suit, his face became more intense, like all else had left his mind except for his goal, whatever that was.

"Follow me," he said, and he started walking toward the plane, his eyes focused completely on the aircraft. Lance followed. As they walked to the plane, the soldiers formed lines beside them.

The plane's back hangar door was down, and two people stood near the ramp leading into the plane. One was Andrew, and the other was a man Lance didn't recognize. He was a military man decked out in uniform. He was about the same age as Lance and was somewhat muscular and a little shorter than Lance. His most noticeable feature was his blond hair, at a length longer than the military usually allowed.

"Ethan, I'm glad you made it," Robert said to the man, his period of intensity over.

The man shook Robert's hand and then looked at Lance and saluted. "Agent Richardson, Lieutenant Ethan Paterson here. I look forward to getting the Historian and ending the Lemurian threat."

"Agreed," Lance responded.

Robert stood next to Ethan and said, "Ethan is someone who has proven himself in the field against the Lemurians. He is my personal pick for the strike force and will accompany you on this mission."

"We look forward to working with him," Andrew said.

Robert stepped away from the plane a bit, looked at

the three men, and said in a quiet, supportive tone, "Good luck, gentlemen." With that, Robert walked away.

Ethan headed into the interior of the plane. As he walked up the ramp, he said, "I have been looking forward to this for a long time."

19

The next day, Lance was on the bridge of a military vessel in the South Pacific. Besides the commotion of some soldiers behind him, it was probably about as quiet as it could be. Despite being on his way to a battle and despite being a little nervous about his conversation with Robert Ramirez, Lance actually felt peaceful. Maybe it was just the water, which was genuinely beautiful, or maybe it was the fact that he was on his way to what could be the Lemurian headquarters, maybe to end their threat once and for all. Lance tried to empty his mind and continue to enjoy the view. Very shortly he would have to once again be ready to deal with his potential death.

While Lance was watching the water, Andrew came up behind him. Andrew didn't say anything. He just put his hands on the rail of the boat and looked out on the water as well.

Lance decided to break the ice and have some conversation with Andrew. "Maybe we should go somewhere in the South Pacific after this is over, for that surfing trip."

"I like that idea," Andrew said. "I know you've been around. Ever been anywhere in the South Pacific?"

"Not really. I've spent some time in the Philippines but haven't been to any of the islands around here. How about you?"

"Me neither. I've been to Australia, though."

"How are the waves in Australia?" Lance asked.

"Pretty good. You know, some people say that the farther away you get from the East Coast, the better the waves are."

"Really?" Lance asked, honestly curious.

"Yeah. Think about it. Ever been to Florida?"

"Yeah, I guess that makes some sense, now that I think about it. I haven't gone surfing since Tara was born. I might be a little bit rusty."

"That's to be expected," Andrew said. "We'll get this son of the bitch the Historian, and after that we'll go surfing, just like the good old days."

"I look forward to that. Speaking of the mission, what do you think about Ramirez's man—Paterson, was it?"

"Yeah, you're talking about Ethan. If it's any consolation, he doesn't seem to be the politician type. From what I can tell, he was just a normal soldier until he had some success against the Lemurians."

"Former soldier with some success—that kind of sounds familiar," Lance said.

"Yeah, I guess so, but he came right out of the army. He has never worked intelligence," Andrew said.

"That's not a big deal for now. We're in a military operation, after all, and the strike force is supposed to be outside of normal intelligence. I'm more worried about what happens after this. I know Ramirez wants him to come back to the strike force."

"I think you can agree that we should focus on this mission for now," Andrew said.

"Yeah, I agree." Lance paused and then said, "Andrew, I don't want to sound rude, but I think I'm going to go to the bunk and spend some time by myself and collect my thoughts for a bit."

"Okay, see you soon," Andrew said.

Lance walked away from Andrew. He figured he had about three hours until the assault started. He thought he might try to get another hour and a half or so of sleep to be more prepared, though he wondered if he'd be able to fall asleep with everything on his mind.

When he reached his bunk, he took out a shoebox from under it and. The box was empty except for a letter Lance had written and a family photo taken shortly before the Berlin attacks. Lance took a look at the picture and put it down, and then he took his ring off and put it in the shoebox. With that, he lay down, and after a while he drifted to sleep.

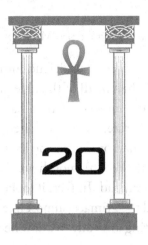

20

L ance was on a boat leading several other men to the island where the Lemurian base was located. The only one he knew, oddly, was Ethan Paterson. Andrew had been asked to lead another group of men that would be working closely with the Chinese army to secure the other side of the island.

Lance wasn't looking out the window of the boat, so he couldn't see the bombing going on, but he could hear it. Lance had mostly worked by himself when he was a field agent. It had been a while since he was this close to a conflict like this. It reminded him of being in Afghanistan taking out Taliban bases.

Lance guessed that the Lemurians had better technology than the Taliban, but he wouldn't know for sure until he reached the island. Lance also thought this battle would be better in a way because there were no civilians on the island.

He knew they were getting close. Some of the other men were starting to get up, and then he suddenly felt the boat hit the beach. Lance started to get up but not too quickly. He wanted to make sure the safety was off on his gun in case he needed to defend himself. Lance had been observing Ethan in all of this. He had to admit that he admired Ethan's intensity. Ethan had not said a word on the entire boat ride. Lance had seen a lot of soldiers in his life, but he had only seen the look on Ethan's face a few times before. Ethan's mouth was in a grimace, but he didn't look overly sad. In fact, it looked like there was happiness behind the grimace, almost like he was masking a smile, not wanting anybody to know he was happy to be in a battle. Lance really noticed Ethan's eyes. They were a light blue, light enough that they looked almost gray, and they were clearly focused. Lance wondered whether that was what he'd looked like to others while in Copper Canyon.

Once the boat landed, Ethan got up quickly and got out after a few of the other men. Lance followed.

The beach would have been beautiful any other day, but the smoke from the bombing was obscuring its beauty. Beyond the beach were some palm trees crushed by bombs. Lance guessed the army had done a good enough job clearing the beach in preparation for their arrival.

One of the men asked, "What's next in the mission, sir?"

Lance said, "Go and scout the area and see if there are any remaining Lemurians, and then we'll release a flare telling everybody the beach is secure." Lance took out this gun. "Move out," he said, gesturing for some of the soldiers to move in front of the him, another necessary evil he had to deal with. The higher-ups in the mission had ordered Lance to ensure his own survival. Ethan didn't seem to mind, though, immediately going to the front of the pack.

After a few minutes of moving along the shoreline, Lance eventually saw a Lemurian antiaircraft gun in the distance. The gun was surrounded by sandbags, with around twenty men inside the trench with the gun. To Lance it looked like something out of World War II.

"Should we call an air strike?" one of the soldiers whispered to Lance.

"No, we take this out first. After this the island should be defenseless for the rest of the military transports," Lance said.

This dialogue feels a little out of place. Should it be combined with the earlier "Ethan, I want you and your men to go to the left ..." dialogue? Here's what I'm imagining:

Lance crouched down to the ground with his men and then hid behind a rock. He whispered, "Ethan, I need you to lead a team of ten of these guys. I want you and your men to go to the left and throw some grenades and shoot them from that angle. Once they move their fire to your side, my group will flank them and take out the turret."

"All right," Ethan said. He then added emotionally, "Lance, I hope we succeed in stopping this today."

"Me too," Lance said, nodding in agreement.

The two groups broke apart, and Lance and his men started walking ...

Lance and his men started walking toward the right side of the trench. They were still covered by a series of rocks and palm trees. When they got close to the side of the trench, Lance paused, waiting for the sounds of grenades hitting the trench.

An explosion hit the far side of the trench, killing two of the Lemurians. Ethan and his men charged out of the brush, firing. The commotion forced even the machine gunners to exit their stations. It was working as planned. All the remaining soldiers in the trench went over to the left to fight Ethan's group.

Lance whispered, "All right, now."

Lance cocked his gun and started marching toward the trench. When he got within fifty yards, he fired. Lance and his men were able to shoot at least seven of the Lemurians in the back while they were occupied with Ethan's forces.

Quickly, however, the remainder of the Lemurian soldiers jumped into a holding pattern, firing from both sides of the trench. Bullets were firing from every direction. Lance shouted a rallying cry. "We outnumber them! Keep firing! Keep marching!"

Lance's men were still proceeding with minimal losses, but then one of the enemy soldiers got up from behind the sandbags with a rocket launcher. Lance screamed, "Rockets! Retreat! Go for cover!"

Before they could retreat, a rocket hit near Lance's group, killing several of his men and knocking him to the ground. Lance lifted his gun, took aim, and shot the soldier wielding the rocket launcher through his chest. Lance got back up and yelled, "Launch more grenades now!"

Several of Lance's men fired grenades into the trench, and within moments a few more Lemurians were killed. Lance, feeling confident of their victory, screamed, "Keep marching! Keep shooting!" His soldiers then got close and shot the remaining three Lemurians, capturing the trench.

With the last remaining Lemurians in the area dead, Lance's group joined back up with Ethan and his men. As Ethan looked over the dead Lemurians, he seemed to be holding back a smile. After a period of silence, he finally asked, "Should we light the flare and signal that it is safe for soldiers to land in this area?"

Lance said, "I need to call Andrew first to see if he's in position, because when I launch the flare, chances are the Lemurians will realize what is happening and will try to recapture this trench."

"That's a fair point," Ethan said.

Lance took out his walkie-talkie and called Andrew. "We've secured the antiaircraft gun. Use the trace on me to find the coordinates. I expect any remaining Lemurians will be attempting a counterattack on our position. We can use some air support."

"Roger," Andrew said. "Hold your position. We are sending Apaches to help clear the area."

"Thanks."

Lance got his group together and yelled, "Ethan take a team and go to sniping position to help us get some cover, everyone else, destroy the antiaircraft gun as best you can. If we fail to hold this trench, we can at least make it no use to them."

Some of the men detonated grenades anti-aircraft guns, destroying them, which made Lance happy. He then took the flare and lit it. The flare shot in the air and exploded. Lance said, "Take cover in the trench.

Get ready. If there's going to be a counterattack, it will be now."

Lance and his men waited for a few minutes in the trench. It looked like they wouldn't be attacked after all. However, after about ten minutes, twenty men began to charge the trench with repeating rifles. Lance told his men to fire, but at that moment, Ethan and his team started gunning down the charging men, sniping several of the Lemurian soldiers.

Lance became confident and yelled, "Fire! Finish them off!" Lance's men successful gunned down the remaining men charging the trench. It seemed the threat was over.

Lance took the time to look over the dead Lemurians and their uniforms; it seemed the Historian had gathered a multicultural force. The men were of a variety of races. Since the men had shown a willingness to die, Lance guessed they weren't mercenaries. Lance wanted to get closer to one of the corpses to inspect what sort of body armor the Lemurians were wearing, but then he heard a noise.

In a clearing about three hundred yards away from the trench, several trees fell down. Then a tank appeared over the horizon. Lance looked at the tank with disbelief. He could not believe this was happening. One of the soldiers next to Lance turned to him and nervously asked, "What are we going to do now?"

Lance nearly panicked but then focused. "Get cover. Maybe we can destroy it with some grenades."

The tank grew closer. In an instant it shot its gun and destroyed half the trench, killing several men. Just when

Lance was about to order a retreat, an explosion occurred on top of the tank, followed by another explosion. Lance refocused. It looked like the tank was decommissioned. Lance was curious how this had happened. Then he looked behind him and saw several soldiers in foreign uniforms approaching. Upon closer inspection, Lance realized they were Chinese soldiers. This surprised Lance. He'd known the Chinese were going to be involved in the mission, but he hadn't expect such close coordination. Then again, these men had probably saved his life, so Lance figured this wasn't the time to quibble.

One of the Chinese soldiers said, "Soldier, please state your name."

"Agent Lance Richardson," Lance replied. "I am in charge of the paratroopers sent to clear out this trench. I also have a few more men up on the hill in a sniper position led by Lieutenant Ethan Paterson."

"Good to hear from you, Mr. Richardson. I'm Lieutenant Jiang Tiong of the Chinese armed forces. It is good time that we got here," the soldier responded in broken English.

"You're goddamn right about that, my friend," Lance said happily. "I'm curious—what firepower did you use to destroy that tank?"

"Sorry, what?" Jiang said.

Realizing Jiang probably did not speak English fluently, Lance rephrased his question. "The tank—what did you use to destroy it?"

"Called in air strike."

Lance would have preferred to know the exact model

of plane that had been used, but he knew he might be pushing his luck trying to explain that to this man.

Jiang seemed to notice Lance's frustration and said, "Sorry, English is not very good."

"Relax, man. I can't speak any Chinese, so I'd kind of be a jerk if I was bothered by your English," Lance said.

Coming down from the hill Ethan started to rush towards Lance and Jiang "I don't mean to interrupt, but we have a mission,", butting into the conversation.

Lance said, "All right, give me a hundred men, and I will destroy any remaining antiaircraft guns around the island. How about you use the rest of the men to clear out the remaining trenches?"

"We've already cleared out this part of the island. You should be good to attack the center of the island," Jiang replied.

"Great," Lance said.

"We have somebody coming who wants to talk to you," Jiang said.

Several of the Chinese soldiers behind Jiang moved aside, revealing Andrew and some other American soldiers.

Andrew smiled as he came closer. "Lance, I'm glad you made it."

"You are a sight for sore eyes, Andrew," Lance said.

"Thank you, Lance, but I have something important I need to tell you. We did some sonar of the island, and we believe the main Lemurian base is underground, below the mountain in the center of the island. There," Andrew said as he pointed to the mountain.

"Jiang told me we've secured most of the island, so we should be able to take over the base relatively easily."

Andrew shook his head. "It won't be easy, Lance. We were able to send some unmanned drones to scan the island, and it looks like there is currently only one way in."

"Where is that entrance?" Lance asked.

"It's an elevator on top of the mountain," Andrew said.

Lance said, "With one small entrance, I can only take a few men. There might be hundreds of men aiming at the elevator ready to shoot at us. We need to develop a plan."

"You knew it would be a dangerous mission, but you are the best. Are you up to it?" Andrew asked.

"There's no reason for suicide," Ethan chimed in. "Do some poison gas. We can clear out the base before we send our troops in there."

"We're not going to use poison," Lance said. "That would be against at least two international treaties I can think of, and despite what the media says about the military, we do have some rules of engagement. Besides, I think I know of a way we can be sure to enter that base and live."

"You've been right before, Richardson, but you better be a hundred percent sure about this," Ethan said. "I don't exactly care about the human rights of the Lemurians after all they've done, and I'd be more than comfortable dealing with any media parasites trying to justify false outrage against us. Frankly, if gas isn't an option, I suggest we just bomb the place with several bunker busters and then sift through the rubble. We might even kill the Historian in the process."

"It's not just about the Historian. We need the base in decent condition. This is our best chance to find information—their contacts, their locations. If we just destroy the place, we might miss our chance to end them," Lance said. "I promise everybody here that I can do this mission."

"Thank you, Lance," Andrew said. "Ethan, continue working with Lance, and I will continue leading the assault here on top of the island."

"Where is the entrance to this bunker?" Lance asked.

"We believe it's about ten thousand yards in front of the trench you took from the Lemurian soldiers," Andrew said.

"How is the battle progressing across the island?" Lance asked.

"Very good. Five more trenches have fallen. We almost have the entire island cleared, and we now have two thousand soldiers on the island."

"Good."

Just then Lance felt the ground beneath him shake. He looked in the distance toward the beach and saw several American tanks starting to come closer to them.

Andrew gestured to the tanks and said, "As you can probably tell, we seem to have more than enough to finish the job up here."

"Well, what do you think?" Ethan asked Lance.

"Very good," Lance said. "I think we should start heading to the elevator."

"Good luck, Lance," Andrew said."

Lance and Ethan headed toward the mountain with about ten other well-armed men. Once they were a few hundred yards away, the tanks started firing from all directions. "Why are they firing?" Lance asked Ethan. "I don't see any Lemurians."

"To suppress any Lemurians that could be trying to converge on our path to the elevator shaft," Ethan said. He suddenly froze and then said quietly, "Lance, I think I see some movement in the brush."

"Okay," Lance whispered as he grasped his gun. "I'll tell the men to fire."

"I can handle this," Ethan responded coolly.

Ethan took out a flask of alcohol and a rag and created a Molotov cocktail. He threw it into some brush, and burning men started to flee in retreat.

"Fire," Ethan commanded coldly, and he and the other soldiers gunned down the men running from the brush.

Ethan looked back to Lance and then said to the soldiers, "Good work, men. Less filth in the world."

Lance was starting to feel a little weird about Ethan's intensity. He was worried about what Ethan could do if pushed, but he felt a sense of purpose within Ethan's anger, something he had not expected in Ramirez's personal recommendation for the strike force. Lance wondered again if he'd looked like Ethan to Dan and the other agents at Copper Canyon. Lance eventually said, "Nice shooting there, Ethan. We could use more men like you."

Ethan said strongly, "Lance, I hate the Lemurians with every fiber of my being. I pray that we end them soon."

"You're a good man, Ethan. Just remember to keep focused. I hate the Lemurians as well, but we don't want to get too wrapped up in the moment. It only takes one mistake to ruin a mission."

"Trust me, I know. I will not compromise this mission," Ethan said.

Then suddenly one of the soldiers yelled, "Stop!"

"Why?" Ethan asked.

"According to drone we sent, we should be here," the soldier said.

Lance looked at the side of the mountain and saw what looked like a mine shaft elevator. He turned to Ethan and his men and said, "All right, scan the shaft for explosives. We don't want to die so anticlimactically."

"I prefer not to die, period," Ethan said.

Two men took out a sonar-like device that could detect anomalies. Lance waited for a few moments, until one of the two soldiers said, "It's clear, sir."

"Great. Now move forward," Lance said.

All the men stepped into the elevator, and then slowly the elevator started to descend. As the elevator descended, Lance busted open the wire panel on the far side of the elevator and started messing with the wires.

"What are you doing?" Ethan yelled.

"You don't think I'm going to let them fire freely at us, do you? I'm rigging the wires to make sure the doors only open a little so we can use them for cover against any Lemurians waiting for us. Then we immediately throw some grenades through the door opening to help clear some of the Lemurians."

"Sounds good to me," Ethan said.

As the elevator crept downward, the men got nervous. They thought they might see the Historian himself. After a few minutes that seemed like an eternity, the elevator stopped, and the doors opened just slightly.

Lance whispered, "Soldiers, launch the grenades through the crack now."

The grenades went off as planned. Lance heard the explosions. However, there were no returning shots at the elevator.

"No one is firing. May we go out, sir?" one of the soldiers asked.

"Fine," Lance said. "But keep you guns up and go slowly. There might still be some Lemurians in there." Lance then worked with the wires to open the elevator doors all the way.

All the soldiers got out of the elevator and entered a large room with their guns still armed. However, there was still no sign of any enemy soldiers.

"Drop your weapons," Ethan said. "There's no sign of any heat signatures on the thermal scanner. There is no one here but us."

"How is that possible?" one of the soldiers asked.

"Maybe they escaped through a second exit we didn't know about," responded another soldier.

Lance added, "Or maybe we were wrong. Maybe we're in a minor base, not the main base in the area."

Ethan moved to a side room off the main room and shined a flashlight inside. "No, this is the place," he said. "Look."

Lance walked over to the room and said, "Jesus." Inside was a modern computer system that would not have looked out of place in Langley. Lance guessed that was what the Lemurians had been using to command the island's defenses. The Lemurian flag was plastered around the room.

Lance looked at Ethan and said, "If this is the right base, we might as well look around and see what we can find."

"Here's that goddamned flag again," Ethan said. "Did you ever find out what the symbol means?"

"It's the name of an ancient Egyptian pharaoh—Menes. We're not sure why the Historian likes that symbol. Some people think he might be a pagan. A lot of pagan groups respect pre-Christian civilizations," Lance said.

One of the soldiers walked into the room and exclaimed, "Agent Richardson, I'm sorry to interrupt, but there's something you must see."

"What?" Lance asked.

"I think you need to see it for yourself," the soldier said. "Come with me."

Lance followed the soldier to the other side of the large main room. The soldier opened a door that led to another room. Inside was a huge screen with a countdown. White numbers appeared on a black background. 33 … 32 … 31 …

The soldier said, "We checked it, sir. There are no weapons attached to it. There's only a signal."

Lance was frozen in fear. He couldn't help but wonder what sick twist the Historian had waiting for him. He was still not over the shock of finding out about the nuke, what he was taunting them with. Lance's breathing grew faster. He was almost having a panic attack brought on by fear and anger. It finally was starting to make sense why the base was abandoned.

The countdown started to end. 3 ... 2 ... 1 ... There was a pause, and the screen went black. It was silent. Nothing was happening. Then a news report came up. Lance knew enough to tell that the characters on the news ticker were Korean, although he had no idea what they said. The screen went black again.

The news feed turned back on. It was still in Korean, but now the story seemed different. A reporter was interviewing a crying woman in a city. Lance didn't understand what the woman was saying, but he could tell she was hysterical. The news feed then cut away to a horrible image: a nuclear mushroom cloud.

Lance went to his knees. Seeing another nuclear weapon go off was something he couldn't handle. He started crying. He was broken. Here he was in a chamber of the Lemurians' base. A few hours ago, he'd thought the war was over, and now the Historian was humiliating him for constantly failing to save people.

The cycle started to repeat, with another newscast in German appearing, following the exact same pattern: a normal news story, than a cut to a live interview of some other people crying and mourning.

Lance was still collapsed on the ground in the face of the destruction. He'd failed. Despite their victory in Mexico, the Historian had still launched the nukes. As Lance sank into his desperation, Ethan yelled, "I'll kill you! We got your base, Historian." Ethan turned to Lance. "He's just trying to get to us. Get up." Ethan turned back to the screen, letting out in an angry bellow, "You hear me, you bastard? We got your base! We'll search it, and we'll find you."

The screen turned black once more. Lance clenched his chest, preparing himself for another city somewhere in the world to be destroyed, hoping against hope he could handle it. Instead the Menes symbol the Lemurians used appeared, along with a doctored voice.

"I don't think you'll find much here, Paterson. I had time to evacuate."

"How the fuck do you know my name? Who are you?" Ethan asked, grinding his teeth to hold back his anger.

"You can't guess? You were just talking about me," the voice mocked.

"Historian." Ethan grimaced. "You will be put on trial. We will stop you, You lied you said we had a month. It has only been a week" Ethan snapped in anger.

"No, I gave the world a chance to stop this and you showed no signs of attempting to comply, but you failed to listen to my warning. A smart leader can change plans when needed" the Historian said, his tone still mocking.

Ethan was huffing, rage consuming him. Lance, still on his knees, couldn't say a word, but hearing the Historian's voice was making rage replace the sadness he felt for the victims of the bombs. Lance thought. The Historian sounded nothing like a freedom fighter. Lance knew more than ever that asking for those regions' independence was a diversion, as he'd suspected.

Lance remained silent as the Historian continued, "You think you can stop this from happening on your own shores? Your failure will be complete soon."

Ethan finished his huffing, though he continued to be

consumed with rage. "I'll kill you! I'll kill you!" he yelled over and over, banging his fists against the walls of the abandoned base. His hands began to bleed with him so caught up in his anger.

Lance wanted to hurt the Historian, to not let the Historian's victory be complete. In his desperation, he could think of only one thing that might work.

"*Victor!*" Lance yelled impassionedly.

There was a long silence, so long Lance wondered whether the Historian had heard him. The screen still showed the Lemurian symbol.

"Say something, Victor Webb," Lance said.

The screen scrambled again, and after a few moments a face started to form, slowly but surely. The outline of a man and an office appeared. Lance could tell the man was the one from the picture Josh found, albeit a little older. He was sitting with the camera close to his face. He had large green eyes and black hair that had not yet turned gray. From his face and upper body, he looked to be in good shape but not overly muscular. Wherever he was living, he was able to take care of himself. With him sitting he could not make out exactly how tall he was, but he could tell he was average height at best.

After a few seconds that seemed like hours to Lance, Webb said nonchalantly, "So you know my name, Lance Richardson. I've always believed in rewarding merit."

Lance was in shock finally seeing the Historian. He didn't know what to do. He stared silently at Webb, the man who had taken his daughter's future. Sometimes Lance felt numb to the loss of his family, but the one thing that always got him mad and broke through the numbness

was thinking about what Tara could have been, knowing that he would never go to her high school graduation or her wedding.

Lance finally yelled, "Webb, I promise I will make you pay for everything you have done. You will pay for everyone you've hurt if it is the last thing I do. I promise on the graves of everyone who died in Manchester and every one of your victims that you will be brought to justice."

The neutral look on Webb's face twisted into a smile. "At some point, I bet you promised your daughter you would always keep her safe. With the record you have, it looks like I have little to worry about." Webb chuckled. He then added confidently, "I wonder, Lance—what do you think Tara's last thoughts were before Raul put that bullet in her head? Do you think she was disappointed in you? Do you think she waited for you until the very end, hoping you would save her? Or maybe she spent her final moments traumatized, so consumed with fear you weren't even a thought in her mind."

Lance felt as if his eyes were glowing red. He couldn't stand that this piece of filth was in front of him. He was sickened that he'd ever wanted to know this man's name. He hated himself for his prior curiosity about the Historian's identity. He regretted having any emotion for this man other than hatred. In that moment he saw only his daughter's murderer in front of him, not a target that might have vital information. His anger had no words. He wanted to hurt Webb, even if it was just to stop his mocking.

Lance raised his gun and fired, breaking the TV. He

made no noise while doing this and showed no emotion, except for a grimace. He wanted to show as little emotion toward Webb as possible, thinking that any visible emotion would give Webb some sense of satisfaction.

The video feed cut out when Lance shot the TV, and Webb's voice disappeared as well. It seemed the transmission was over. Lance didn't know if destroying the TV had stopped the transmission or if Webb had just ended it because he wanted to. But Lance didn't care at that moment.

Ethan finally walked over to Lance, seeming to recover from the shock of Lance firing his gun. He said, "Lance, we still have the base. He admitted that he had to evacuate. We will kill that man. We can still avenge them."

There was some truth to what Ethan said, but Lance could not feel victory in this situation. After everything he'd seen here today, it seemed obvious. Today Victor Webb had won.

21

Houston, Texas, 11:00 p.m. one hour after island attack

Jacob Lanser was preparing for a final assault on the Lemurian team that was going to launch a nuke on Houston. Through wiretapping and the interrogation of some captured Lemurians, he'd been able to trace the nuke to the sewers beneath Houston. Jacob had secured info that it would be a suitcase nuke that would be easy to move quickly. Jacob already had a plan in place and was wondering what could still be done before the final strike. If there was anything his years of working in intelligence had taught him, it was that it couldn't hurt to rally his men.

Jacob walked in front of his men before the sewer entrance. The place had a noticeable reek, but Jacob ignored it for the moment because he had something bigger to deal with.

"Men, we believe the Lemurians will launch the nuke at midnight in the sewers, the second the cease-fire is over. What I am about to tell you is very important. Tonight our lives are expendable. We must secure this bomb at all costs. The lives of millions are at risk. Every move we make tonight is to ensure Houston's survival. We win tonight, and history will remember us as heroes."

"So we should just give our lives?" one of the soldiers said.

"Yes," Jacob said. "Don't throw your life away if it isn't necessary, but securing the bomb comes first. Besides, if that bomb goes off, you won't live for long anyway. If anyone does not feel they are capable of handling this, you can leave now. I promise there will be no legal action against you."

Jacob paused briefly. The men all stayed. Jacob looked at the men and said, "Thank you. Now let's stop that bomb."

Jacob led the men into the sewer, and they walked along a pipeline. They moved slowly, striving to hide their movements from any Lemurians they might encounter.

"Men, be quiet," Jacob said. "Any signal that we're here might cause them to detonate the bomb early and kill at first sight. We can't risk this bomb going off."

Jacob and his men walked through the pipeline until they heard men talking in the distance. Jacob, taking the lead, raised his hand to signal the men to stop and listened carefully.

"Antonio, where is Candellario?" a Lemurian soldier asked in the distance. "I thought he would be here for this."

Another man, Antonio presumably, replied, "Webb told him to be outside of Houston for this. He claims Raul is too important to get captured or killed if this goes wrong."

The first man said, "So Webb thinks Raul is worth more than us?"

"Boris, you know he is. Just be glad Webb is giving us this opportunity. It shows he trusts us."

"You're right," Boris said in a businesslike manner. "We must finish this."

Jacob, listening to this conversation, thought, *These guys are very loyal. Can't believe Candellario isn't going to be here. I thought this would be our chance to stop him.*

Jacob signaled for his men to follow him to the end of the pipeline. In the circular space where the pipes met, some men were congregated around something. Jacob knew it was the bomb. Jacob whispered, "Men, this is it. We stop this now. It looks like there are ten men. The two closest to the bomb need to be killed first. Then we surround the bomb and fire like hell at the rest. Once we attack, someone might try to rush to the bomb to activate it even though the cease-fire isn't over yet." Jacob then confidently added, "Time to go."

Jacob and his men charged, firing as they ran. They killed the two men closest to the bomb immediately; however, the remaining men were armed and started firing back, killing three of Jacob's men instantly. Jacob yelled, "Surround the nuke! Keep firing!" Jacob's men did as commanded. Circled around the nuke, they kept firing at the enemy soldiers until eventually, after casualties on both sides, there was only one Lemurian soldier left.

The last soldier knew he had no shot and ran down another pipeline. Jacob's soldiers tried firing at him, but Jacob said, "Forget about him. I can disable the bomb, but I need all of you to cover for me." The men surrounded

Jacob as he crouched over the bomb. They'd made it there in plenty of time. According to the timer, the bomb was set to go off in twenty-four hours. Jacob quickly cut the appropriate wires to disable the bomb and then said, "It's done, guys."

Jacob had won for the moment. He thought the bomb might contain some radiation, so he had a couple of his men scan it just in case. The bomb was truly destroyed. Jacob pointed to two men and said, "You two stand here. Contact the Houston Police Department and get the FBI to come take the bomb." He turned to the remainder of the men. "The rest of you follow me. I'm going to report back to Washington. I'm sure the administration will be happy to know about this success."

Jacob headed back down the sewer pipeline again. It still stunk to high heaven, but Jacob wasn't bothered by the smell. After months of failure, he'd stopped the bomb. The Historian was still out there, but wherever he was, he probably wasn't going to be happy about this.

"What are we going to do next, sir?" one of the men asked as they walked. "I mean, I'm glad we stopped the bomb, but what is the next step from here?"

"Having the bomb is a huge help. We can test the neutron count, and that might give us an idea of where the Lemurians got the material needed to make a nuke," Jacob said.

"All right, glad I can help nail these bastards," the soldier said.

"Good work today, Private Walker. That goes to all of you as well," Jacob said, turning to the others.

When they got out of the sewers, Jacob walked briskly

to the waiting jeeps, ready for the drive back to Ellington Air Force Base. Jacob slid into the driver's seat of one of the jeeps, and Private Walker got into the passenger seat.

While in the car, Jacob thought it would be a good time to call Robert Ramirez, the president's chief of staff, to tell him the good news. When Ramirez picked up, Jacob said, "Robert, the bomb has been stopped. Houston is safe."

Ramirez responded calmly, "Thank you, Jacob. I needed some good news today."

"What happened?" Jacob asked.

"Have you had any access to the news?"

"No, but I've been busy stopping an atomic bomb going off in downtown Houston, so give me a break."

"No need to get defensive, Jacob. Ten minutes ago, bombs went off in Hamburg and Busan."

Jacob cursed under his breath. "How is Lance?" he asked nervously. "How did the operation on the island go? Have we found out anything else about the Lemurians?"

"The Historian is named Victor Webb. We don't know much about him except that he was an American aid worker thought dead. We don't know how he arose to be the Lemurian leader," Ramirez said solemnly.

"I honestly don't know what to say right now. It's good that we finally identified the Historian, but hearing that there were two more bombs … I just don't know what to say about it anymore. This is a tragedy. I just want to stop them. Where do you think we should go from here?"

"Go back to Langley. We need your help to get a new plan in motion to finally end the Historian," Ramirez said.

"I will," Jacob said and hung up.

"Anything wrong, sir?" Private Walker asked.

"Two nukes went off, one in Germany and one in South Korea," Jacob said in an angry huff.

"Shit." Walker grimaced.

"We'll get them. We stopped them here, and we'll stop them again," Jacob said.

Jacob continued to drive for a while with mixed emotions. He felt happy about his success, his feeling of uselessness gone, but he kept thinking about the casualties that must have occurred in Hamburg and Busan. It seemed that the Historian, or this Victor Webb, was always a step ahead.

Jacob's thoughts were abruptly cut off as the jeep started to spin out of control. Two of the tires had been shot out. As Jacob tried to stabilize the jeep, he yelled, "Walker, be prepared!"

Walker grabbed his gun and aimed out the window, but he was shot immediately. The final two tires were shot out, stopping the car. Jacob ducked below the windshield and loaded his gun. If he was going to go out, he'd do it fighting.

Jacob slowly exited the jeep, attempting to see what was out there. He raised his gun. A bullet bit into his shoulder, and then he was on the ground.

A group of men approached Jacob. The leader, a tall masked man who towered over Jacob, asked one of the others, "Antonio, is this the guy?"

"Yes," Antonio replied.

The leader then said to Jacob, "Mr. Lanser,

congratulations on your victory. However, it will not last long."

"Who are you?" Jacob asked.

"I'm surprised you cannot recognize an old enemy," the man taunted. He then took off his mask, revealing himself to be Raul Candellario.

"Candellario!" Jacob exclaimed. "I thought you were too much of a coward to be in Houston tonight."

"I was just outside the range of the suitcase nuke you destroyed; I wanted to see Houston explode and know my work was completed. When Antonio here escaped from your attack, he radioed me for backup and told me that a very important member of the CIA was here."

"Looks like you failed," Jacob said defiantly. "You will not see Houston explode. I stopped you, you worthless piece of shit."

Raul gave Jacob a sick smile. "Yes, Mr. Lanser, you've stopped me. However, it looks like I'm going to get a consolation prize."

"Go ahead—kill me," Jacob said bravely. "At least I'll die saving others, something you've never known."

"I'm not going to kill you," Raul said. "Victor wants to do that himself."

"Bastard!" Jacob screamed.

Raul then said sternly, "I am getting bored of his whining, Antonio. Take care of this for me."

Antonio walked up behind Jacob and hit him with the barrel of his gun, knocking him out.

22

After the failed island invasion, Lance and Andrew returned immediately to CIA headquarters in Langley. It was more than a day after the nukes had dropped in Korea and Germany, and everyone was still in a panic at headquarters. As Lance walked down one of the corridors, he spotted Andrew and called out in a nervous rage, "Andrew, have we found Jacob?"

"The bomb in Houston has been secured, but Jacob is still missing. We've found the body of one of the men who was with him. As of now, it looks like an abduction is the most likely scenario," Andrew said, a nervous tone sneaking through his calm demeanor.

"Shit," Lance simply said. He didn't know which would be worse, Jacob being dead or Jacob being at the mercy of the Lemurians. Lance was at a loss of words in regard to Jacob. As morbid as it was, he thought it might be better to focus on the good news for now. They had secured one of the Lemurians' bombs, and they might be able to figure out where it was built, giving them a good lead. With these conflicting emotions in his mind—the hope of the bomb lead and the fear of Jacob's capture—Lance thought it would be best to focus on delegating the tasks.

"With Jacob missing in action, who's in charge of the strike force?" he asked Andrew.

"As of now I'm acting leader, until we reach a more permanent solution," Andrew said quickly, without much confidence. It was clear Jacob's mission was taking a toll on him.

"Is Sarah doing all right?" Lance asked with concern.

"She's at home with some family. We've brought Ethan onto the force and have promoted Josh in order to keep up with the workload."

"I can't fault her for that." Lance sighed, collecting his thoughts. He wondered what the next step should be. He figured he could simply ask Andrew for some advice. Andrew seemed down, but Lance still trusted him for good advice. "What do you think we should do in the short term?"

There was a pause, and then Andrew said, "Head to the command center. I know this is tough, but we have to build on the momentum of finding the bomb and identifying the Historian."

"Yeah, okay. I was thinking we should redouble our efforts to find Anubis, the hacker Robert claims to be Erin Cahill," Lance said in a gruff, serious tone. After everything that had happened, Lance wanted to make as much progress as possible, anything to get his mind off of Jacob's potential capture. "Okay, Andrew, I'll talk to you later."

"All right," Andrew said.

Lance left Andrew and walked to the conference

room with the reliable world map and some TVs. Lance was feeling a little sick seeing the reports on the bombs going off. At this point he figured there was no point to looking at the victims. All Lance thought about was stopping future disasters. There was nothing he could do now for the people of Busan and Hamburg.

Josh was working on his computer, and Lance went toward him. When Josh noticed Lance, he asked, "Are we having another meeting? I've heard about Jacob being missing."

"We are. Now that we know Victor Webb is the Historian, I think we can find out more about him, with the entire department looking. You should probably work on finding anything you can about Anubis. She was right about the Historian. It can't hurt finding out more about her."

"Her?" Josh questioned.

"Yeah, Robert Ramirez claims that he knows Anubis and that she's a hacker named Erin Cahill. Did you ever hear of that name while you were in the hacking community?"

"I've never heard of her, but that honestly doesn't mean much. I think sometimes you're so happy to have a former hacker working for you that you overstate my importance," Josh smirked.

"Trust me, I read your file; I know the biggest job you did was hacking some game company. You're here now because you were right, and in these times that counts for a lot," Lance said sternly.

"What is the priority then, Cahill or the Historian, I mean Webb, I guess?" Josh asked.

"You no longer have to work in secret. I told you that you'd be rewarded, and I'm a man of my word. You will have any resources necessary to find out more information on Victor Webb. As of now you are head of this effort."

"I'm honored, Lance. I'll remember this," Josh said with emotion, looking at Lance with wide eyes, looking truly appreciative.

Lance was happy to gain Josh's approval; he was a good man despite his past. "Just stay calm, all right? There's a lot going wrong right now. I've spoken to that bastard Webb myself, and I've never been more certain that we have to stop him at all costs. I will not rest until the Lemurians exist only as a history lesson."

"That might take a while," Josh smirked. "Even today there are still those freaks that try to follow Hitler's example."

"Always giving it to me straight, Josh," Lance said, returning the smirk. "I'll settle for the day Webb's dead and the only Lemurians are a few losers rotting in prison, trying to sell some two-bit drugs."

"Agreed," Josh said.

Lance left Josh to his work and thought about where he should go next. He was curious how Ethan was holding up. Ethan had handled Webb attacking the cities worse than Lance had. Lance was surprised at how well he himself was handling the situation. He didn't even feel more than basic sadness for those events. Lance was becoming more desensitized to the horror. He didn't want to feel that way. He'd felt like that in the past, and it had taken a lot of time to reverse that, mostly with Rachel's help.

Lance walked toward the center of the room near the monitors, interested in seeing the updates on the situation. Just then, Dan rushed into the room, headed toward Lance. At first Lance thought maybe Dan was worried about him. He hadn't seen Dan since his return from the island. However, as Dan got closer, Lance realized the look on Dan's face was one of great fear. As soon as Dan got close enough, he immediately said with clear fear in his voice, "Lance, come with me. There's something you should see for yourself."

Lance didn't feel the need to ask any follow-up questions. He trusted Dan enough to believe that something important was happening. Lance followed Dan down a secluded hallway to a small, rarely used conference room that was currently crowded. Lance recognized some of the key faces. Andrew was there, and so were Franco and Director Samson. Lance also recognized General Jason Goddard. Lance had a brief sense of worry that was only compounded when he looked at the far wall, where a TV projected an internet feed of Jacob in the middle of a room on his knees, visibly gagged.

It was horrifying to watch. One of Jacob's ears had been removed, one eye was black, and there were visible scars on his forehead. It almost seemed as if his captors had made sure his face would be just recognizable enough for the public. Jacob was still wearing the SWAT uniform he'd been kidnapped in. The Lemurians hadn't seemed to dress him up in anything, unlike Islamic terrorist groups. The video was very quiet except for the sound of Jacob's breathing.

Lance hated this pause in activity and the silence of

the room. It was bad enough that Jacob was captured, but now he was stuck looking at the captured Jacob. Every moment Lance was in the room, he felt trapped in a personal purgatory. After a few minutes that seemed like hours, a Lemurian soldier wearing a mask walked in and stood behind Jacob. The soldier took off the mask, revealing the familiar face of Victor Webb.

Webb removed Jacob's gag and quickly asked, "Do you have any last words?"

With the gag removed, Jacob was able to get some of his breath back, and he then yelled in a panic, "This is a tactic! Don't listen … Don't listen!" Jacob twisted toward the camera and yelled at the top of his lungs, "Fight back … Fight back!" He kept yelling. Then there was a loud bang, and Jacob fell down.

Webb slowly walked toward the camera, not saying anything, and knelt down, obstructing the view of Jacob's corpse. Everybody in the conference room was dead silent except for Franco, who, of all people, started to cry a little bit. Lance didn't blame him. He almost wished he was crying himself, but he was too absorbed in the situation. He just sat there, intensely looking at Webb, waiting for him to say something. Finally, Webb said in a calm, stern manner, "My name is Victor Webb. I am the leader of the Lemurians." With those simple words, he started to walk away, and the video feed ended.

Lance just stared at the blank screen. He couldn't believe that Jacob Lanser, his friend and the man who had trained him, was dead. The Historian couldn't get away with this. Two weeks ago Lance had thought he might have finally cornered the Historian, but now two cities were destroyed and Jacob was dead. Eventually Dan asked calmly, "Has this been released to the public?"

"Webb leaked it online," Samson said. "We intercepted some early leaks, but it is only a matter of time before the general public knows what happened."

"He spoke so little," Andrew said, sounding confused. "He didn't gloat about the bombings. He just told us his name. He didn't even tell anyone why Jacob was important."

"He didn't need to," Lance interjected angrily, causing the other men in the room to look at him. "We're going to do it for him," he said more calmly.

"What are you talking about, Lance?" Dan asked.

"Everybody in the world is going to ask who the man Webb killed was, and that, combined with the panic over two more nukes going off, is going to play into Webb's hands. People are going to lose faith in the government. We knew his identity, so he revealed it to the world before we could. He still looks like he's in control. Every day we don't tell the world who Jacob was, the people are going to grow more restless. The last thing we need right now is more looters and protesters. As much as it hurts, we need to be honest."

"I agree with Lance," Robert Ramirez interjected. "I've seen hundreds of politicians try to keep something hidden only for it to be exposed later. If you want to limit the damage, tell everyone about the nuke Jacob stopped in Houston. Jacob is a martyr. He died saving millions. There should be streets and bridges named after him. That could combat some of the fallout."

"In America ... What about the rest of the world?"

Dan asked. "Do you think that could stop increased fallout abroad?"

"I think the international community will be happy with the progress, but it won't have the same effect. I honestly expect increased strife in Europe, but remember—as morbid as it is, we need to focus on our nation first," Ramirez said.

"So are you saying we take advantage of Jacob's death while his corpse is still warm and his wife probably hasn't heard the news yet? That doesn't feel right," Lance said.

"Didn't Jacob himself say that he was going to do whatever it took to defeat the Lemurians?" Robert snapped. "You're willing to accept collateral damage but not play politics?"

Lance quickly silenced his objections, accepting Robert's position. He realized he might be rejecting the idea only for emotional reasons.

Franco had stopped crying, but he was still clearly upset. Samson stood up, taking control of the situation in the room. He said confidently, "Lance, Robert is right. Robert, you have my blessing to conduct a political strategy, but the most important thing going forward is to find and kill that bastard Victor Webb."

"I already have contacts trying to dig up more about Webb's history," Lance said in a businesslike manner. "All we know now is that he was a former aid worker who faked his death."

"Tell your men to get in contact with the NSA. We need every analyst in American intelligence researching that man. Tell them to get in contact with Eliza Churchill.

Anyone who found out anything about Webb is welcome to the team."

"If that's the case, we should tell them about our friend," Lance said, looking at Robert. "Anubis figured out the Historian's identity somehow. We need to know more."

"I told you that there's no way Erin will work with us voluntarily. There was a fallout between her and the government," Robert said.

"We won't give her the choice," Samson said. "This is war, and whether she wants to give us information or not, it's not optional for her. Anubis will be declared an enemy of the United States if she does not help us." Samson banged his hand on the table.

"That's not a good idea. Anubis gave us vital information of her own free will. Is that really what you want to do to someone who helped us willingly?" Lance asked.

"Do we have any other choice?" Robert replied begrudgingly. "She won't work for us, and we need that information," he said with some intensity.

"All right, let's get a strike force together and find this hacker. I understand your point, Lance, but we need to find Webb, and this is our best lead," Samson said.

"In Afghanistan I had to talk to some pretty tough guys to form anti-Taliban militias, and recently I think I've proven myself by convincing that Lemurian militant to give up Candellario. If I can do that, I'm sure I'll be able to recruit a hacker I've already talked to before," Lance said confidently.

"All right, it's settled. We need to get a strike force

together to track Anubis down," Franco said. He looked to Andrew and said, "Kekso, you're taking over for Lanser until further notice. Get the team together."

"Agreed," Andrew responded in a businesslike manner.

"Hold on," Dan said. "Jacob is dead, and since we saw him murdered, we've only talked about Webb."

"Jacob was my friend too, Dan, but we can't bring him back. The best way to honor him is to stop his killer and the Lemurians," Lance said with some sadness.

"How about just a moment of silence for him? I know the mission comes first, but I think after what happened we at least owe Jacob a moment of silence."

"I think we can all agree to that," Lance said. He lifted his hand and gestured. "Gentlemen?"

The other men in the room nodded, agreeing without needing to speak. Lance put his head down, closed his eyes, and reflected on the day. He was momentarily alone with his thoughts, away from the briefing. Jacob was gone. He truly had been a good friend to Lance. When Lance's sister-in-law had attempted to sue him, Jacob had supported him, helping make sure that he kept receiving benefits and keep things out of court. Lance shook his head, and several tears started to fall from his eyes. The moment of silence seemed to increase the sadness for the other men in the room as well. Franco started to cry again. Eventually the men began to leave the room.

As Lance entered the hallway, Dan walked up behind him. "What should we do next?" he asked.

"I dunno," Lance said. "I guess we should get the strike team ready. Do you want to come and get Anubis?"

"Andrew spoke to me beforehand about being the official second-in-command of the strike force now that he's in charge. Sarah also might want some time off because of the obvious. I think my place is here for now."

Lance was surprised that Dan had surpassed him in rank so quickly, but this thought didn't last long. He remembered his recent history. With Jacob's identity being leaked in the next few days, the last thing the suits in Washington needed was to have anyone as controversial as Lance on top. He understood this reasoning, and he wasn't in this for a promotion anyway. "Congratulations," he told Dan sincerely.

As Lance started to walk away, Dan said, "We probably have a few more days before the misson Is there anything you want to take care off?"

"Yeah, I have to call what's left of my family. Webb knew both Ethan and I 's name the second he saw us. I have to assume he has a good amount of information about our families. I think they should have some guards, maybe be put in witness protection," Lance said.

"I think if Webb was going to kill your family, he wouldn't have taunted you like that. It would have been more effective to kill them first. What benefit does he get giving you a heads-up? I think he's just trying to get into your head," Dan said reassuringly.

"That could be true, and purely as an analyst, I agree with you, but I'm not in the mood to take any risks with my family. Tonight I'm going to call my uncle, and I think I should call Cassandra too."

"Can you do that? Doesn't she is still bitter Jacob was

able to use his connections to stop that restraining order?" Dan asked.

"Yeah, but she is my sister-in-law, and I do love Jean and Sam. I still have to protect them, even after everything that has happened. I have my problems with Cassandra, but she doesn't deserve to be killed by the Lemurians and my niece and nephew certainly don't," Lance said. "I suggest you do the same. Call your mom and dad. Tell Jim to call his family too. If Webb knows about my uncle, he can probably find your partner's family very easily."

"All right. Stay safe, Lance."

"I'll try the best I can," Lance said begrudgingly.

The two walked off in different directions. Lance still felt the ever-present fear, despite wishing things would improve. He clung to something that was more hopeful—the fact that the nuke had been captured and that maybe Webb's location, or at least where Webb built his weapons, could be found. The thought of talking to Cassandra had brought up a new emotion, though, one that Lance had not felt in a while—a fear, not about his own survival, but a fear of being hated.

23

Pomerene Hospital, Ohio, one month after the Berlin attacks

anny Smith was walking through the halls of Pomerene Hospital, sweating in the hot August heat. It was his first time visiting Lance since the tragedy. As he wiped the sweat from his face, he had an almost good feeling, something other than anger and fear, for the first time since the start of the attacks. Danny had been afraid simply driving to the hospital. The hospital itself was surrounded by armed guards, but the roads leading to the hospital were abandoned. Most people had left after the first series of attacks on small towns across the United States. The Lemurians were fulfilling their promise. Worse than the Lemurians were the looters that sprung up, picking through the carcasses of abandoned neighborhoods.

Danny was glad that the hospital seemed to still be in good shape. It seemed that not everything was going crazy in these times.

Dan started walking up the steps to the third floor, where Lance's room was. Dan was hoping that Lance would want to speak to him. He had gotten in contact with Lance's uncle Tony, who had visited Lance earlier. Tony had said Lance was in an almost catatonic state, barely even talking, except for an occasional yes or no. Dan couldn't blame Lance; he'd only just woken up from a medically induced coma, never mind the death of his family.

As Danny climbed the stairs, he worried about being useful. He'd dealt with victims of terrorist attacks in his work at the CIA but never with a victim he knew personally. That scared Dan, something he wasn't proud to admit to himself.

As he reached the second-floor landing, he saw several doctors moving around one person on a stretcher. It was hectic but no more so than any other hospital. In these times that was something to appreciate—something not being worse than normal. Dan had only just heard about another attack in the town of Primm, Nevada. He couldn't help but wonder whether it was another Lemurian attack or maybe those goddamned looters taking advantage of the situation.

Danny tried to get in a better mood as he continued up to the third floor. He tried to think of something positive to talk about. He knew Lance liked baseball, and there was going to be a baseball season next year. That would be something positive he could talk to Lance about. Danny wondered how many visitors Lance had except his uncle. He didn't know if Lance had any. Lance's parents were dead. His mom had died when he was young, and his dad had sadly lost his battle with cancer about two years ago. Lance didn't have a lot of people in his life left.

Danny was scared. He was someone Lance trusted and would potentially be happy to see at this time in his life, but Danny had no idea what to say to his friend. However, whatever he did would be better than no one showing up.

Danny was now in front of Lance's room. He took a deep breath and walked through the door. Lance was asleep in his bed. Dan sat in a chair beside the bed. He was glad he had more time to collect his thoughts. He had time to look at Lance. Sometimes when thinking of the tragedy of Tara's and Rachel's deaths, he forgot that Lance had survived a shot to the head. Dan was honestly impressed by his friend's survival, though that probably wasn't something Lance wanted to hear right now.

Lance's left eye—or, more accurately, where Lance's left eye used to be—was covered by a bandage, but other than that obvious exception, Lance looked a lot better than Dan expected. He didn't have any cuts or bruises, and his brown hair even looked neatly groomed, with no cowlicks or bed hair.

Dan had always been impressed by Lance and still was, even now after the tragedy. Lance surviving a shot to the head had almost confirmed everything Dan thought about him. Lance was still defying the odds. He used to boast to Dan about the Taliban soldiers he'd killed in Afghanistan, telling stories of personally gunning down seven in one battle, although this boasting had mostly stopped when he became a family man. Dan still wondered how much of it was true. Seeing his friend still alive after that gunshot gave the stories a greater ring of truth. It was taking a while for Lance to wake up on his own, and Dan wondered if he should wake him.

It probably wasn't the best thing, though, so for now he would just continue to wait.

Dan sat there for what seemed an hour. Finally Lance started to wake, slowly stretching his arms above his head. "Lance," Dan said calmly, keeping his distance so Lance wouldn't panic upon seeing someone in his room. "Lance," he repeated.

Lance opened his eyes and looked at Dan. There was an extended pause. That worried Dan. He thought it'd be best to say something. "It's been a while."

"Dan, I wasn't expecting to see you," Lance said with a clear sense of nervousness. He eventually settled down and said, "Good to see you."

Dan didn't want to ask Lance how he was. It seemed the answer was too obvious. He quickly said, "You look good."

"Thanks." Lance got up a little more. He looked like he wanted to get out of the bed.

"Are you sure that's a good idea?" Dan asked.

"Yeah, you're here. Let's go for a walk. I have no idea how long I've been out, and I want to get out of this room, get some air," Lance said gruffly.

"Okay. Do you need some help?" Dan asked as he reached his hand out.

"No, I'm fine," Lance said. "I just want to get out of this damn room."

As Lance got up, Dan moved behind him, hoping that he'd be able to help if it looked like Lance was going to fall.

"Where would you like to walk to? The cafeteria?" Dan asked.

"No, let's just go outside. There's a nice garden on the left side of the hospital," Lance said.

As Lance and Danny walked down the hallway toward the garden, Lance didn't say a word. Dan worried about an uncomfortable silence forming. He realized that he hadn't asked about Lance's loss. Dan was conflicted. He didn't want to bring up bad memories, but it felt like he should ask about it. Not mentioning it felt wrong to him. Dan reached his hand out to Lance and said, "Lance, I'm sorry about what happened. I don't know what you must be feeling, but I'll always be there for you. You are not alone."

Lance paused for a long while and then said, "Thank you for the offer, Dan, but I don't think you can do anything for me." He started to breathe heavily, nearly panting, and said, "Let's just go to the garden for now." With that, Lance continued to walk slowly to the garden.

Dan had a feeling he would just be hitting a brick wall if he pressed the issue any further, or, even worse, he might make Lance snap. Dan tried to think of something else to say, something to change the subject. It didn't seem like a good idea to let Lance stew in his thoughts. "Did you hear that there's going to be a baseball season next year?" he asked.

"Really? That's great. I was disappointed when I heard that they canceled the games for the year. I have to say this is some unexpectedly good news. I thought the MLB was going to continue to cave as long as these attacks happened. I mean, it was bad enough that they stopped us from taking coolers into stadiums after 9/11, and then they started canceling games."

"Yeah, I think you'd agree that people need some good news right now," Dan said, moving so that he was walking next to Lance instead of slightly behind him. They were almost to the front doors of the hospital. Dan turned toward Lance and asked, "Which direction is it to the garden?"

"Go right," Lance said quickly. As they got to the doors, Lance froze. He started to breathe more quickly, like he was worried. He continued to breathe faster and then finally said, "Dan, let's go back to the room. I changed my mind. I don't want to go outside."

Dan was surprised by this sudden turn. Lance was in better shape than he'd expected, much better than the catatonic state he'd feared Lance would be in. But he could tell Lance was worried, so in order to not cause a problem, Dan simply said, "Okay, let's go."

Lance turned around quickly and walked at a fast pace away from the door. Danny tried to walk beside him, but Lance sped ahead. He could tell that Lance was nervous for some reason. Tailing Lance, Dan said, "Slow down, man. You're still in recovery."

A woman's voice then yelled in clear condemnation, "Lance!"

"Lance, someone is calling," Danny said, thinking maybe it was a doctor. Maybe he'd been in the wrong letting Lance go outside the room. Despite Danny calling to Lance, Lance continued to walk ahead, ignoring both the woman and Danny.

"Lance!" the woman called again as she grew closer. Dan no longer thought she was a doctor or a nurse. She seemed to be more than just upset; she sounded enraged.

Dan finally got a look at the woman. She was about five feet six, a little chubby, and she had naturally red hair. She wasn't wearing makeup, and her hair was messy. It was clear she didn't care how she looked.

Lance was still walking away. The woman screamed, "Answer me, Lance! Are you too much of a coward to even face me?"

Lance stopped and turned around. He seemed to have finally had it. His expression was one of pure rage. His face was red, with visible veins, and his eyes were opened wide. His mouth was pulled into a bitter smile, and his hands were clenched in angry fists. As Lance started to walk toward the woman, he said in an elevated tone, "You have some nerve, Cassandra, coming to see me here." After a few angry huffs, he added, "You arranged my family's funeral while I was still in a coma. Did I not have the fucking right to see my family be buried?"

The woman's face went red as well, mirroring Lance's. Dan could clearly tell this was a mutual feeling of hatred. She yelled, "No, you piece of shit, if it wasn't for you, they would still be alive today!"

"Fuck you, Cassandra. You knew Rachel longer than I did. Did I make her join the CIA? The attack wasn't even a strike on me. Have you watched the goddamn news, seen all the casualties, do you think they are attacking the entire country just to annoy me? And you have the audacity to come here and insult me, on top of everything else that has happened. Ruined my chance to at least attend their funeral."

"It can't be a coincidence they died on the first day of the attacks, Lance. They were going after you for some reason. I know you, Lance Richardson," she snarled with disgust. "You must not have thought there would be consequences for everything you've done."

Lance walked over to Cassandra and looked down at her. "There is no evidence for that. You are using the death of your sister and niece to get at me. Rachel would be disgusted with you if she was here."

"Go to hell!" Cassandra yelled quickly.

Lance had finally had it. Hatred consumed his face. His breathing grew faster, and his fists started to shake. Lance had nothing new to say. He just looked at her for what felt like an eternity, until he finally snapped. Lance raised his fist and quickly punched her to the ground.

All the people nearby were already looking at the two of them, and when Lance threw the punch, the area went as quiet as an abandoned church. Despite all the anger Lance felt toward Cassandra, he didn't want to hurt her. The loss of everything and her insults had finally caused him to snap.

24

Lance was sitting at the table in his apartment. He had just finished drinking a beer. He was nervous about making these calls and had figured a drink could give him some more courage. There was some truth to the saying liquid courage, after all. He decided to start with the easier of the two calls he had to make—the call to his uncle. Lance was ashamed that it had taken him so long to get in contact with his uncle Tony. It had been two months since he'd last called, and now the reason he was calling was to give his uncle some bad news. Despite his thoughts, Lance figured it was just time to make the call.

Lance dialed and listened to the phone ring. Uncle Tony answered and said in a friendly voice, "Lance, it's been so long. How have you been doing, buddy?"

"All right, I've gotten back to work," Lance said quickly.

"Are you sure that's the best choice, Lance? I'm happy you're doing something with your life after everything that has happened, but do you think it might trigger some bad memories?" Uncle Tony asked, his voice a mix of concerned and friendly.

"I'm always going to be affected by what happened, but I believe the best thing for me now is just to keep my mind focused. I think I'd be worse off if I spent too much time alone. Also, I hate to admit it, but having a chance to stop these people is helping me get by. I know it isn't a good thing to say, but I want revenge," Lance said. There was a sternness to his voice but also some sadness to it.

"You have every right to be angry," Uncle Tony said. He added, sounding a little worried, "I don't know what to say, Lance. I can't imagine what I would do if I was in your shoes. Your dad died before his time, but he still lived a good fifty years. Tara was so young."

"You don't need to tell me," Lance said.

"What are you doing with the CIA right now? Anything you can tell me that isn't classified?" There was some guilt in his uncle's voice, and he was clearly trying to change the subject.

Lance felt a need to address the elephant in the room. "Yes, there is, and you might want to sit down for this, because this is news that will affect you."

"Okay, tell me, Lance," his uncle said quickly.

"We have credible intel that the Lemurians might attack the loved ones of the people in our strike force. The Lemurians know my identity, and they might seek to hurt you," Lance said, his fear clear in his voice.

"What should I do next?" Uncle Tony asked.

"A CIA agent is coming to see you soon. He will go over a list of options, including security guards and potential relocation. I understand that it's annoying, but it is very important that you go," Lance said in an impassioned plea.

"Okay, I'll go. I trust that it's for the best. Hell, I'm a marketing executive, and you're a CIA agent. What am I going to do—tell you you're wrong on a security issue? I've known you my entire life, Lance, and you've never lied to me."

"Well, I did break that lamp in your house when I was nine, but except for that, I'd like to think I've been generally good to you," Lance joked, trying to lighten the mood.

"That's true," Uncle Tony responded happily. "How long do you think this is going to last?"

"I honestly don't know. I wish I could tell you more."

"Okay," Lance's uncle said somewhat sadly.

"I'm sorry I did this to you. I'm sorry you have to leave your home," Lance said with regret.

"Hey," Uncle Tony said strongly, "never apologize for stopping these monsters. I want you to get that Historian bastard When this is over, how 'bout you and me go to an Indians game, for old times' sake?"

"I would like that," Lance said happily. Unseen to his uncle, some tears had filled his eyes. It was the best Lance had felt in a while. It meant a lot to continue to have support from somebody after all these years.

Lance hung up with his uncle, and now it was time for the call he was dreading. Lance wasn't afraid of breaking the law. He knew he wasn't going to get in trouble; a quick call to Zach Franco or Robert Ramirez could end any problems with that. Lance's fear was greedier in nature. Lance had finally had a good moment with a member of his family. He hated that his next conversation was probably going to be one where he was insulted, where his past could come back and hurt him. However, Lance still believed it was best just to get it over with, so he picked up the phone and dialed Cassandra's number.

As the phone rang, he started to breathe more heavily. Even Lance could tell he was nervous. After the third ring someone picked up. "Hello," a young girl said. It was Jean, his niece.

"Hello, Jean," Lance said, trying to sound happy through his nervousness. "It's your uncle Lance."

"Mom says I'm not supposed to talk to you," the young girl said nervously.

"I want to talk to your mom. If she has a problem, she can tell me about it," Lance said sternly, perhaps a little too sternly for a child of eight.

"Okay, I'll get her," Jean said nervously.

Lance then realized he had an opportunity to talk to his niece, a chance to connect with her. "Do you agree with what your mother says about me?" he asked.

"I don't know," the girl replied nervously. "I miss you sometimes, but Mom says you're bad. That's why we don't see you anymore."

There was a loud, swift sound, as if the phone had been snatched away, followed by Cassandra bellowing, "What the hell are you thinking, Lance? Hang up now before I call the police!"

"You've said it yourself, Cassandra: I'm in some fucked-up stuff in the CIA. Do you think the local police scare me?" Lance yelled back.

"Why are you calling? I think it's clear enough what I think of you," she snarled.

"I'm not calling you for reconciliation; I'm calling

because I still care if you and your family live," Lance said harshly.

That seemed to get her attention. "What do you mean?" she asked with worry.

"The Lemurians know who I am. They might seek to hurt you or your family," Lance said with concern.

"I knew this would happen. You got Rachel killed, and now you're going to be the death of me as well." Her voice was a mixture of anger and panic.

"Can you stop hating me long enough to let me finish? I'm sure you watch the news," he said. "All those people in Germany and South Korea—how high are the casualties now, hundred thousand? Are you going to blame me for their deaths as well? I'm calling because I want to save your life."

"All right," she snarled, "I'm listening."

"I have good reason to believe the leader of the Lemurians might know you are at least somewhat related to me, and so I think he might target you to get to me," Lance said.

"You have brought nothing but misery to my family, bringing Rachel into your world," Cassandra snapped.

Lance was angry. He knew Cassandra was wrong. It was tearing him apart listening to her. It was bad enough that he'd lost Rachel and Tara, but now he had to deal with Cassandra's unfair words. He wanted to mock her, to remind her of her divorce, to say *something* to hurt her. Maybe he could comment about her probable failure to please her husband. Lance once again returned to hatred. He hated Webb, but he'd never felt betrayed by the Lemurians. This woman, someone he'd used to care for, had forbidden him from seeing his niece and nephew. Maybe he should just let Webb kill her. It would be justice in a way. She would die because she couldn't get past her hatred of him. However, Lance remembered his niece and nephew. He also knew that even after all Cassandra had done to him, she didn't deserve to die.

After a period of silence, Lance blurted out, "I don't want you to die, Cassandra, and no matter what you think of me, I love Jean and Sam, more than you know." Lance started to breathe heavily. "Cass," he sighed, "I can count the number of people I love in this world on one hand, and Sam and Jean are two of them. Whatever you think of me, know that is true."

There was a silence on the other side of the phone. Finally Cassandra asked in a resigned calm, "What happens next? What are the next steps?"

"A CIA agent will come to your house within the hour. They will explain your options, including security details or, if you want, witness protection," Lance answered.

"Okay," she said in a resigned way. It seemed a part of her knew Lance was right.

"You've made the right choice, Cassandra," Lance said thankfully. "Thank you for listening."

Lance heard some breathing, and he thought Cassandra was going to say something. There was silence for a long time, until finally she hung up.

The past few days had been undeniably the worst since the start of the war. Jacob was dead, and Lance continued to dread the daily casualty reports coming out of Germany and South Korea. With people dying from radiation poisoning, the death count would continue to rise for years. However, for one moment, Lance felt some happiness. He'd achieved his goal. It looked like he might have helped some of the people left in this world that he loved.

25

Ethan and Lance were on a plane on their way to Planesville, the eastern Indiana town where they thought Anubis was hiding. It was going to take another hour to get to the town, which they expected to be deserted. Nerves began to overcome Lance. He was afraid of failure. He knew that Webb was succeeding. It seemed crazy that anyone would think challenge the entire world. Lance was used to the rhetoric of the Islamist militants, but he'd never thought they had a real chance to conquer the world for Islam. They were violent but deluded. Lance feared Webb on a different level, and he wasn't afraid to admit it. It was partly because no other terrorist had hurt him on the same level as Webb, but it was more than that. Webb had come out of nowhere and mocked the greatest powers in the world. Webb was confident—Lance had been able to hear it in his voice—and whatever he had planned that gave him his confidence scared the hell out of Lance.

On top of everything, Lance was still concerned about Ethan. Robert was good at his job, but Lance worried he had ulterior motives in choosing Ethan. Lance wasn't sure

Ethan was up to the task. Ethan had taken seeing Webb on the island worse than Lance had, even after all that Lance had lost.

Lance looked toward where Ethan was sitting. He seemed more relaxed than he'd been on the island, but he was still intense. Lance thought that maybe he could finally get more information on his new comrade. "Ethan, I never got to tell you how impressed I was by you on the island. You seem pretty committed to all of this."

Ethan looked at Lance and said, "Victor Webb has killed millions of innocent people. Any sane person would hate him. There is nothing more useful anyone can do than fight the Lemurians."

"I can see why Ramirez likes you," Lance said.

"What are you saying, Richardson?" Ethan asked, annoyed. "Am I suspicious because he likes me? You can look at my file—I killed ten Lemurian sliders when they attacked Olean. It was only rational I got promoted after that."

"Forgive me for being suspicious. You haven't known Robert as long as I have. You being his personal choice and you being from outside the intelligence community is going to make some people nervous," Lance said.

"Some people or you?" Ethan asked.

"Both," Lance replied solemnly.

"We need to be on good terms, so I'll tell you why Robert Ramirez picked me," Ethan said in a businesslike manner. "I wasn't completely honest with you about my history with Webb. Of course I'm mad about his cruel attacks on innocent people, but I also have a more personal reason for joining this fight. Before I joined the army, I was a police lieutenant in northern New York. About a year ago, after some nearby towns had been attacked, there were reports of looters taking advantage of the anarchy, so I thought it would be wise to form a group to guard the homes in Olean. It was sort of like a modern-day militia, made up of a few police officers and some volunteers. One day, I was on patrol guarding my own neighborhood with three other guys. Everything was quiet until several snipers shot my men. I jumped behind a car on the street and hid. Soon, five Lemurians appeared. Apparently, they thought they'd already killed me, because they didn't leave any snipers in position. I launched an attack. For the next twenty minutes I had a shoot-out with the men. I was eventually able to kill them all," Ethan said angrily.

"You took out five Lemurians by yourself—that had to impress people," Lance said.

"That wasn't the reason for Robert liking me," Ethan interrupted. "After I killed the Lemurians, I ran right to my house, hoping my family was okay. In my fear I lacked judgment and forgot to call in backup. I rushed home alone, broke into my house, and screamed for my family. There was a man standing in my kitchen. I pointed my gun at him and said, 'Put your hands up, or I will shoot.'

"The man turned to me and said confidently, 'I don't think you want to do that.' He then whistled, and several men came out holding my family at gunpoint."

Ethan had some tears in his eyes. "My wife and my nine-year-old son, Stan, just looked at me with fear in their eyes. Stan was mewling like an animal caught in a trap. I tried to get him to quiet down. I didn't want him to go on screaming. I hated seeing his pain and didn't want those Lemurian bastards to have any sadistic joy in this. I told my wife and son to calm down and let me do the talking. I turned back to the leader, and he said, 'Drop your gun. I know from the pictures on your wall that this is your family, so don't bother lying to me.'

"I dropped my gun and said, 'Surrender. I killed your men, and I've sent for reinforcements.'

"The man laughed. He stuck his hand in his pocket, pulled out some police officer badges, and threw them at me. 'Do these look familiar?' he taunted.

"I screamed, 'You son of a bitch!'

"The man pulled out his gun and said, 'I don't think you want to do that.'

"I felt defeated. I could only ask, out of curiosity, 'Why did you invade my house?'

"The man answered, 'After I killed some of your police friends, I stole this walkie-talkie you were using. I know you helped leader of this so-called militia and where lived.'

"I was powerless. 'What do you want?' I asked the man. 'You can kill me. I helped lead the men against you. Your boss will be happy if you kill me,' I panted. 'Just spare my family,' I begged.

"The man said, 'You know what? I'm not going to kill you. I've killed enough cops today.'

"I thought I might be able to escape this with my family intact, but then the man said, 'But I am going to give you something to remind you of this day.' He turned to one of his henchmen and said, 'Sayid, bring me his son.'

"I charged at him without thinking. He quickly dodged my punch and hit me in the gut, knocking the wind out of me. His henchman took my son to him, and he lifted my son into the air above his head."

"I can still hear my son screaming," Ethan said with clear tears coming out of his eyes. "Daddy, Daddy, stop him! Do something!"

Ethan took a shaky breath and continued, "The man then said, 'After today, every time you look at your son, you will realize just how helpless you are to stop us.'"

Ethan turned to Lance. "He broke my son's back over his knee, paralyzing him. Every time I go to sleep, I hear my son's cries from that day."

Lance felt a sense of shame. He had no right to judge Ethan for the way he had been handling everything. Lance had mourned his family to the point that he sometimes forgot the atrocities the Lemurians had inflicted on others around the world. He felt a similar intensity to Ethan, and it sickened him that he hadn't even considered that Ethan had been personally affected by the Lemurians. He'd pinned Ethan as someone who, although competent, was probably just a yes man for Ramirez, a necessary pick to please the executive branch. Lance wanted to make Ethan feel better. He remembered back to Dan visiting him in his apartment, how Dan had tried to tiptoe around the death of his family, not wanting to upset him. Now Lance had forced someone else to live their worst memories. Lance said, "Ethan, I'm sorry. You don't have to tell me anymore."

"The story isn't over yet," Ethan said defiantly. Lance raised his eyebrows, surprised by Ethan's rise of intensity. "The men left after breaking my son's back. I cried for a while, but then I ran out the door with my gun. I wanted to kill that man. I was consumed by rage. I was going to end that man on that night. I ran and ran and ran, attempting to find him ..." Ethan started to huff. Going through this whole story seemed to be getting to him.

"Did you join the military because you want to find that man?"

"No," Ethan said quickly. "I joined because I already killed him," he added with strength and pride.

Lance was taken aback. Ethan continued, "Eventually I found them in the woods. They were putting on some stolen cop uniforms. They probably thought it was going to save them." Ethan laughed. "I jumped them and killed everyone. I shot the man who crippled my son through the heart. The last thing that man saw before he died was me smiling. Ramirez heard my story and wanted someone like me on your team. He wanted someone who would give the Lemurians hell."

Lance was silent, not knowing what to say. Ethan's story was unbelievable. Lance didn't know whether to be impressed or horrified. Ethan had succeeded where Lance had failed; he'd killed the man who hurt his son. But Lance couldn't help but notice the look on Ethan's face. Ethan was full of hatred. Lance knew more than most that Ethan's feelings were more than justified, but he couldn't help but still feel uncomfortable around Ethan, whose eyes showed a mix of hatred and joy. Even after everything, sadism was something Lance wished to avoid.

"Did you accept Robert's offer only to kill Lemurians, to satisfy the need you feel to finish that job?" Lance asked with fear. "I hate Webb with every fiber of my being, but we can't lose sight of why we're doing this. I'm doing this to save people."

"Ending the threat would save people. Webb is still out there, breathing and having a life, while thousands of people across the world are dying from radiation poisoning. It sickens me. Stopping that man might make me be able to—" He stopped himself with a clear look of worry on his face.

"What?" Lance asked.

"I killed that man, but he was sadly right about one thing: every time I look at my son, I cringe. He reminds me of that horrible day. I'm not proud of it, but it's true. This has affected my marriage. As we speak, my wife is writing up divorce papers. In addition to wanting revenge for my son, I partly joined the army to get away from my home situation."

Lance took in Ethan's story. It was brave of Ethan to admit all of this to him. Someone else might hold Ethan's failure around his son against him, but Lance had seen fathers fail for far less understandable reasons. "You think that killing Webb, stopping them once and for all, will make you able to face your son again?" Lance asked sympathetically.

"Are you a religious man, Lance?" Ethan asked, shifting somewhat off topic.

"No, not particularly. I've always believed in focusing on my life right now and dealing with death when it comes."

"Well, despite all that has happened, I have to say that being here in this strike force almost feels like divine intervention. Just when I was going to give up on ever making it up to my family, Robert came to me and gave me a chance to help. I get a chance to avenge their suffering. I don't know for sure why he came to me, Lance. I just think he wanted someone not connected to the establishment, someone he can trust, and after that night in Olean, I was as good a guy as any. Would you turn down the chance if you were me? Damn, being part of this group means I might be the one to shoot Webb himself and make him pay. I truly have a chance to make things right."

"For all we know, Webb might kill us today," Lance said. "You shouldn't base your life on one possible outcome. Even if you are successful with everything and you shoot Webb himself, the damage might be too much for you to ever reconcile with your son if you don't start soon. I suggest that, after we get Anubis, you try to talk to your family and see if you can reconcile. You don't want to risk your son hating you for the rest of your life."

"It's at that point already. I honestly don't know if I can keep it up anymore. I don't think I can face my son knowing I failed. If I can't kill Webb or see him die, I hope I die trying, because I believe I'm beyond redemption if I can't avenge my son," Ethan replied.

Lance got up and walked closer to Ethan. "If you let Webb kill you before you ever get a chance to make up with your son, then you will only complete the victory he started that day. You've got to man up and deal with it."

Ethan shrugged. "When I was a teenager, I was shy around girls. My friends gave me the advice 'Be confident.' I knew they were right, but I couldn't be confident, no matter how much I tried. Do you think I don't know that I'm not doing the right thing with my son? There is a sickness in me that I can't control. Being where I am now is my best chance. This is the only thing I can think of doing. I think I owe it to my son to try to avenge him."

With a sympathetic look, Lance said solemnly, "From one father to another, please try Ethan. My daughter is dead, and it might sound horrible, but I would die for her to only be crippled."

"I …" Ethan trailed off, seeming to feel some guilt.

"Promise me, Ethan: just call him. I don't know how you're going to get over this, but maybe you can just call him. I don't know, but maybe just hearing his voice and not seeing him crippled will help you."

"I'll try," Ethan said, pushing through.

One of the men from the front of the plane walked toward Lance and Ethan and said, "Richardson, we are nearing what we believe to be Anubis's location."

"How much longer?" Lance asked.

"About five minutes," the soldier replied.

"All right, we'll be ready," Ethan said quickly as the soldier walked off.

"We're going to succeed today, Ethan," Lance said strongly. "Then you're going to talk to your son," he added with some newfound camaraderie with his unlikely friend.

"I'm still looking forward to ending these people, Lance. No matter what happens with my son, I don't think that is going to change," Ethan said.

"Nor should it," Lance said.

Ethan stood up and looked at Lance as a true friend after this talk. "You have truly helped me a lot today, Lance. I'm going to talk to my son after this. Now let me help you avenge your daughter."

26

In the back of the plane Ethan and Lance were bracing for the impact with a team of soldiers around them.

"Have we scouted the area?" Ethan asked.

"We've sent several drones over the area," one of the soldiers replied. "We've detected little movement near Planesville, but there are some cars on the roads outside of town. We're not sure if they belong to remaining civilians or looters and squatters."

"All right, let's prepare for this," Lance said.

Lance felt the impact as the plane landed. He wondered where exactly they'd landed, since there probably wasn't any airport in this town. The plane's back door opened, and he looked outside.

They seemed to have landed in a park on the outskirts of the town, near some buildings to the left of them. "Let's look in these buildings," Lance said. "We traced Anubis's signal to this area."

Lance and Ethan took the lead with the soldiers walking behind them. Lance finally had a chance to look at the town. The place was incredibly empty, not a soul moving or any sign of life. There was some broken glass in the street and a collapsed billboard—signs of the war.

"This place is sickening, isn't it?" Ethan yelled.

"What do you mean?" Lance asked with some sadness.

"Two years ago this was part of the heartland, probably had a bustling main street, and now it's no better than a ghost town."

"I know it sucks, Ethan, but for now keep the talking to a minimum," Lance said. "Webb might have a few henchmen around here. We shouldn't reveal our location."

As Lance walked through the streets of the town with still no sign of Anubis, he started to fear that Webb had beat them to her. He might have had plans to either kill her or, even worse, capture her and do to her what he'd done to Jacob. Like Ethan, Lance was also having problems seeing this town in its current condition. About fifteen hundred people had lived here, and now it was deserted. Talking about it only hurt him more, and he didn't need any more pain in his life right now.

Lance then heard a gunshot. He turned around and rushed in the direction of the shot to see Ethan and a few of the soldiers pointing a gun at a woman.

"What's going on here?" Lance yelled.

Ethan said, "I saw this woman in an abandoned building. I thought she was going for a gun. I don't think she's a Lemurian. Once I fired, she dropped a whole bunch of jewelry. I think she's a looter."

The woman said with a sigh of relief, "You aren't Lemurians"

"Be quiet," Ethan commanded.

"Listen, Ethan, we should give this woman a chance to explain herself," Lance said.

"Thank you, sir. My name's Molly. I'm one of the last people left in this town since the attacks. Please, I'm not with them. I just grabbed for the gun because I was afraid."

"Were you looting?" Lance asked.

"Yes, we're desperate," Molly replied frantically.

"Jewelry isn't exactly food," Ethan said sarcastically.

"I lost my job. I worked as a clerk at a supermarket. I can't do that now that the town has been abandoned. I needed to do something to get money," she pleaded.

"Ethan, she's not on trial. We came here to find Anubis, not to catch some looters," Lance said. "Drop the gun. I don't think she'll hurt us. She is clearly unarmed right now." Ethan lowered his gun, and Lance turned to Molly. "You said you're one of a group of survivors. Where are the rest of them?"

"We're barricaded in the town hall," Molly said. "I was sent out to get some supplies for the rest of us."

"In your group is there anyone who seems to be using the computer a lot, someone who could be a hacker?" Lance asked.

"There is one guy. He isolates himself. He's kind of a weirdo. He refuses to help any of the people in this town," Molly said.

"Refusing to help in the looting—sounds like an all right guy." Ethan looked toward the woman in a disapproving manner.

"Robert said that Anubis was supposed to be a woman, but I suppose any lead is worth looking into. Robert could always be wrong," Lance said to Ethan. Then he asked Molly, "Can you take us to the other survivors?"

"I will do anything that will help. I'll take you to the rest of my group," Molly said.

"Thank you," Lance said, surprised by how quickly he'd gotten a lead.

All of them started to walk to the center of the town with Molly. Lance scanned the area, thinking that the abandoned main street would be a good place for snipers. If Lance could find Anubis, he figured the Lemurians could also have similar success. "Get to the side of the street, you and you," Lance ordered, gesturing to two of the soldiers. "Get on my right flank, and keep a watch for snipers. Molly, get behind me."

Near the center of the abandoned town was a building with some lights on. "There it is!" Molly happily yelled.

Lance kept looking around. Just as he began to feel some relief, he heard an unsettling sound.

A mortar shot went over their heads and hit the building that Molly claimed was hiding the other survivors. Several flames began bursting out of the building. Lance and the soldiers around him raised their guns up.

"Oh my God!" Molly screamed frantically as a second mortar hit the building.

"Get to cover!" Lance shouted. "The Lemurians are here!"

Several more mortars hit the building, causing the entire front half of it to start collapsing. The people inside began to scream as they were burned alive.

As Lance and his soldiers ran for cover, Lance saw an abandoned corner store. The door was already open. He knew he could get inside. While rushing toward the store, Molly was shot through the head. Lance dashed into the store and jumped behind some abandoned shelves. He whispered to Ethan, "Contact backup. This might be an ambush ..." Lance stayed in position. He was worried and kept his guard up, listening as hard as he could, wondering where an offensive would come from.

About ten minutes went by, and there were no additional shots. Lance wondered if the Lemurians were playing mind games with them, trying to draw them out. Eventually, in the silence, Lance turned toward Ethan and said, "I'm going to go to the front of the store to see if Webb's men are in position."

In a crouch, Lance crept toward the front of the building. He grabbed a can of soup that had been left behind on the floor whenever the store had been abandoned, and he threw it quickly out the door to see if any of Webb's men would shoot at the movement. When nothing happened, Lance went toward the door and finally put his head outside to scout the area. A masked figure with thick body armor was coming toward him. The figure had a gun in one hand but was holding both hands up in the air in a nonthreatening gesture. In a voice muffled by the mask, the figure said, "Don't shoot. I will not hurt you."

Lance aimed his rifle at the figure and said sternly, "It is time for some answers. Who are you?"

"My guess is that you guys wanted to find Anubis." The figure dropped the gun and unmasked, revealing a short brunette in her early to mid-twenties. "Well, if that's the case, then you found her."

27

Ethan and the remaining soldiers approached Lance and the woman. Ethan asked angrily, "Who the hell is this bitch, and why are you just sitting out here? You're exposed."

Lance calmly answered, "This woman claims to be Anubis. From the gun, I think she's the person who shot Molly."

"I am Anubis," the woman said. "I can prove it."

"I will give you a chance to prove yourself, but I want some other answers first," Lance said.

"Very well," the woman said.

"Why did you kill the woman with us and those people in the building? What did they do to deserve that?" asked Lance sternly.

"They were looters. Before you all came here, I was spying on them. They were no innocents merely looking for food. That woman and her group killed some of the last remaining people in this town that didn't run off when the Lemurians first started attacking. They planned to pick this town dry. Disgusting," she scoffed.

"They killed some survivors?" Ethan questioned. "Do you think they were Lemurians?"

"No, worse—just people trying to benefit from this war. They weren't with Webb. Lemurians don't give two shits about finding jewelry," she responded with disgust.

"Were they doing anything to hurt or threaten you? I hate looters, but people still deserve trails," Lance said in a manner of slight condemnation.

"What about for committing treason?" she snapped quickly. "Looters sicken me and deserve no pity. You know why we're losing this war, Lance? It's because the Lemurians at least stick together. While the Lemurians are out there committing Sandy Hooks every day, looters attack homes, exploiting people living in fear. These people that you think deserve a trial are helping the Lemurians. They make us waste our time on them. Plus, I can guarantee you there are Lemurians in jail who just said they were looters to avoid suspicion."

"Agreed," Ethan chimed in confidently.

The woman made a lot of good points—good enough that Lance didn't want to get drawn into a discussion on ethics with her. But he still needed proof that she was Anubis. Ramirez had provided pictures of what she looked like, and a DNA test back in Virginia would end all doubt. For now, it was important to keep focused on the job above all else, so he didn't waste time on a debate. It took him a second to notice what was arguably the most important thing this young woman had said. "How do you know my name?" he asked.

"I was able to find your number, Lance. Do you think

I couldn't also find out what you look like?" she said in her consistently confident manner.

"Impressive, but for all I know you could be a Lemurian with good intelligence. Do you have any tangible proof that you are Anubis? I cannot take a risk trusting you."

"Maybe I don't want to be trusted. Are you all here to arrest me? That's no way to reward someone who was willing to help you," she said, looking directly at Lance.

"If you're Anubis, this isn't an arrest. I came in person to make an honest appeal. I know nothing about you except that you gave us good information about Webb. Even if there was anything in your past worth arresting you for, what would we gain by taking you out of the field after you gave us intel?"

"You might want to interrogate me," she replied. "Find out what I know, if I've been hiding anything from you."

"I think you know that the war isn't over yet, and judging from your success, I think having someone like you on our side as a partner would be more beneficial to the both of us."

"I told you, Lance—I don't want to work for the CIA. Why would you waste your time coming here?"

"I don't believe you're the kind of person that would condemn someone for trying. Besides, despite your success, you gotta realize you're making yourself a bigger threat and thus target to the Lemurians. Working with us might be good for your protection. Who knows—maybe you can even get the CIA running more the way you like it, if you provide us with something good," Lance responded in a confident manner.

"Will I really be an advisor? If I join you, Agent

Richardson, I want some power in your group. I don't want to be some token hacker or someone outside the group to blame if something goes wrong. I'm not going to sit by if I'm not listened to," she said sternly.

"You have my word. If you were able to find me before, you have to know some things about me, including that my word means something."

"All right, I'll come, on the condition you give me an apartment in DC and make sure there are no security guards near me. I don't want to see any guards. I don't want to feel like I'm a prisoner."

"Did you not just hear him? You might get assassinated!" Ethan yelled at the woman.

"Consider it a miracle that there are any terms in which I would agree to this. I promise to work in any location you see fit, but I am not going to sleep surrounded by government agents. If you are worried about my protection, I assure you that all I need is access to my guns," she finished in a businesslike manner.

Lance did not like this, but he couldn't risk not having Anubis on their side. "Okay. I'm glad to have you on board. We have some intelligence that your name is Erin Cahill—is that correct?"

"Yes," she said. "I'm guessing your source for that was Robert Ramirez."

"You're off to a good start already, having figured that out," Lance answered honestly.

"It will be interesting to see Robert again," Erin said with some sentimentally breaking though her businesslike manner.

"Ms. Cahill, do you have any goods in this town

that you would like to take to Virginia—clothes, personal items?" Lance asked.

"Anything of any value to me I have in my pockets. I could use some more clothes. If the CIA will give me money to buy some new things when I get there, I can honestly leave now," Erin said.

Lance didn't know what to make of this. He found it hard to believe that she had so little desire to keep her property. Maybe she had a storage locker somewhere that she could access later, or maybe she was purposely leaving important things behind as a deliberate deception—if the Lemurians found her things, they might think she was dead, or maybe it wasn't the Lemurians she was trying to deceive. Lance finally said after some thinking, "Okay. We have a plane that is ready for us to depart."

Lance, Erin, and the group started to walk back to the airplane. Relatively speaking, this unlikely trip had gone well for the most part, Lance thought. Walking behind Erin, he had a chance to really look at her now that the threat seemed to be over. She was really short, possibly on the border of being five feet tall. Lance would be surprised if she was more than 110 pounds. He knew from the briefing that Erin was supposedly twenty-six, but she looked younger than that. He could tell that her size and age didn't slow her down. This woman had gotten intelligence that no one else had been able to get, and any snide comments about her appearance would not take that away.

Erin turned around and said, "I never got the chance to tell you how I appreciate you, Mr. Richardson. I know what happened in Copper Canyon, what really happened and not the official press release."

"How do you know that? Did Josh Saunders tell you?" Lance replied.

"Josh Saunders, ha," she said. "That's who you got on the job trying to find me?"

Lance was happy that Josh didn't appear to be leaking info, but he couldn't help but wonder what made Erin give that response. "What do you have against Josh?" Lance asked.

"He's a good hacker, but his claim to fame is taking down Xbox Live a few years back. You need someone better than that to target Webb," she responded.

Lance felt he should defend Josh, but he didn't want to get into a fight with a new contact.

They walked up the ramp onto the plane. Lance looked around to make sure the area was clear. Erin sat down next to Ethan. Lance thought it would be good to continue the conversation and find out as much about Erin as possible, so he took a seat near her but not next to her.

"You still didn't answer my question of how you knew about Copper Canyon."

"I hacked the Mexican Army. I was able to piece the story together," Erin said.

"That story apparently impressed you. I'm not above flattering my own ego, so tell me: Why do you think I deserve praise?" Lance asked.

"You were willing to do whatever it took to defeat the Lemurians, and it worked out. If you weren't there, Lance, the mission would not have succeeded. Candellario might still be launching attacks every week, but you showed me that maybe I could be wrong about the government, that maybe there are people in the government who will do what is necessary."

"You seem committed. I'm glad, and I'm not going to lie—having someone tell me that I was right is always reassuring. But we can never be overconfident. Webb's taken out three cities now, and thousands have been killed. Who know what that man is planning right now," Lance said. He then thought that he was being too emotional around this woman, so he stopped speaking.

"Amen to that. Maybe if we're lucky, it will be one of us to put a bullet in Webb's head," Erin said.

"I don't think it will be one of us. It's probably going to be some jarhead we never even meet. Personally I don't care as long as he's dead."

Erin chuckled, showing an unexpected crack in what had been a stone-cold exterior.

Lance then said, "I want to know what we're getting into with you. Earlier, you suggested you had something that might hurt Webb. I think now is the time for you to tell me."

"It's from the same source that gave me Webb's name. I think if we help him, he might be willing to come forward and give us Webb's location."

"That's great news!" Lance exclaimed. "But my guess is that this source is someone questionable, and that's why he came to you instead of an agency."

"You're right, and let's just say that dealing with him will truly test our resolve in finally doing what is necessary to stop Victor Webb. I had a feeling that the Lemurians had something to do with the decline in Islamic terrorism, and Webb gloating about how he captured some of the world's most notorious criminals pretty much confirmed that involvement. I went to the dark web to find any terrorist websites still running. I first posed as a sympathetic individual. Then I revealed my identity as an anti-Lemurian hacker who wanted to find Webb. Once I promised to convert to Islam and join them, they gave me my contact. After talking to him, I got him to agree to help you find Webb."

"I'm guessing that conversion was a lie."

"Of course, but I might need to buy a Hijab once I get to DC if I have to Skype with him in order to keep the ruse going till he surrenders, but there is one more thing you guys should know. I don't want to rely on him, but I have no choice. As far as I know, he is still alive, and he claims to know where Webb himself will be soon."

"How can you be so sure that this contact is not with Webb and trying to lure you out? Promising you Webb's location seems way out of the capabilities of a normal person."

"Well, he said he's willing to walk up unarmed and surrender himself to an American military base of our choosing. Now that I'm with you guys, I can see if he is truly willing to keep his word."

With an increased sense of dread, Lance asked, "Who is this person, Erin?"

Erin looked directly into his eyes and said, "Ibrahim al-Hirrshi."

28

Zhou was walking in a cave; he was finally going to see Victor again. He'd just come back from a mission in Malaysia, where he'd set a few small plots into motion. Victor had told him to keep the momentum going. It had taken everything they had to get that nuke into South Korea—a strong victory—but they could not rest on one attack. They must always keep going, and the last thing he ever wanted to do was let Victor down. On his trek down into the cave, he saw Raul Candellario with four soldiers around him. Zhou had always liked Raul. He was a good solider and had followed the Lemurian mission well since he'd been brought on. It seemed they were both heading in the same direction.

"Great to see you, General Candellario!" Zhou shouted. "Are you going to see Victor?" he asked.

"Yes. As we move into the next phrase, Victor needs to know who the clear players in the CIA are at the moment," he said, sounding more nervous than Zhou was used to seeing from Raul.

"Are you all right?" Zhou asked as the two of them continued on through the cave.

"I got to be honest, Zhou—I'm a little worried about talking to Victor. I haven't had the best track record in the past few months."

"You got Jacob Lanser, and Victor told you not to be in Houston when the bomb was set to go off. You can't blame yourself for it not going off."

"It's not just that. The Copper Canyon operation was more devastating for us than we thought. I really don't have the resources anymore to conduct anything more than small-scale attacks in the states," Raul said with sadness.

"We were heading into the next phase anyway. The nukes scared the Americans enough."

"You're probably right, but I have to think about the past and where to improve. We didn't get here by not learning from our mistakes."

"That's true. How are Esperanza and the kids?"

"They're good. She and the kids are in a safe house along the Bolivian border. I look forward to getting them into better living conditions soon."

"I can understand that." Zhou looked around as they reached an iron door blocking the back of the cave. "Do you feel the guards are necessary, Raul? We're pretty close to dealing with Victor."

"You're right. It might be best if we keep this meeting between you, me, and Victor," Candellario said. "I won't be here for long, however. I'm going back to South America. With the problems we've had in the United States, I think it might be time to rebuild some of our support in South America."

"You ready to head in now?" Zhou asked.

"Yeah. Men, stay here and guard the door while I'm in the meeting."

Zhou noticed how obedient Raul's men were, immediately moving into a guarding formation outside the door without saying a word. Zhou then opened the door.

Victor was sitting in the back of the room with a few guards around him. He was focused intensely on a set of maps and didn't even notice that Raul and Zhou had entered. It seemed Victor was planning where to put troops for an upcoming battle.

"Victor," Zhou said to get his attention.

Victor looked up with his big green eyes that, in the right light, had an almost gray tint to them. He smiled. "Come sit down."

Zhou and Raul both went to the table with the maps. "How have you been?" Zhou asked.

"I'm stressed as always, but I'm happy about the bombs going off successfully and the reaction to Lanser's death," Victor said.

"What makes you happy? Have you gotten any positive intelligence?" Candellario asked.

"It seems the bombings have had a strong effect. There has been a no-confidence vote against the German chancellor, and there have been riots in almost every European country. This should make it easier to get agents in Europe."

"There is no doubt that is good," Zhou said.

"The global intelligence community is probably going to find out we can make our own nuclear material soon," Raul said. "The Americans captured the nuke for Houston and are going to study it."

"Then we have to keep moving forward and put more on their plate to make sure the world's intelligence agencies can't unite behind an individual target," Victor said.

"That does seem for the best, Raul," Zhou said kindly, sympathetic to Raul's predicament.

"Is there anything else you need from me, Raul? You didn't come all the way to Afghanistan just to give me an update," Victor added solemnly.

"I've already told Zhou, but I plan to start a second offensive, focusing mostly on South America. I would like to get some more recruits for this, and I want you to put me in contact with Khaled. I wonder if he can spare some of his men to help me."

Webb took out a card and said, "Go to this address in Panama City. If you can't go, send one of your best men. You'll find someone there who can put you in contact with Khaled."

"It will be hard to get one of my men to this address undetected. It's in the middle of Panama City. Can't Khaled be more accommodating?" Candellario asked.

"You know he has take every precaution necessary. Every intelligence agency in the world is after us."

"All right, thank you, Victor." With that, Candellario got up and left rather quickly. He seemed disappointed that he couldn't get help more easily.

With Raul gone, Victor sat back in his chair with a drink in hand and asked, "What about you, Zhou? Is there anything you want to discuss with me?"

"I honestly could just use a friendly talk. How have you been, Victor?" he asked happily.

"I have mixed feelings. I can't believe we've gotten so far. After all these years, I'm close to actually doing it."

"Are you nervous at all?"

"Of course I am, and you should be too. We have the entire world against us. We would be insane not to be at least a little afraid."

Zhou chuckled. It seemed Victor could always make him laugh, even now, when the world was after them. Reflecting, Zhou asked, "Do you ever think about them?"

"Who is them?"

"The people in Busan and the rest. I know it was necessary, but it brings me no happiness thinking of the children we killed that day."

"Or the children we are going to kill," Victor added.

"How do you do it? You don't look tired. How do you sleep?"

"Remember the lessons I gave you about all the kings and queens of the past, the founders of every nation, and what they did. They all put blood on their hands to improve the world. Do you think our goals are less noble than theirs?"

"We have done a lot, and we're not done yet. I know what we have to do is important, but what if we fail? Then all of this—all of these deaths—will have been for nothing."

Webb finally got up from his chair and went toward Zhou, his face growing more serious. Zhou felt that he'd made Victor mad at him. Victor breathed heavily and said sternly, "I had those thoughts once, but I've been able to focus on this mission. You have every right to question me, but I have to be truthful—I can't have anything less than one hundred percent confidence in the mission. I am willing to have millions if not billions of men, women, and children die for the smallest chance of success, because if we don't succeed, everyone on earth is going to die."

29

As Lance and Danny walked down the corridor of the base at Langley, Lance asked Danny briskly, "Are we really going to do this?"

"You're the one that brought her to the president. If you're unsure about finding Hirrshi, you could've told Erin to fuck off. That probably would have ended it," Dan joked.

"I was ordered to bring her back. It was a miracle I was able to convince her to work with us. Besides, maybe doing this is the right thing. Webb has killed a lot more people than Hirrshi in a fraction of the time. But part of me will never accept making a deal with him. Do you think he'll even cooperate?"

"Anubis, or Erin, was able to back up her claim. He surrendered peacefully and claims to know where Webb might be."

"But he wants a pardon, Danny, and the president is going to give it to him. You weren't there when he was at his strongest. You didn't see some of his attacks. Eleven years ago he killed forty in a suicide attack in Alexandria, Egypt. To do this he told two young women with Down

234

syndrome they would go to heaven if they listened and did as he said. That was an act of pure evil. Anything he can do to help stop Webb is not going to make that go away. I understand that it will be for the greater good if his help leads to Webb's capture, but it is still tough for me to know there will never be justice," Lance said angrily.

"You're the one who told me saving people's lives is the most important thing. I know this is going to be trying, but it's the only thing that can give us a shot."

"I guess that's true, Dan, but I still need to vent. With the things Hirrshi has done, I'm never going to be completely forgiving. Rachel was always good at keeping me from doing something drastic."

"I wish I'd known her better. The way you talk about her, she sounds like a truly great woman," Danny said.

"I remember one time we caught this guy who was planning to launch an attack on the DC subway system. Jacob got a deal for him to be put in witness protection and serve no jail time if he gave us the rest of his crew. I thought this was outrageous. This guy would have killed more people than most serial killers if he'd succeeded, yet he got to keep his freedom. Then Rachel came to calm me down and remind me one asshole going free was better than dozens of dead men and women. That was always something special about Rachel. In this job many people become more cold, but Rachel made me better," Lance said. "I'm not going to do anything she would disapprove of with Hirrshi. Rachel was the best person I knew, and even in death I am loyal to her."

"If you want a prediction, I think dealing with Hirrshi

will work out. If his intel is accurate, Webb's days are numbered," Danny said.

Lance and Danny proceeded to the office they'd given Erin. Lance opened up the conversation with "Erin, are you liking the arrangement? The office and salary good with you?"

The young woman responded, "Everything is quite good. I think it's time I fulfill my side of the bargain in regards to Hirrshi. I just spoke to him. He's willing to give us everything he knows in exchange for a complete pardon."

"Did you get any leads as to what exactly this guy knows that will be helpful?" Lance asked calmly.

"He mentioned that he knows more about Webb's operation, in addition to having an idea of where Webb could be right now," Erin replied.

"We cannot be one hundred percent sure with Hirrshi," Lance said.

"He said he's lost everything. Webb has effectively destroyed his organization and is trying to assassinate him. This is his only chance for survival." Erin paused and said, "Please don't think that I think any more of this guy than any of you. I know he is a coward who was pushed into making an undesirable choice—nothing more. Letting this guy keep his life is a small price to pay for killing Victor Webb."

Lance gave her a perplexed look. "Small price to pay ... Do you know what this man has done? The deaths of fifty thousand people can be traced back to him. That's nothing to scoff at. It is a necessary evil, but today we will have to pardon one of the worst terrorists in history. No matter what the reasons are, it's not going to be easy to let this man walk."

Erin responded, "Hirrshi was a nuisance, but you and I both know he was never going to destroy this country. He was a killer but nothing more than that. Webb will destroy our way of life and everything we know and hold dear. We still know little about him, and you said yourself that we must believe what he says. If letting one old terrorist go will stop the worst killer in human history, I won't lose any sleep over what we are about to do."

"I understand," Lance said. "But we must not let it get that easy for us. Webb is willing to do whatever it takes to commit his anarchy. The fact that we have standards is what separates us from him."

"Maybe the fact the he is so willing to do anything is why he's winning," Erin replied smugly.

Lance became enraged. "You sound like him! Are you implying that we should fight more like him after everything he's done? We can't have those ideas here. I don't want to help aid the ideals of the number one enemy of this nation."

Erin looked angry for a second but then calmed down. "You know, Lance, you're right. I can't deny that Webb and I are alike in some ways. We're both smart, we both worked around the US government successfully, and we both are willing to have the ends justify the means. However, there is one thing that separates us and makes us enemies. Webb's final goal is to destroy our country and everything we hold dear, and my final goal is to save it. I think that is the only difference needed for us to work together, Agent Richardson. Remember what I told you in Indiana: I have done research of my own. And I'll tell you what, Lance, I know you are a lot of things, but I never thought you were a hypocrite. After Copper Canyon and Farud Hadi, I never thought you would insult someone for doing what it takes."

"Hey back off him," Dan interjected in defense.

After that Andrew Kekso walked through the door and said, "Al-Hirrshi is waiting for a debriefing. I think it's best if you two show up for this."

Dan, Lance and Erin put aside their argument and joined Andrew, Robert Ramirez, Aaron Samson, Sarah, and Danny Smith in the conference room. Seeing Sarah back was a pleasant surprise for Lance. He hadn't expected her first time back since Jacob's death to be in the presence of someone so inflammatory. Lance was no stranger to the fact that doing something, anything, was better than being alone with your thoughts.

At the front of the conference room was a presence that was unmistakable—Ibrahim al-Hirrshi, the killer of thousands. He seemed tired and beaten. He'd even cut his beard to survive. Lance figured that must have broken some religious vow, but Hirrshi probably would have some bullshit justification if called out on it. It might have sounded archaic to Lance, but he felt that an evil presence lingered.

To Lance's amazement, he was still thinking about Erin, despite Hirrshi being in the room. Lance was upset that he'd had to finish the conversation with Erin on bad terms. He would have to deal with that later, but as always, he had to focus on the mission. He hoped Erin would not give him any problems during the meeting.

Lance had a chance to look at his old enemy. Hirrshi looked older than Lance remembered, his hair filled with a little more gray than the most recent pictures Lance had seen of him. He looked miserable and angry, but his brown eyes were still intense. He was wearing Western-style clothes, not the robes Lance was used to seeing him wear in his videos.

After a few minutes of awkward silence, Andrew started the conversation. "I think it is time we get started, Mr. Hirrshi. I assume Erin told you of this deal, and you know very well why we are even considering it. If this was two years ago, we would have killed you on sight, but these are trying times, and we know you want revenge on Webb. Right now it is in both of our interests to cooperate. You will get your freedom when we kill or capture Victor Webb."

Hirrshi looked around with some consideration and finally responded, "I want you all to know this: I couldn't care less how many Americans Webb kills. If Webb wins, we trade one blasphemer for another. I want to be free and stop running, so you won't get a lick of information from me until there is absolute proof that all of my transactions are forgiven I need solid proof. This women clearly lied about joining me" he said as he gestured to the uncovered Erin.

"I'll convert the second we find Webb, I just can't wait" she said sarcastically "What do you get in heaven do I get seventy two male virgins, oh that's going to be fun"

Ramirez stepped in seemingly trying to cut Erin off and said, "I have your proof right here—papers for a pardon. The president is willing to sign these, granted you have information on the location of Victor Webb."

Hirrshi examined the papers for a bit. "Good enough. I am a man of my word. Allah rewards honesty and fighting against the infidels. What in particular do you want to know?"

Lance took the lead. "Erin reported that Webb has attempted to kill you. What are your thoughts on why that is the case? Did he want to add your face to the people he showed in that video?"

"I'm sure he would have put me in the video if he had succeeded in killing me, but I don't think that was the main reason. Three years ago I began to hear reports of mysterious deaths of my fellow mujahideen, and I tried desperately to find the reason. Mujahideen seemed to be dying in record numbers under mysterious circumstances, and many more had gone missing. At first I assumed the CIA, the Mossad, or some other Western intelligence agencies were getting better. However, you showed none of your usual tells."

"What do you mean our 'usual tells'?" Sarah asked.

"Your leaders love to gloat when one of my brethren is slain. I saw no strategic reason for not telling your people. If anything, the Western masses would relish in the destruction of their enemies, and your politicians would be rewarded. Also the assassinations were done pretty crudely—poison, pipe bombs, not Western precision strikes."

Andrew asked, "Why do you think Webb took out Islamist leaders? If he was building his army with soldiers comprised of many known terrorist groups, wouldn't he try to recruit your kind to his cause? You seem to have like-minded goals."

"My guess would be that even Webb could see that allying with these guys would be impossible," Samson said. "They would never accept a deal with a non-Muslim, even if he got more help."

"The West has many enemies, but we do not all think alike," Hirrshi said.

"What do you mean by that?" Lance asked.

"I have personally met Victor Webb, and he is not my kind of man. He is more immoral in the eyes of Allah than most. He'll have sex with anything, does not pray, and thinks our tales and hopes and paradise are useless," Hirrshi replied.

Lance, with some anger, said, "I like how his slaughter of innocents seems to have no effect on you."

Andrew said, "Lance, I hate him as much as you do, but we need what he knows."

Hirrshi responded with glee, "Thank you. You are quite a smart kaffir."

Andrew added with clear disdain, "Just tell us how you met Webb and what the circumstances of that meeting were."

Hirrshi said, "About eighteen months ago, right after the failed bombing in Paris, my organization was in disarray. We were not immune from the assassinations I told you of. I was more fearful than I have ever been. However, at this time, we got what I thought was a break. An agent of mine who had gone missing returned and told me that he'd escaped an assassination attempt against him and knew who was attacking us. He said they were a group of ex-Mossad agents working outside the Israeli government, and he knew a place where we could ambush and kill them."

"We all know that was not the case, so what happened there?" Andrew asked.

"I was enraged by all the damage I thought these men had done, so I wanted to be there to kill them personally. But when we got to the ambush site, all my men were shot and killed, and I was shot in the back of the head with a tranquilizer bullet. I woke up in a warehouse in Peru two continents away from where I started. A man approached me there, the one we now know to be Victor Webb."

"Webb had you in a compromising position. Why did he not kill you there? He showed no hesitation in killing your friends," Danny said.

"Webb told me he had a plan to change the structure of the world's government, making a new nation that would be a superpower of the world. He spread his profanity, such as his belief that sexual deviants should be accepted and not killed. He said that he disagreed with my practices, but since we had a common enemy in the West and the American government, it was possible we could work together, at least in the short term."

Dan quickly left the room without saying anything. From the scraping of his chair and the slamming of the door, he was clearing enraged. Such behavior would normally not be appropriate, but Lance didn't think anyone would hold it against Dan for leaving.

Hirrshi continued with a look of disgust on his face, "I refused, of course, and Webb decided to kill me to make me an example to others who resisted his advances. I could have been one of the faces Webb released."

"How did you escape? You're obviously not dead," Andrew said.

"After Webb captured me, I was saved by someone in Webb's organization who claimed to still be loyal to me and who said he'd simply joined for his own survival. I arranged to have contact with him once I had plans for revenge. Later I told some of my most loyal remaining men to immerse themselves in Webb's organization and agree to follow him. I have eyes among the Lemurians. That is why I have an idea where Webb will be."

"All right, Mr. Hirrshi, tell us where Victor Webb is right now, or you won't get anything," Ramirez said proudly.

Hirrshi said, "My contacts currently tell me that Webb is an a town called Herzejot, Afghanistan, near the border of Turkmenistan. It was a small town at first but Webb's built up as a base. Figures that Webb has the nerve to desecrate Muslim land. I would suggest focusing most of your intelligence on that region."

"Samson, does that make sense?" Ramirez asked.

"Large parts of Central Asia are pretty dark in terms of communication right now, and we assume it has to do with the Lemurians. It seems like a place where he might hide," Samson replied.

Ramirez responded, "All right, Mr. Hirrshi, you will be put in custody for a bit, and then if your information is accurate, you will be released."

Hirrshi said confidently, "No, you will have to take me on this mission if you want to find Victor Webb. One of my men can lead us to a passage where Webb himself will be, provided you give me a transmission radio once we get to Afghanistan. I am going to be there personally on your mission. I will leave with my agents after it is done. I am not going to trust the US military to ever let me go."

"You are going to be a pain till the end, huh, Hirrshi?" Sarah said, annoyed.

"I have been kind enough to put up with being in a society that mocks the Sharia and Allah, with infidel women showing their flesh and people breaking the rules of Allah. I have nothing but disgust for all of you, and I look forward to the day you all burn in hellfire. The only reason I'm helping you is for my pardon. I am not going to explain myself to sexual deviants and whorish women. In the caliphate, filth like you would face Allah's wrath," Hirrshi said with glee.

"Good thing your caliphate will never come," Sarah taunted.

"I have no remorse for anything I've done. I will now be free knowing that I will never pay for killing filthy American swine." Hirrshi started to laugh maniacally.

Growing angrier, Lance stood up and started to walk toward Hirrshi. Andrew quickly got up too and stepped in front of Lance.

"Don't give this man that joy. You know Rachel wouldn't want this," Andrew said.

Hirrshi didn't say anything. He just sat there with a smug smile.

Andrew snuck behind Hirrshi and stuck him with a needle. The terrorist let out a scream and started to thrash around. He made an angry swing toward Andrew but quickly fell down on the floor. Andrew said, "Just because we have to tolerate his existence doesn't mean we have to listen to this maniac anymore. We got what we wanted."

"Do you think that will hurt our chances of him cooperating with us? He's a piece of shit, but we might need his contact if we are going to find Webb," Sarah said with concern.

"I don't think that will be much of a problem. He'll whine when he regains consciousness, but I believe he still wants any chance of freedom," Samson said.

"Are we going to take him to Herzejot?" Lance asked.

"Probably. Who knows—it might be good to have him there. Webb's men will probably recognize him, and maybe he'll get shot there and spare us the problem of pardoning him," Andrew said.

Eliza Churchill of the NSA entered the conference room just then and said in a solemn tone, "We need to accelerate this invasion."

"I've started to get used to hearing bad news, so just let it out, Eliza," Lance said strongly.

"Webb is launching an invasion in Central Asia. Lemurian flags are rising outside of Afghanistan and Pakistan. He seems to finally want more than an insurgency. They have started fighting in the streets of Bishkek, and there are also reports of a growing insurgency in South America."

Erin walked up toward Lance and said, "He's finally doing it."

Lance stood in silence for a few moments, thinking about Webb's confidence in that goddamned bunker under the base and then becoming enraged. "If Webb is going to start the invasion, I think it's finally time to end this. Eliza, contact me when we launch the attack. I will be there."

"Are you sure you want the strike force to be there? The military wants to take the lead in this operation."

"This strike force is responsible for fighting against Webb. I think you want a professional to escort Hirrshi into Herzejot. Do you honestly think there is anyone better than me?"

"All right, Lance. It will probably take a few days to prepare. I promise that you can go to Afghanistan. You've done enough to earn that."

"Thank you, Eliza," Lance said, and then he stormed off to his locker. He must have some built-up anger over the attacks and having to deal with Hirrshi. He was looking forward to going home, but he knew it might not be good for him to go home angry. Thinking of mistakes, he thought of Sarah of all people. He felt bad that he hadn't talked to her since Jacob's death. He thought that was something he should do. With him going to Afghanistan, he might not get another chance.

He went back to the main conference room to see if Sarah was still there. When she wasn't there, he next headed up the stairs to Jacob's old office. As he got closer, he saw her sitting at Jacob's old desk. Once he was close enough to start a conversation, he started with a simple "Hey, Sarah."

She looked up at him from Jacob's desk. "Hello, Lance," she replied simply.

Lance could tell she was trying to force some

happiness, but there was sadness to it. He thought it best not to bring up the issue of Jacob's death immediately. "It's sickening that we have to work with that piece of shit, huh?"

"You of all people should understand what we have to do to stop Webb," Sarah quickly said.

Lance didn't like how the conversation was going. He already had Erin mad at him; he didn't want to keep getting into arguments with people, so he said, "I understand, but that doesn't mean I have to like it. Are we even confident that he will be honest?"

"He surrendered himself. We can check all communication coming out of Afghanistan and see if any of it reveals Webb's position. We should trust our intel. We trusted Landshire's info on Candellario, and it paid off."

"That's true," Lance said, though he still had some doubts. Landshire was a follower, and Hirrshi was an important terrorist leader. Lance didn't want to add any more conflict to his life, though. He moved closer to Sarah, to look her in the eye. Her eyes started to water, but she did not yet break into a cry. It seemed that she was able to guess what he was about to say. "Are you all right, Sarah?" he asked simply.

She started to cry. She rose from the desk and hugged Lance, crying into his chest. "I don't know what to do, Lance. Every time I close my eyes, I see what Jacob looked like before he killed him."

"Even I don't know what that is like. I sometimes debate if it's better that I didn't see how Tara died or if it's worse, since now it's left up to my imagination."

Sarah stepped back and looked at Lance with empathy. Right now she was someone who might possibly understand what he'd gone through. She said, "We are going to kill him, Webb. He'll pay for Tara, Rachel, Jacob, and all the rest."

"I don't think we can truly make him pay. He's caused too many deaths to ever make it even. All we can do now is stop him from hurting others."

"That sadly might be true," she said, "but I think it helps just to think that there will be justice."

"Jacob at least gave Webb a black eye before he went out, stopping that nuke. Ramirez told me they're probably going to name an airport after him or something. He will be remembered."

"I'm happy to hear that. We never had kids, so I'm glad his name can live on somewhere."

"Sarah, is there anything I can do for you, besides kill Webb?" He chuckled.

"Just know that the door's open, Lance. I always can use someone to talk to. Or maybe come over—I can cook for you. I always liked to cook for Jacob."

"That would be pretty easy. I always liked your cooking. Your chicken parmigiana was very good at Christmas."

"Jacob loved it too. You want to know something? Jacob didn't become obsessed with Italian food until after I married him. Before he met me, he had steak and mashed potatoes every day. Maybe he'd get some meatloaf if he was feeling adventurous. Then after we were married for a few years, he would go on and on about how he knew Italian food and how much of an expert he was."

"Really?" Lance responded in a joking manner.

"But you know what?" Sarah said with a sigh. "He might have exaggerated a bit, but he really did try. He even learned to cook a pretty good lasagna. Sometimes he would sneak home and surprise me with dinner."

Lance smiled at Sarah, and she started to frown a bit. It seemed joking about Jacob brought her mourning to the forefront, although she didn't cry. Lance hugged her and said, "People are going to view him as a hero, you know."

"Yeah," she said simply, talking into Lance's chest. Lance wondered whether he should talk about Afghanistan to Sarah, tell her that he was going to end Webb, but he quickly decided against it. Sarah knew where he was going. As far as he was concerned, their conversation was up to Sarah. He asked, "Do you want to go somewhere and talk? Maybe you can tell me more stories about Jacob."

"I'd like that," Sarah said.

Lance and Sarah sat down and continued to talk into the night.

30

Lance Richardson was sitting in a military transport above the skies of Afghanistan. He was anxious. Andrew Kekso was going to be giving a briefing on the mission soon, and emotions were running through Lance's head. This was the closest he might ever get to defeating Webb and getting revenge for his family. But Webb was not going to give up and would probably try to avoid being captured alive, no matter what. There was still a part of Lance that wanted to make Webb face justice, but he certainly wouldn't reject a chance to kill him. Once again Lance thought of his mortality. The thought that this might be the last day of his life sprang into his head. Stopping Webb and avenging his family would be a worthy end to his life, but he felt a fear of death within him, as well as a sense of nervousness about what would come after this. What would he do after meeting Webb? With heavy feelings, he left for the briefing.

The meeting was held at the front of the military transport. In addition to Andrew, Dan and Erin were there, sitting near each other, as well as Ethan and some British and Russian allies. Lance felt it might be good to talk to Erin before the assault started. Lance wanted as little on his mind as possible before the attack. Andrew then started the meeting.

"Hello, everyone. I want to thank our allies in the British and Russian armies for helping with this operation. We all know the importance of the mission, so I will quickly head straight into the battle plan. We have reliable intel that Webb himself is in Herzejot. Webb has started his invasion and has conquered the areas around this city by a hundred miles in each direction, so a full-blown invasion of Webb's territory will give him plenty of time to escape or go back into hiding. Currently, we have several dozen of the best military transports available. We will fly over the range of Webb's defenses and land our troops. Once there, we head into Herzejot and conduct a quick raid to capture Webb. After that is done, we arrange a quick evacuation."

Ethan said, "I assume the armies are going to launch some air strikes before we get there, to weaken any resistance we'll face. Who knows—maybe all we'll have to do is identify Webb's body."

"We have launched several air strikes, but we aren't confident in them being enough to kill Webb. We sadly need Hirrshi's man to locate him," Andrew replied.

A British lieutenant said, "Mr. Kekso, after the Manchester attacks, no one wants to get Webb more than us, but we all know how you got that information. How can we know that this info from Hirrshi is really accurate?"

"I concur," said the Russian representative. "You need to have more evidence than Hirrshi's word."

"We have also monitored all communication for a hundred miles," Andrew said. "We were surprised to find a lot more activity than normal for a smaller city in the developing world. After intense hacking, we found a secret of Webb's. He has created his own cellular network through the use of various towers he has built, like the one on the island. He has been communicating with his allies using this network. We cannot rule out that Webb has been able to launch a satellite into orbit."

"We're not just asking if the city is occupied," the Russian said. "We need clarification that Webb himself is in there. With the Lemurians attacking around the world, we don't have the willpower for an occupation of the city."

"With the discovery of Webb's cellular network, we've been able to crack several codes, allowing us to decipher a conversation between Webb and recently known Lemurian Zhou Chang. Zhou is believed to have been involved in the nuke in South Korea and is Asia's equivalent of Candellario. From this conversation it is obvious Webb is in Herzejot. I will play it, so everyone can hear it." Andrew played back the recording for the group.

"Zhou, what is our status?" Webb asked.

"For the most part the invasion has gone under way successfully. However, Russia has been able to take back some of their land," Zhou replied.

"That is to be expected. This invasion is just the beginning. Eventually we will make the killing blow. For now I will stay in Herzejot the next few days to help organize the invasion."

Lance finally broke his silence. "What do you think he

means by 'this invasion is just the beginning'? What can he possibly plan that is more than a full-blown invasion?"

"Nothing, because Webb is going down. Today his plans are over," Andrew replied.

The group applauded Andrew for the response and then scattered across the military transport. Lance went back to his seat on the plane and continued his contemplation of the mission. Erin was sitting nearby working on a laptop. Lance figured this would be as good a time as any to try to deal with any problems between them.

"Cahill," Lance said formally. He did not think they were on good enough terms right now to address her by her first name.

"Come to apologize to me?" she asked immediately.

"I'll admit that I should not have been disgusted by what you said. That was hypocritical, and I do apologize for that."

"Thank you," she said quickly.

"But I still feel that I have to be honest with you. I think you were too eager to do anything to stop Webb. While it sometimes is necessary to do bad things for a greater good, it should always be a struggle, or else you have become someone who does more harm than you're worth."

"Did you have these thoughts after you killed Farud Hadi? He was fourteen, Lance," Erin said sternly.

"That's the thing—I didn't. I didn't care that he was fourteen, and I didn't care what anyone would think of me. He was coming to kill me, and if I didn't do what I did, I'd be the one dead. It is as simple as that. Taliban reinforcements were coming, and I figured the society he lived in had brainwashed him to be a monster. How else can someone be willing to die to force women into captivity in their homes and to kill anyone who doesn't follow their god? Someone like that is not worthy of life. His society killed any hope of him being someone worth caring about long before I got there."

"Do you still think that?" Erin asked.

"To a degree. I think since then part of me wanted to change. I feared the person I could become if I stayed in the army any longer. I looked to join the CIA after it was over. I figured at least I wouldn't be on the battlefield, and I would still have the chance to serve the country."

"But do you still think you did the right thing back there?"

"I don't know. I've thought that I could have shot him in the knee and taken him prisoner. Maybe he could have been deprogrammed. The Saudis haven't had much luck rehabilitating terrorists, though. Let's say I am far from optimistic. It probably doesn't even matter what I think now. He was trying to kill me at the time, and I did not have the luxury to think it through."

"Lance, you seem to have an understanding of how necessary our work is. Can't you see why I was angry? I thought you would be on my side. It might have been presumptuous of me, but you know I did not want to work for the government and when you criticized me it felt like I lost an ally. You've been at this longer than I have. Aren't you disgusted by the people who would call you a war criminal for collateral damage, after you have done everything to stop civilian deaths? Aren't you sick of being insulted by the same people who are silent after all the deaths people like Hirrshi have caused?"

"I do get angry, Erin. I'm surprised how well I took being in the same room as Hirrshi. Maybe my conversation with Webb made me numb to insane rhetoric, but Hadi is not the only thing that haunts me. I sometimes have regrets about the person I was. After 9/11 I wanted to nuke Afghanistan. The thought of civilian deaths wasn't on my mind. Rachel helped me move past that, but I am always afraid of going back to that. Right now, I know Webb is below us. Do you think there isn't a part of me that wants to destroy everything to make sure we get him?"

Erin sat in silence looking at Lance. It seemed that Lance was successfully getting to her in some manner. Lance wondered what to say next and then said honestly, "I just feel that we need hope that we can be better than him and others like him. There is a point where you have a society not worth saving. I'd like to tell you I had some strategic reason for shutting you down, Erin, that it was part of some plan, but in the end it's just me. I need to feel better; I have to feel that I am doing something good, and seeing the ease you had in letting Hirrshi get away with it hurt me, that I was releasing a monster on the world. You know, after I lost my family, I was never suicidal. I thought maybe it was just me being faithful to my wife's wishes, but maybe I saw suicide as being too easy on myself. It could have been my own ego keeping me alive. I think I might have been angry with you because you stopped me from thinking I was some great guy for a bit."

Erin had a confused look on her face, as if surprised

about how Lance was feeling. She finally asked, "Are you going to get Webb soon?"

Her tone was sympathetic, as if she felt sorry for Lance in a way. Lance didn't like it. The woman who had been so angry toward him mere moments ago now had some pity in her voice. He was happy to change the subject and said, "I'm ready for this. We are taking him down."

"All right, good luck, Lance, and I mean that," she said sincerely.

Lance was still not completely satisfied with his status with Erin, but being pitied was better than being hated. Lance went back to his bunk and suited up for the mission. While putting on additional body armor, he saw Dan in the distance. Lance was glad. It would probably do some good to have a friendly conversation before the mission. It always paid to have positive thoughts on your mind before a mission.

Danny saw Lance, walked over, and said with a friendly yet concerned voice, "You were more quiet at that meeting than normal. Are you okay?"

"All right as I can be. I got a lot on my mind. Webb is down there—we know it this time—and he is not going to go quietly," Lance said.

"Today isn't the first time we've dealt with monsters, especially for you, yet you always seem to make it out alive."

Lance asked out of nowhere, "Dan, what was the best moment in your life?"

Dan smirked a little. "Why do you want to know that, Lance?"

"We may be heading into a tough fight, and if there

is any chance these are our last moments, I want to at least spend some of them talking about something good," Lance replied.

"I have a few moments that stand out, but the one that is coming to mind was the twenty-first birthday of a friend of mine. It was back in college. We went to this nice little bar near Belcher Street after a party, just to get a few drinks. I sat down and had a drink and looked around, absorbing the moment. A lot of happy friends stared back at me. It sounds simple, but to me it showed that I'd made it. I was shy in high school and didn't have a lot of friends, but at that moment I knew the past was behind me."

"That's a good story, Dan. Would you like to know about my moment?" Lance asked.

"Sure," Dan replied politely.

"It was when I walked into the delivery room after Tara's birth—that moment I first saw her and got to hold her. I swear she smiled at me the first time I held her. I couldn't help but smile, and Rachel looked at me and said happily, 'I think she likes you, Dad.'

"Dan, you know more than anyone that I have killed men. It should not be easy, to know that you've ended a life, even if the person is terrible. Until recently with the Lemurians, I never thought that I would want to kill someone just for my own satisfaction. There are times I wonder if I am truly a good man or just another killer. It takes effort to keep your humanity in this line of work, but that day I truly felt loved. I had two people that made me feel alive."

"That is a good memory, Lance," Danny said.

Lance then said sadly, "Then Webb took them away."

"I'm sorry, Lance. I shouldn't have made you talk about Rachel and Tara. There was no need to salt the wounds," Dan said with a hint of regret.

"No, don't be sorry, Dan. I volunteered to share," Lance said with a little remorse. "Webb took their lives, but it doesn't change anything I did with them while they were alive. Those feelings and memories are all I have left, and I'm not going to let Webb take them too. Telling people about who Rachel and Tara were keeps them alive longer."

Dan said, "That is very true, and today we make sure he never does this again."

Andrew Kekso walked over and said, "Gentlemen, are you ready? We're almost on the east side of Herzejot. You're going to have to parachute out of the plane and sneak in while we draw Webb's forces away."

"All right, we're ready. Has there been any attack on Webb's forces yet?" Lance asked.

Andrew said, "We've had some firefights outside of where we believe Webb is right now. He's going to make a move soon with his reinforcements."

"Who is with us for this mission?" Lance asked Andrew. "I want to know the men I'll be leading."

"It's a combination of Russian, American, and British troopers. You, Ethan, and Danny are going in the same unit, so you will have some familiarity. The men in your group are the best in the field, despite having some possibly disagreements."

"What do you mean?" Lance asked.

"Ramirez says that the best-case scenario is capturing Webb alive, but many of the British might be against it after what happened in Manchester. Many of these men lost family members. Take him alive if possible, but ending Webb is the main objective."

"Webb took my family, Andrew. I'm surprised you're trusting me to even try to keep Webb alive."

"You have proven yourself; you didn't kill Candellario or Landshire. If we take Webb alive, it will stop him from being seen as a martyr, and if we can break him and get information from him, it could be the end of the Lemurians."

"Thank you for the kind words," Lance said. "I won't put my revenge before the good of this country and the citizens of this world."

"Thank you, Lance. I know this is hard for you after what he has done. If you're lucky enough to capture Webb, you can do whatever you want with him."

"Trust me, as much as I don't want to admit it, I'll keep that in mind if I get the honor of capturing him," Lance said, trying to mask some anger.

After saying his piece to Andrew, Lance moved to the back of the plane with Danny and said. "Are you ready, Dan?"

"I think it's time for us to end this and help achieve peace after all this anarchy and justice for all that Webb has done. I promise you, Lance, if Webb is in my line of sight, I will shoot him in the legs myself. He will not get away."

Lance looked into Dan's eyes and said, "Thank you for everything, Dan. You're a good friend."

After that Ethan interrupted them, saying, "We're over Herzejot. Everyone ready?"

With a look of intensity, Lance said, "More than anything."

With that, the three men jumped from the plane and once again headed toward war-torn landscape and Victor Webb himself.

31

Thoughts rushed through Lance's mind as he headed toward the ground. He once again went back toward the fond memories of his past, the touch of his wife, the laugh of his daughter. He felt a sense of empowerment. He had lost them, but now he had a chance for vengeance. He hoped to make Webb and the Lemurians pay for what they had done.

Lance heard Danny's parachute go off and realized he'd gotten lost in his thoughts. Lance pulled his parachute's rip cord, slowing his fall to the earth. The landscape looked like Mars. It was nothing but red and brown with only a glimmer of green scrubs. He heard gunfire in the distance. Once on the ground, Lance turned to Danny and Ethan and asked, "You guys good?"

"Yeah," Ethan responded, with Danny giving a nod in the background.

"Where is Hirrshi?" Lance asked sternly.

"He was transferred to the custody of the British special forces," Ethan said. "They should be closing in on our position while the Russians lead the assault on the other side of the city."

"All right," Lance said. "Dan, use the rifle with the thermal scope and see if Andrew and the main forces are doing a good enough job drawing Lemurian forces away from the east side of the city."

Dan looked through the thermal scope and said, "The diversion seems to be working for the most part. There are some units still there but nothing we can't deal with if we use stealth."

Suddenly the British landed with al-Hirrshi in tow. There was some silence until Lance asked, "Who is in charge here?"

"I am," replied a man with dark-red hair. "My name is Cameron Colton."

"Is Hirrshi intact?" Lance asked.

Hirrshi smugly walked in front of the Brit and said, "I am."

Ethan raised his gun and said, "Know your place, Hirrshi. The only reason you're still breathing is that you are of use to us right now."

"I regrettably know that," Hirrshi responded.

"All right, we have differences, but for the next few hours we are united by our hatred of Victor Webb. So, Mr. Hirrshi, where is this contact?" Lance asked.

"I was able to contact him by radio. He knows to head to the east side of Herzejot, about a mile from the city, at a location known only by me. He will have a stolen transport with Lemurian uniforms stored in it. From there we can sneak into Herzejot and proceed to kill Victor Webb," Hirrshi said.

"Uniforms?" Ethan questioned.

"I can confirm that intel," Dan said. "According to

some agents behind enemy lines, Lemurians have actually started to govern some of the cities they control."

Lance looked at the rugged terrorist and said, "That plan sounds as solid as any to get into Herzejot. Lead the way, and we will get this deal over with."

"My pleasure," Hirrshi responded rudely. "However, there is one problem: we will have to split up."

"Why?" Lance asked.

"For one thing, I plan to escape after we get you into Webb's city. Having fewer men around me will guarantee me a greater chance of leaving without getting shot."

"Do you really think we're going to change our strategy just to make you happy?" Dan asked.

"No, but the vehicle my contact is bringing won't fit all of us, so I suggest the rest of you capture another vehicle and wait to learn Webb's location," Hirrshi replied.

"Fuck you, asshole!" Ethan yelled. "Lance, are we really going to let this guy call the shots?"

"If you want to find Webb, you've got to," Hirrshi smirked.

Lance moved closer to Ethan and, in an attempt to calm him down, said, "Ethan, I know this is tough, and trust me, a few years ago I would be more angry than you are, but this is our best chance to end Webb, to bring him in front of the world and make him pay for what he has done. Today we can show all Lemurians that their leader is nothing compared to us. This is our chance for justice for everyone he has hurt—my family, your son, and all the people we will never know."

Lance pointed in front of him and said to Hirrshi,

"After you." With that, Hirrshi took the lead and started walking.

As they were walking, Cameron Colton came over to Lance and said, "It stinks that we have to listen to this wanker if we want to find Webb."

"I can understand your concern, but I promise you that if we had a better way, I would gladly do it," Lance replied.

With a puzzled look on his face, Cameron said, "Mr. Richardson, I know you wouldn't do anything to hurt this mission. There might not be any person on this planet I respect more than you."

Lance, though trying to be humble, let out a little smirk. "Thank you," he said in a simple manner.

"Do you want to know why?" Cameron asked.

Lance debated how to answer. He wanted to focus on his task, but he did not want to create any additional problems with his crew, so he asked, "Why, Cameron?"

"I know what happened on that island. Webb let hundreds of his men die, just to torment your team. Just the fact you're here must put a frown on that smug face." Cameron grew angrier. "That demon, that filth, thinks he can kill any person he wants. He will pay!"

Lance nervously said, "Focus, Cameron. The goal is to capture him alive. I want to end this too, but we might slip up if we get too bogged down in our anger."

"Lance, Victor Webb ruined my life. I had two younger brothers in Manchester when the bomb went off. I helped raise them myself, and now they are gone. You're the only person Webb considers a threat, so you have my full support. I will trust any order you give me. You are my best chance to stop him."

"I'm glad you have faith in me, but I'm no hero, just a soldier with a few lucky breaks," Lance replied.

As the group began to walk across the mountains outside Herzejot, Ethan suddenly had an angry outburst. "What is your endgame, Hirrshi?" he yelled.

"I've told you—my freedom," Hirrshi responded.

"How do you think you're going to get away? What is stopping us from killing you the second we get what we want?" Ethan asked.

Lance interjected, "Ethan, you know the importance of this mission. Don't let your personal feelings get involved."

Hirrshi retorted, "Relax, Richardson. I enjoy the repartee. Mr. Paterson, you think I don't have a plan. I have full confidence that I will stay alive when this is done."

Ethan raised his gun toward Hirrshi in a threatening manner. "Don't be so sure."

Thinking quickly, Lance stepped in and said, "Ethan, go with Cameron. Stay away from Hirrshi for now. If you get out of hand, everything we've worked for might go to hell."

"Relax, Richardson," Ethan said. "I can handle myself."

"With everything riding on today's attacks, I can't take that risk. Go with Cameron. That's an order," Lance said solemnly.

Ethan gave Lance a look of disapproval but walked away. Hirrshi laughed smugly. "That's right—go away."

Infuriated by this smugness, Lance ran over to Hirrshi and punched him to the ground. He then took out his handgun, put it on Hirrshi's neck, and snarled, "You are going to be very quiet now, you waste of human life. We both know the only reason you're still alive is that you've got something we want. That man there is just saying what we all are feeling. The only reason I don't shoot you myself is I want to limit how many people Webb kills. That's the only thing controlling my rage. However, if you can't behave, it might be a bit harder for me to control myself." Lance paused and took stock of his anger. He calmed down and sternly added, "Are we clear?"

Hirrshi, a grimace on his face, nodded, got up from the ground, and walked forward with no fight. It seemed that Lance had been able to restore order.

Lance walked back to Cameron and ordered, "Cameron, take your team and Ethan and go stake out a position. Dan and I are going to go with Hirrshi's man into the city. Try to steal another vehicle. Maybe clear out a building covertly so we have a safe house in the city if things go wrong."

"All right, I'm on it," Cameron replied confidently.

With that, Lance and Dan walked to Hirrshi. Lance said, "All right, Ibrahim, this is the moment we've both been waiting for. As much as we disagree, we need this plan to go smoothly if any of us is going to get what we want."

"Despite my beliefs, I am not blind to what needs to be done. My friend secured a jeep and is about a hundred yards ahead behind a series of large rocks," Hirrshi said.

"All right, let's head out." Lance pointed his gun at Hirrshi and said sternly, "You first."

Hirrshi walked ahead and then said, "Listen, Lance, I know it's not for the same reason, but I want Webb to die just as badly as you. I spent my entire life supporting jihad, and now Webb had destroyed my life's work. I am not oblivious; I know you have had success fighting him. Despite our history, I know this is the best chance to kill him, and I am not going to backstab the man who is most likely to end him."

Lance looked at Hirrshi. After some thought, he said, "I believe you, and on this day, I will not kill you if you help us find Webb, but after this is over, I will not let up on stopping you and everyone like you."

"I would not expect anything else."

Dan then turned to Lance and said, "I think I see the jeep."

As Lance, Dan, and Hirrshi walked closer to the jeep, the door started to open. Lance said to Hirrshi, "Go first. Contact your man."

Hirrshi walked to the jeep, and a man got out of it. "Samir, is that you?" Hirrshi asked.

"Yes, sir. It is great to know that the sheikh Ibrahim al-Hirrshi is still alive."

Lance and Dan then started to walk toward the two men, and Hirrshi said with a hint of regret, "Yes, I am back, with a bit of a handicap."

"Shame we have to work with the Western pigs," Samir said.

Dan responded, "The feelings are mutual. The only way any of you are going to get any freedom now is if we get through the operation against Webb, so limit the small talk."

"Well, one of us is going to get his freedom right now," Hirrshi said. "Now that Samir is here, I have done my part." Hirrshi turned to Samir and said, "Samir, my supplies."

Samir took a bag from the back of the Jeep. "Here. These supplies should allow you to make the hike away from here."

"What is going on here, Hirrshi?" Lance asked.

"Lance, you may not respect me, but I didn't get this far being an idiot," Hirrshi replied. "I am leaving now. If you kill me, Samir won't help you into the heart of the city to find Webb."

"Defiant to the end, huh?" Lance said.

"What do you expect?" Hirrshi returned smugly. "It is my turn to finally collect my part of the dea—"

Hirrshi was shot in the head before he could finish. The bullet wound was large enough that the left part of his brain fell to the ground.

"You infidels, you'll never get Webb now!" Samir screamed just a moment before another bullet killed him as well.

"Danny, get behind the jeep!" Lance screamed. Dan dived for cover, and Lance followed. Lance then took a grenade out and launched it at where he suspected the shooter was.

After the explosion, a voice called out, "Richardson, are you trying to kill me?"

Lance recognized the voice. "Ethan?" He looked around the edge of the jeep and saw Ethan with a sniper rifle in tow. "What are you doing here, Paterson?" Lance asked angrily. "I told you to go with Cameron. With Hirrshi and his contact dead, there is no way we can find Webb now."

Ethan responded, "Listen, Lance, I may be less experienced than you, but I would not put this mission in danger. Cameron and I found out where Webb is through an audio transmission. He is in a blue mosque near the center of the city. Once we had this info, I agreed to come back and make sure Hirrshi didn't escape."

"Did it occur to you Webb might be leaking false reports, knowing that there are troops near his city?" Lance asked.

"What makes you think Hirrshi was telling the truth?" Ethan retorted.

"Hirrshi wanted his freedom. It was a selfish motive but an honest one," Lance said. "We can't trust Webb to make mistakes, but we could've trusted a selfish man to look out for his own best interest."

With a look of dread and disbelief, Ethan said, "You actually were going to let him go. If I didn't kill him, you were going to let him go free."

Lance looked at Ethan with apprehension. He was about to answer but then stopped, afraid to utter his next words.

"Answer me, Lance," Ethan demanded.

His face stony, Lance blurted out with little emotion, "Yes, Ethan, I would have let him go, in order to get to Webb."

Ethan ran up to Lance and punched him, causing Lance to fall to the ground. Looking at Lance on the ground, Ethan screamed, "How could you have let that animal go after everything he did—the children he slaughtered, the graveyards he filled? How could you betray all those people?"

After this insult Danny jumped in to defend Lance. "How dare you accuse Lance! Lance has given us the best leads about the Lemurians. Even after losing his entire family, he has been able to keep his mind and keep fighting. Lance would have never even thought of doing something so drastic if he wasn't sure he could still find Webb."

"You two are starting to sicken me. Is there any point at which we draw the line? Are we willing to do anything to stop Webb? Lance, that man killed thousands of people just like your family. Do they not deserve justice, because they had the misfortune to be killed by the second-worst killer of our time?"

Having recovered from the blow, Lance looked up at Ethan and exclaimed, "Ethan, I have never judged you for being inexperienced, but don't you dare criticize me for the decisions I made until you have seen the things I have gone through. You're right—I was going to sacrifice the justice of many people. But there is no great answer, no perfect decision that makes everyone happy at the end. For twenty years I have fought killers and terrorists. People like that have been around since the dawn of humanity. I know we aren't going to destroy them completely. People like Hirrshi and Webb were here long before me, and they'll be here long after I die. There is no complete victory in this job. All I do is cut my losses and make sure I save as many lives as possible. Webb, in his short time, has caused more deaths than Hirrshi ever did, and that number is only going to increase the longer he is free. I can't save the people that Hirrshi killed, but maybe I can stop deaths now. That is the choice we have to make in this war."

Ethan gazed at Lance with a look of contemplation. He simply said, "You made your point. Maybe this is something we shouldn't discuss until after the mission."

"I can accept that," Lance replied. He then turned to Danny. "Danny, check the jeep to see if there is anything that can help us get into the city."

"All right." Danny opened the door and inspected the interior of the jeep, seeing nothing of use in the front. Turning to the back of the jeep, he found a tarp covering something soft. He called back to the others, "Whatever this is, it's obvious Samir thought it was important."

Lance took off the tarp, revealing a set of sand-colored camouflage uniforms. They were similar to what soldiers in the American army would wear but with the Lemurian Menes Hieroglyph on the shoulder. This was Webb's work. With that in mind, Lance blurted out, "Well, looks like the reports about uniforms were accurate."

Dan took one of the uniforms and said, "Just give it to me. I think I'm going to die a little inside having that uniform touch my skin, but in a few hours Victor Webb could be just a bad memory. Who knows—I might be able to sell it to a museum after the mission is over."

"Good idea," Ethan said. "I'm honest enough to admit I might as well make some money out of this when it's over. Now give me a uniform. No way am I going to let Webb have his country."

The men put on the uniforms and got in the jeep, with Lance driving. As they proceeded toward the city, Lance gave some orders. "Ethan, you need to give Dan the frequency of Webb's communications. We need to try to intercept more of his transmissions."

"All right," Ethan said. He took out a piece of paper and wrote down the frequency.

"Okay, now call Cameron," Lance said. "I want to see how his team's progressing in securing another vehicle."

With that order given, Lance had some time to think about what he was doing. This was Webb's city, the start of his potential empire, Lance felt a new level of fear with the realization that Webb was actually doing it. In this moment of desperation, Lance thought of Rachel and Tara, the loss he'd felt that day. He must finish what he'd started. He must stop Webb, and today was as good a time as any to do just that.

As they approached Herzejot, Ethan said, "Spoke to Cameron. He says he was able to take control of a small settlement outside of the main city. Probably was a farm before Webb rolled in. After we nab Webb, we'll head there."

"Now, that shouldn't be too hard, capturing the leader of the deadliest terrorist organization in the world, in the middle of this own army," Dan said. "You know I trust you, Lance, but there has to be more to it than that if we have any chance of succeeding."

"Ethan said that he's in a converted mosque in the city. Once we're near it, I will call Andrew and tell him to conduct some drone strikes near but not on the mosque. Hopefully there will be enough chaos that no one will be paying close enough attention to realize we're not with the Lemurians," Lance said.

"Well, if we have any chance of success, we need to get into the city. Keep driving, Lance. It might be easier to get better info to find Webb once we're closer to the city," Ethan said.

"All right," Lance said. "Danny, keep the scanners open. I'm going to try to enter the city. See if there is any useful information."

"Okay," Danny said, and Lance started the final drive into the city.

"Richardson, it should be stated that if Webb looks too guarded for us to attack, we need to call in a strike to end him," Ethan said. "I know Robert said that getting Webb alive is the best-case scenario, but we cannot miss this opportunity."

"Agreed. I promise the both of you that we will take Webb out if there is no other choice."

Ethan seemed to be getting over his anger over Hirrshi and said agreeably, "All right."

As Lance drove into the city, he lowered his helmet in an attempt to further obscure his face. Danny and Ethan followed suit. They entered the city streets. They were lucky so far that no soldiers had tried to stop the jeep. Lance took this time to look upon Webb's conquest. The city was poor, the relic of years of war that had started before Webb. However, despite that, Lance felt Webb's presence. There were soldiers wearing Lemurian uniforms, and the conquered city had more technology and power cables than would be expected for such a poor, remote area, showing that Webb had been successful in building the city to his liking.

From the back of the jeep, Dan exclaimed quietly, "With all the machinery Webb has added to this city, he must have some important information stored here somewhere. I bet somewhere in this city there is information revealing the location of every Lemurian base. I know the main goal is Webb, but we should look around while we're here, write up anything else that looks suspicious."

"We'll do our best," Lance said, "but for right now we need to look for that mosque."

"It's Afghanistan. There might be more than one blue mosque here," Dan said. "Anything in particular I should listen for in the Lemurian transmissions?"

"Focus on troop positions. Common sense says that Webb will be where the most soldiers in the city are," Lance said. "For now I'm guessing our best chance is to go into the center of the city."

Lance kept driving into the city. So far their luck had held. None of Webb's men seemed suspicious, but the fear was still there.

Ethan then said, "Three different battalions of Lemurian soldiers have headed to a large blue-and-white mosque near the center of the city."

"Okay, looks like that is where we have to go," Lance said.

"We're finally close to getting that bastard," Ethan said.

"Just remember—we also have to confirm he is there and sneak past hundreds of Lemurian soldiers," Dan said.

"We've succeeded before, but now we're finally close to Webb himself. This is our opportunity to end this war once and for all," Lance exclaimed strongly.

Lance continued to move toward the center of the city. Eventually a soldier stopped him with a hand gesture and started walking toward the stolen truck. Lance was nervous. Ethan started to reach for his gun, but Lance gave him a stern look, signaling that it wasn't a good idea to bring the guns out just yet. Lance took in their surroundings. There were dozens of soldiers around them. He knew that if they fired first, they would have no chance of survival. Their only chance would be to hold the approaching Lemurian at gunpoint and hope the other soldiers would hold their fire. However, as Lance was thinking about this, the soldier stopped and pointed to a detour to his side. Lance was immediately relieved and followed the detour. Their cover was seemingly still intact. Lance continued driving until they got to an area near the mosque with many military vehicles and looking like over a hundred soldiers present. He parked the jeep and turned to Ethan and Dan. "Where do we go from here?" he asked simply.

Ethan said, "Lance, I don't think we can possibly get Webb alive in this city. There are too many of his soldiers. Let's just report the location of this mosque to the troops, have them bomb it, and leave. This might be the only chance we have to end it."

"The city is surrounded with antiaircraft turrets. If we don't confirm the location Webb might realize how much danger he is in and escape" Lance said. "We're not completely certain Webb really is in that mosque. If we do this and it's a failure, we might make Webb be even more careful, and this entire mission and every life lost on it would be for nothing."

"He is protected, but I don't think Webb has strong enough weapons to stop all of thedrone strikes. If there is a chance Webb is here, It's worth a shot," Ethan said.

"I agree that it would be suicide trying to get into the mosque and capture Webb on foot," Lance said, "We need tell Andrew to strike near Mosque, in hopes that Webb evacuates and we can get him. Robert and I don't agree on much, but I think it is important to get Webb alive. We've seen what his organization can do, and in my experience with terrorist organizations, killing the leader won't make a dent for long. I don't want Victor Webb to die and become a hero, the Karl Marx of whatever movement he's trying to start. I want every Lemurian to know that without his soldiers and force, Webb is a coward, and for that we must get him alive."

"I honestly can see your point," Dan said, "but I don't think it's possible. We have to take the easiest route on this one. How do you possibly expect us to take Webb alive in the middle of his own army? You may want to humiliate Webb, but if this fails, Webb will keep killing. Bombing this Mosque is our best chance at ending him."

"You know terrorist groups Dan, someone else can takeover, Webb's death is not the end, Taking a chance like this to possibly kill him isn't the best way to stop then"

"I hate to give Webb any credit, but look at what the Lemurians did with him in charge," Ethan said, sounding frustrated. "He came out of nowhere with nukes. Losing him will hurt every one of them. Whether he's dead or in prison won't matter."

"All right, Ethan, contact Andrew and tell him we have Webb's location. They'll have an air strike ready. It's time we ended this," Lance said.

"You're doing the right thing, Lance," Dan said as he put his hand sympathetically on Lance's shoulder.

Lance put the jeep in reverse and started to drive away, figuring they needed to put some more distance between them and where the bombs would fall. "Dan, get out some binoculars and focus on the mosque and the surrounding area. We need to see how the Lemurians around the mosque react. I got a feeling the Lemurians will act pretty crazy if Webb is dead. Ethan, keep listening to the transmissions. Any confirmation would help."

"Roger," Ethan and Dan both said.

It was now time to wait. After a few seconds that felt like an eternity, Lance heard the planes coming toward their location. The sound rushed toward them, but shortly there was a sound that was less comforting: the hit of a missile on one of the bombers. In the distance, a Missle crashed into the ground, and debris started flying. Before Lance could get a handle on the Missle stike, a plane started falling to the earth. He didn't even have time to catch his breath before several drone then fell behind his postion. Fear started to engulf Lance. If this attack failed, there was no good alternative. Planes continued to fall around the city. Lance was shocked that Webb had enough technology to stop planes so effectively. Once again it seemed they had underestimated Webb. The planes and drones did not stop. They kept going toward the city after a lull. A drone even crashed about one hundred yards away from their jeep.

Lance started panting, consumed with fear. Webb was more prepared for an aerial assault than he'd thought possible, and even worse, what if Webb wasn't even there? Maybe Webb knew the team was in the city and had altered the messages over the airwaves to misdirect them from his location. Webb could be leaving the city right now. Maybe Lance had come all the way back to this godforsaken country for nothing.

Before panic consumed him, Lance heard a welcome sound. A drone strike got through. A missile hit near the mosque, causing the front part of the building to collapse. Lance thought this would be their moment. The damage was clear. Ethan said from behind him, "This could be it."

"Dan, look to see if Webb reveals himself. Ethan, if you can intercept any new messages," Lance said.

Lance looked toward the back of the mosque. If Webb was really there, he would exit through the back. More Lemurian soldiers were gathering around the site, sparking greater confusion. The men got out of the car and went toward the mosque. Lance heard a Lemurian soldier yell, "Men, we have to retreat out of this district! Bombs are starting to come!"

Lance thought it would be best to go undercover with some of the soldiers swarming toward the back. He signaled a move, and his two companions followed. The trio, still in the stolen uniforms, headed to the back of the mosque and immersed themselves in the other soldiers. There were what seemed like dozens of soldiers at the back of the mosque, but Webb was not there. Once more pressure started to build within Lance. Webb was not showing up. However, as hope started to elude Lance, four well-armed men left the mosque. They were wearing all-black uniforms with the Lemurian symbol in purple spreading out on the shoulder. It was obvious that there was something special about these soldiers. The four soldiers spread out in a guard formation, and then Lance saw him—Webb himself.

Lance was finally able to take a good look at Webb. He looked a bit different in person. He wasn't as confident. He was sweating and clearly nervous. It looked like Webb was ordering a jeep; he was ready to move out.

Lance knew that an attack on Webb directly would fail. He thought of calling in a strike, but with the three of them so close to Webb, it would become a suicide mission. As Webb got into a jeep, Lance thought of a plan. A Lemurian soldier gestured toward their group to get into one of the military transports. Lance leaned toward Ethan and Dan and whispered, "Listen to the solider. When we are in the transport, follow my lead."

Dan and Ethan nodded. They got into the indicated transport, Lance beside the driver and Dan and Ethan in the back. The only Lemurian in the transport was the driver. Lance knew what he had to do, but he wasn't going to do it until he was confident there would be no witnesses. Lance sat in silence, trying not to draw suspicion as the Lemurian started driving. Lance didn't hear more bombs, but civilians were running through the streets, trying to get cover. Maybe they were just scared. He didn't blame them. The Lemurian driver was still silent. He was a fairly young man. Lance would estimate him to be in his early twenties—younger than he would like for a man he was about to kill.

The convoy was lining up and leaving the city. It was time for Lance to start with his plan. Pointing, Lance said to the driver, "Look—there might be an American jeep about a hundred clicks left." When the driver leaned over toward Lance to get a look, Lance put him in a choke hold. "Dan, take the wheel!" Lance dragged the driver onto his lap while continuing to choke him, and Dan quickly jumped into the driver's seat and continued to drive in formation. Lance choked the man until he died and then threw the body next to Ethan.

"Put me next to the corpse, huh?" Ethan said in a joking manner.

"We'll either be dead or gone by the time he starts to stink," Lance responded. "We need to keep going forward."

"We have control of the vehicle. Where do we go from here, man?" Dan asked.

"It looks like we are back to plan A, we have a chance to capture this guy. This convoy is headed toward the mountains to hide. If Webb reaches those mountains, he can escape," Lance said. "Webb's in another transport two ahead of us. We're going to follow him and see if we can get a chance where we have enough space to ram him. Maybe we can chase him out of the city. Ethan, contact Cameron and activate our tracker he should be able to tell where our position is. We'll need his team to come and provide backup."

"All right," Ethan said.

Dan continued driving in the convoy. Webb's jeep was

up ahead, and the sounds of fighting surrounded them. The road was still lined with some buildings, making it too narrow for Dan to charge Webb's jeep.

"How are we going to get him?" Ethan asked. "This transport can probably take a beating, but if all the Lemurian troops aim at us, we won't have a chance."

"I have a plan. If we stay close to Webb's transport, they won't risk heavy fire with rockets or grenades. They won't risk killing their leader. Dan, next chance you get, make a move to get close to Webb's jeep," Lance said. He then crawled into the back with Ethan. "Ethan, lower your window and get ready. I'll need support. I've got grenades in case we need more heavy fire."

There was nothing Lance could do but wait until Dan made his advance on Webb's vehicle. Lance was feeling a combination of fear and exhilaration. There was still a chance to stop Webb. This was beyond justice in his mind; he wanted to make Webb pay. The man who had taken everything from him was now in his sights. Lance was angry, his conversation with Webb on the island still on his mind. He remembered Webb's arrogance, his confidence that he could do anything and no one would stop him. Today Lance felt that he could finally stop Webb.

"I think I'm picking something up," Ethan said. After a minute he was able to make the sound clearer, and Lance heard Webb's voice. Webb still sounded confident, but Lance could tell there was some fear in him.

Webb said over the transmission, "Men, several battalions and I are leaving the city and heading to the caves outside Herzejot. Within an hour reinforcements will arrive from around our land to give support. Hold out, and we will win this day."

"He's panicked. He knows he can lose," Dan said.

"That might be worse. If Webb was overconfident, it would be easier to surprise him," Lance said.

"Just trying to look on the bright side," Dan replied.

"I know, Dan, but we have to consider every negative possibility. This mission is too important."

Lance kept thinking about the mission. Once the convoy moved out into the wasteland, it would be the best time and place to attack Webb's transport. For now they were on a narrow road, but Lance could see the end of the road up ahead. It was close. Lance was nervous. It was almost time. Lance collected his thoughts.

The convoy left the city and entered the desert. Lance assumed they had two miles before the convoy headed to the mountains. Lance looked two vehicles ahead of them, trying to get a good look at Webb's transport. They would only get one chance at success.

Dan made his move, breaking from formation in the wide-open space, and hit the accelerator, headed toward Webb's jeep.

For a few moments, there was no reaction from the Lemurian soldiers, who must not have realized they'd been successfully infiltrated. However, when Lance, Dan, and Ethan were about thirty yards away from Webb's transport, gunshots rang out. Bullets ricocheted off the transport, which was holding for now. Lance and Ethan ducked and were able to avoid the bullets that entered through the open windows. Dan was closing in on Webb's transport. Webb's jeep also broke formation and drove away from the rest of the Lemurian convoy, headed into the open expanse outside the city. Dan finally was in position with Webb's jeep ahead of them.

Several jeeps were following behind them, and Lance yelled, "Ethan, take out those jeeps. Aim for the wheels, and use the grenades. The wheels are strong enough to stop bullets."

Leaning slightly outside the window, Ethan threw some grenades at the Lemurians behind them. The explosions slowed down the vehicles. One completely flipped over. In the chaos, Ethan was clipped on the shoulder. He pulled himself back into the transport, clutching his arm.

"You okay?" Lance asked him.

"I'll be all right. A bullet just clipped me. Right now we need to deal with Webb."

"Yeah, good work, Ethan. You bought us some cover."

Dan sped up, going as fast as he could go, and was able to get next to Webb's transport. Out of some regretful curiosity, Lance looked at the transport next to him, and there he saw Webb. Webb looked frantic. He was talking to his driver and waving his hands, as if explaining something to him. However, Webb then turned his head and saw Lance. For the first time the two adversaries finally saw each other face-to-face. Webb looked into Lance's eyes, and all franticness disappeared. Webb had a look of intensity that few ever had. The grimace on his face had an undercurrent of desire, and every inch of his face looked committed to a task. Lance and Webb started to draw their guns and point them at each other in a standoff.

Dan quickly stepped on the brakes to dodge Webb's potential shot, causing Webb's transport to make up ground.

"Speed up again!" Lance yelled from the back. "If Webb makes it into the mountains, he'll disappear again."

"I'm going!" Dan yelled in angst.

They started to get close to Webb once more. Then something unexpected happened. Webb aimed an RPG at them, pointing it out of the window of his transport.

Lance exclaimed, "He wouldn't! We're too close! Shooting our car would cause an explosion they'd be caught up in."

"We all know what that man is willing to do," Ethan said.

"Ethan, shoot him! We can't let him fire that RPG!" Lance shouted in a panic and lifted up his gun.

Ethan and Lance took some shots at Webb. They missed a few times but then got a successful shot on Webb's shoulder, causing him to drop one of his hands off the RPG. However, against all odds, Webb was able to hold the RPG with the remaining hand and fire.

The shot hit behind them, and the resulting explosion flipped their jeep over.

As Lance crawled out of the overturned jeep, he spotted Ethan. "Are you okay?" he asked.

"I'll survive," Ethan replied. "I think I broke a rib."

Danny was unconscious and still in the jeep.

"Help me get him out of here," Lance said to Ethan.

Ethan and Lance went in through the back of the overturned transport and lifted Danny from his seat. Lance smashed the back door with the butt of his gun while Ethan held Dan over his shoulder. When they broke out of the ruined transport, they were confronted by an unwelcome sight.

About ten Lemurian soldiers were waiting for them, rifles aimed. In the middle of the group of soldiers was the unmistakable Victor Webb. The arm Ethan had shot was limp at his side. Webb didn't have a rifle and was instead pointing a pistol directly at Lance with his good arm.

Webb broke his silence and said sternly, "It's over, Richardson."

Lance, with his hands up, said with defiance, "What are you going to do with us, Webb?"

Webb responded angrily, "I am going to kill you, Lance." With that, Webb shot Lance in the stomach, causing him to fall to the ground.

"Lance!" Ethan exclaimed.

The Lemurian soldier next to Webb said, "Sir, give the order, and they are all dead."

"No," Webb said. "We can use the other two, for information. We have to find out how the fuck they got this close. But after all the trouble Lance Richardson has caused me, I want to finish him personally." Webb, with his pistol in hand, walked closer to Lance.

Ethan screamed, "You can't do this!" He tried to reach for his gun to make one last stand, but one of the Lemurian soldiers shot him in the leg, causing him to fall as well.

Lance lay on the hot ground of Afghanistan. He'd never believed in destiny, but a part of him could not accept it would end like this. After chasing Webb halfway around the world and surviving everything that Webb had thrown at him, he could not believe this was his end. Webb drew closer and aimed his gun at Lance's head.

"Well, Lance, after everything you've done, you are going to be nothing more than just one more casualty in this war," Webb exclaimed happily. He added harshly, "And when I win this war, no one will remember you."

With Lance's death looking inevitable, One of the Lemurian soldiers fell down, causing Webb to look at the horizon. British jeeps were approaching—Cameron and the other team from earlier.

Webb moved the gun away from Lance and shot at the jeeps swarming them. He killed one soldier successfully, but the British soldiers quickly wiped out Webb's soldiers. They then moved out of their jeeps, surrounding Webb and the corpses of his soldiers.

Pointing his rifle at Webb, Cameron said with fury, "How does it feel to be on the other side of the gun, you son of bitch? Put your hands up and get away from Richardson. I dare you to give me an excuse, Webb."

To Cameron's surprise, Webb actually moved back. He got on his knees and started to beg, pathetically repeating, "I yield. I give up. I surrender. I surrender."

Lance was still in pain, but through it all, he still could feel some happiness at hearing Webb beg. If this was his end, it was better than earlier, better than letting Webb finish him quickly. The last sound Lance heard before he passed out was Cameron knocking Webb out with the barrel of his gun.

32

Two Weeks Later

D an and Lance were walking down the streets of Georgetown, DC. For the first time in a while it seemed the city was back to normal. There were still some homeless, but with people starting to return to their homes outside the cities, things were almost like they were before the war. Lance was still walking slowly, and Dan was getting out a little in front of him.

"Slow down, Dan. I just got out of the hospital," Lance said playfully.

"All right, I'll slow down a bit for you," Dan said, turning back and smiling.

"Figures you finished that mission knocked out and were still the person in the best shape at the end."

"You know me—I've always been lucky," Dan said.

"Yeah, you've been lucky to know me." Lance snickered. "How much longer before we get to the bar?"

"About another block," Dan replied. "Lance, I know it must have been scary having Webb shoot you, but I bet it was worth it to see Cameron fucking Colton smash Webb's face in."

"Hell yeah, buddy," Lance said with a happiness reminiscent of his early twenties. "Last I heard, Webb needed stitches for that."

"Still can't believe we did it, that we captured him alive."

"It doesn't seem real to me either. I know that bastard Candellario is still out there, probably with some other Lemurian freaks, but today is a good day. Let's just get that drink. We'll get the rest of them soon enough."

"Here it is—Rí Rá Irish Pub," Dan said.

"Sounds good."

"I'll open it," Dan said as he opened the door.

The bar was nearly empty, something Lance wouldn't expect on a Friday night.

"Come back here, Lance," Dan said as he headed to a corner booth.

As Lance walked to the booth, he saw a familiar red-haired man. It was Jim, Dan's partner, whom Lance hadn't seen in a while. Next to Jim was Andrew. More people started to surround Lance. There was Erin, Andrew, Sarah, Ethan, and a woman he did not recognize.

"Lance!" Ethan said as he patted Lance on the back. "Did Dan tell you we were coming?"

"No, I wanted this to be a surprise. I think we all could use the break after the past two years," Dan said.

"It's good to see you all here," Lance said happily. "How did you arrange this, Dan?"

"Jim's uncle is pretty rich, so I was able to get a table reserved pretty easily."

"Nice to know that I'm finally making some good connections in DC," Erin said.

"Thank you for helping arrange this, Jim," Lance said. "Do your connections happen to cover some free drinks?"

"I think that will be doable. Everybody will get a Guinness soon."

"Can you order me a margarita instead?" Andrew asked.

"No," Dan said quickly,". You're not going to buy a beach drink at an Irish pub."

"If by 'beach drink' you mean something that actually has a little flavor, then hell yeah I'm going to get a beach drink!"

"I'll order it for him," Jim said. "After all, this is supposed to be a celebration. Don't give him a hard time."

"Thank you, Jim."

"It's good to feel useful for something. I feel out of place being in the middle of the Justice League here."

"Getting us some free drinks is more than good enough. Don't be hard on yourself," Lance said.

The drinks came, and the partygoers got their get-together started. Lance was enjoying his beer despite not being the heaviest drinker. Today was a good day so far.

Ethan finally had the chance to walk over to Lance with the woman Lance didn't know.

"It's good to see you looking well, Lance," Ethan said. "I was happy to hear that the bullet missed your stomach."

"Me too!" Lance said happily.

"I'd like you to meet Samantha, my wife," Ethan said.

Lance was taken aback a bit by the introduction but was surprised only for a moment. He was happy that

Ethan seemed to be taking steps to work on his marriage. "It is a pleasure to meet you," Lance said.

"The feeling is mutual," Samantha replied.

"Are you enjoying living in DC? I never asked Ethan if he liked living here."

"He does, but I'm only here for the weekend, so I can't give you an honest opinion."

"I'll tell you one good thing about moving here, Sam—the food is ridiculously better," Ethan said.

"Well, that's surprising." Samantha chuckled sarcastically.

"Why is that? Do you live far away from a good supermarket or something?" Lance asked.

"No, there's just no variety. The most exciting thing I get to eat back in my corner of upstate New York is chicken fajitas at the local diner," Ethan said.

"You a connoisseur of food, Ethan?"

"I try to be. Before the Lemurians, I thought I was going to retire soon. I was planning on learning how to cook better. That seemed to be the only way I'd get any decent variety upstate."

"Honey, I'm going to the ladies' room. The beer went right through me."

"All right, that's fine."

"It was good meeting you, Lance," Samantha said as she went to the restroom.

Once Samantha was gone, Lance said quietly, "Good job, Ethan."

"No, thank you, Lance."

"How is your son doing?"

"Stan's fine. He was a lot more forgiving than I deserved."

"Sometimes kids can surprise you."

Ethan looked a little uncomfortable. Lance could tell that even though he was trying, it was still a tough situation for him.

Lance noticed that Erin was drinking alone not talking to anyone, so he asked her, "You like your beer, Erin?"

"Yeah," she said in a happy tone that caught Lance off guard. "I didn't know you had a son, Ethan. How old?"

"Eight. I had the chance to see him for the first time in a while a few days ago," Ethan said.

"What did you do with him?" she asked.

"We just talked and caught up. We watched a few movies. He'd actually never seen *Toy Story* before."

"That was one of Tara's favorites," Lance said.

"I never got into those movies," Erin said. "They always made me feel guilty."

"What? How?" Lance asked, surprised.

"The whole point is about how your toys are alive and are sad about being thrown away. Even as a kid that annoyed me. When I was five, I was thinking, *Are my baby toys sad right now?*"

"It's just a metaphor, Erin. You're taking it too seriously," Ethan said.

"I don't know. It just bothers me, even as an adult. I think it might be a conspiracy. Maybe Disney doesn't want people to throw away their toys for some reason. They need to keep the brand up."

"Wouldn't it be the opposite? Wouldn't Disney want

you to throw your toys out so that you'd buy more?" Lance asked.

"You know, that is honestly a good point," Erin said.

"You need to stop being so paranoid, Erin. It's not good for you."

"That might be true for most people, but being paranoid seems to work for me. I survived against the Lemurians living by myself for six months, and now I have a great job, one that pays me pretty well, I might add."

"Now you're the one making a good point. I guess I can't fault someone for doing something that works."

"Lance," Danny said, coming over, "Jim wants to know the look on Webb's face when the guns came."

"Is it true that he pissed himself?" Jim asked, joining them.

"I hope it's true!" Sarah said. Lance knew she was trying to joke, but there was a clear hatred in her voice.

"What about me?" Ethan asked. "I had the better look at Webb. Lance was lying on the ground with a bullet in his gut."

"Okay, what did he look like?" Sarah asked.

"I don't think he pissed himself, but he got close to crying."

"Really?" Erin said.

"Oh yeah. 'Please don't shoot me,'" Ethan said in a mocking manner. "He must have said 'I give up' like twenty times."

"I think it might have been closer to five times," Lance said.

"He's in solitary now. That's all that matters," Sarah added coldly.

"Anybody have any plans for after the war?" Ethan asked the crowd. "Tonight's nice and everything, but I think we could use some time to ourselves after everything that has happened. What about you, Erin?"

Erin looked nervous at being called out and blurted, "Uhh, I don't know yet."

"Well, I can finally work on preparing Jacob's funeral. I felt bad planning it before knowing that we don't have a body, but I think with Webb captured we can finally have closure," Sarah said.

"I'll be there, Sarah," Lance said sympathetically.

"Thank you, Lance." She tried to smile and said, "Come on, anybody have some plans that are more cheerful? Jacob would want us to be happy tonight."

"Not much for me," Ethan said. "Maybe I'll spend the next month exploring DC and getting to know the area better, and maybe I'll finally try Lebanese food."

"Jim and I were thinking about going to Quebec. I've always wanted to go to France on a vacation, but France's economy was hit harder than most in the war, so it might be good to settle for the next best thing."

"I say give France a go anyway, Dan," Andrew said. "When the economy is bad, it's normally a lot cheaper."

"Do you have any travel plans, Lance?" Sarah asked. "You deserve a break more than most."

"I'd like to go to Minneapolis to visit my niece and nephew pretty soon. As for something else, how 'bout we arrange that surfing trip to the South Pacific, Andrew?"

"Sounds good to me."

"I'll get back to you on that after I come back from Minneapolis."

"You used to travel a lot with Rachel, right, Lance?" Steve asked.

Dan immediately glared at Jim, mad that he'd brought up Rachel. To alleviate Dan's anger, Lance said quickly, "Yeah, Jim, we went all over Japan, Mauritius, Italy, Peru, Australia, all sorts of places. We did a lot of traveling before Tara was born. We figured that it would be good to travel a lot before we had a kid."

"Any good stories?" Ethan asked.

"A few—I'll tell you one. Rachel and I were in Australia. We were planning on driving from Brisbane to Sydney, and we stayed at a farm for a night on the way."

"Wait, you stayed on a farm? There wasn't a motel on the way?" Erin asked.

"Eh, we wanted to be adventurous. It was a weird farm/bed-and-breakfast place. But anyway, that morning Rachel got me to go and see the farmer shear some sheep. There were some sheep in a pen, and the farmer asked me if I would like to see if I could capture one of them."

"The sheep pissed on you?" Ethan asked.

"Let me finish. Rach was like, 'Try it, Lance—I know you've faced worse,' so I said okay. As I jumped into the pen, the farmer said, 'Watch out; they jump.' I don't know why—I'm normally smarter than this—but I thought, *Bullshit*. I ran forward and tried to pin this sheep down without a care in the world, but when I started running, the sheep started to stampede. Before I knew it, one of the sheep jumped and hit me in the chest, knocking me over, and the rest of the sheep ran over me."

"Shit, man!" Ethan laughed.

"Did you have any injuries?" Erin asked.

"No, I got lucky, but it is funny. In Afghanistan I once held out against seven Taliban and and then I get my ass kicked by a group of sheep that were probably going to a petting zoo later."

"I guess the moral of the story is to never underestimate farm animals," Dan joked.

Later Dan and Lance were walking toward Foggy Bottom and the nearest subway station. "Tonight was a good night," Lance said. "I think everybody could use some fun in times like this."

"That's true," Dan said.

They continued walking, and as Lance looked at the back of Dan's head, he thought about his friend and what he would do after the war. Dan was almost ten years younger than him. He still had opportunities that were lost to Lance.

"Dan?" Lance said. Dan looked back, and Lance continued, "I know you said at the bar that you want to go to France when you have the chance, but have you thought about the future, after the war?"

"Jim and I are thinking of having a kid," Danny said quickly.

"Really? Are you thinking of adopting?"

"No, I would like to find a surrogate mother. It might be selfish, but I want a kid who is biologically mine."

"You answered that question quickly. Has this been on your mind a lot?"

"I've always wanted a kid. I thought it was too dangerous with me being in the CIA, but after surviving that mess in Afghanistan, I think it might finally be time to take a risk."

"That's as good a reason as any."

Dan stopped walking and took a breath. "Lance, when this kid is born, I might need some help. It would be helpful to call you and get some advice."

"I'd like that."

"What about you, Lance? Is there anything special you have planned after this, you know, besides seeing your niece and nephew?"

"I think I might stay on the job for a bit, help track down the Lemurian holdouts. I still think it's best I keep my mind occupied."

"Whatever happens, it will be your decision."

"Ha." Lance chuckled. "You're right, but I still feel that there's one thing I have to do before this is over, before I can ever move on with my life and even attempt to plan ahead for the future: I've got to stop the rest of the Lemurians."

33

12 years ago Langley, Virginia

Walking down the halls of Langley Agent Lance Richardson reflects on the capture of a suspect making a suicide bomb in the suburbs of Richmond, VA. There was fear of a large-scale bombing of Washington DC, a few hours ago, the place was in a panic, but now it looked like any office. But Lance knows that sometimes a quick victory comes with a price. Past the hallways of agents going on their day Lance stopped at Jacob Lanser's office and took a quick knock and opened the door "Jake" he said

"Agent Richardson, you can go home there is nothing more to do here. We were all worried about the possible attack, but you can get some rest" said Jacob.

"I'm grateful" replied Lance" but I must say the victory seemed kind of quick, can you give me some details about how we found the suspect"

"We made a deal with a member of his cell and that is all you need to know,"

"Did we let him go"

"You don't need the details Lance, I want you on my team, but you are no longer in Afghanistan you have to get used to the rules and make compromises, I will just tell you we made a deal with the suspect and that attack did not happen. For now, that is all you need to know. Now go home Lance and get some rest"

Lance was worried about Jacob not telling him the terms of the deal, but he was not angry enough to fight Jacob on this, he did want to stay employed after all. So he just left without words.

Lance started to walk towards his call and picked up his cell phone "Dan are you there"

"Yeah, what's up"

"How are you getting home today"

"Subway, you"

"I took my car, but I want to Uber myself to a bar and catch a drink do you want to come with me, I can uber myself to work tomorrow."

"It's Friday I can go for a drink, meet you out in the parking lot.

…

Lance walked out to this parking lot and waved to Danny "Hey Dan"

"Hey Lance, how are you"

"Its horrible to admit, but I' m a little bummed out. I feel that Jacob let some terrorist filth go in order to stop this attack. The terrorist was found in Richmond. We still had time, we did not have to give in to this guy. I don't think I am going to sleep tonight not knowing if this terrorist is out there free even after attempting to kill our citizens."

"I understand, it can sicken me too"

"Thank you, but I'll be honest it wasn't to much of a shock that you would agree with me"

"Hey, I trust you and I'm not exactly looking forward to letting a guy go who probably wants me dead"

"How about letting someone go, that knows information that can save hundreds of lives" a feminine voice from a distance adds

Lance turns around and sees a brown-haired young woman "I have not seen you around here before"

"I 'll give you the information that you want Lance Richardson. The suspect is named Amir Hasan, he is an Egyptian citizen, who will spend five years in prison and will be allowed to go back to Egypt afterward in return for ratting on his friends."

"How do you know this" Lance asked

"Because I interrogated this witness and helped make this deal to save lives" the woman said

"You're the new interrogator" Dan interjected

"Yes and I think I am doing a good job" she responded confidently"

"They were not launching the attack yet, we had time to trace their communications. We can find the terrorist cell somewhere else, hell give me some time alone with Mr. Hasan and I'm sure he would have given up the goods without a deal"

"Torture is against the law" the women snapped"

"'The threat is enough, I would have told him about what I did to his friends in Afghanistan"

"That is your problem Richardson, talking to someone is different than fighting them, you need to know their motives, if you told them that you killed some of his allies he would just be more silent to spite you. I saved the lives of hundreds of people today and it's insane that you and your little friend here are sad, we never get the perfect answer, but we stopped the loss of life today and sometimes that is all you can do"

Lance just looked at the women, he was taken back by her sincerity. Maybe his hatred for Islamist terrorists clouded his judgement "Your right, it was good that you stopped this attack, what your name, sorry I did not ask earlier"

"Rachael"

"Well Rachael, I am glad you are on this team"

34

When Lance entered the Langley building, there was a pleasant surprise for him. About fifty CIA agents led by Danny Smith were waiting for him. The agents gave him a lengthy round of applause. Danny walked out in front of the agents toward Lance and shook his hand, saying, "It seems that a lot of people wanted to welcome you back."

Lance looked back at Dan and said, "It's good to be here today, Dan. I feel that the world is finally getting better."

"I agree, but there are a lot of unanswered questions about Webb and the Lemurians. We still have no idea how they got their technology, how they formed, how they took out the satellites, or who makes up most of their remaining leadership."

"How do you think I'll be able to help?" Lance asked. "A further debriefing?"

"I'd be willing to do that."

"We'll have more details when we get to a more private room," Dan said.

As they walked toward the center of the building,

Lance ran into another welcome sight: Erin Cahill, talking to a group of CIA agents. Erin turned to him and said happily, "Hello, Lance."

Lance noticed the change from her previously unhappy demeanor. "Hello, Erin. I'm glad you stuck around to see this war end."

"I am optimistic about our chances. I've tried encouraging some optimism as Anubis, telling people that it looks like Webb is losing the war. I got some good responses; people are moving back into their towns. We're starting to take back every bit of this country."

"That's good to know."

Dan moved toward the duo and said, "I'm glad the both of you are doing better, but Lance and I need to get going."

"All right, I'll talk to you soon, Lance," Erin said happily.

As Lance and Dan continued to walk to the main hub of the building, Lance asked, "Are there any more details you can give me about why I'm needed?"

"Eliza is coming over to the force from the NSA. With Webb captured, Sarah is taking some time off to prepare for the funeral."

"It's more than earned," Lance said.

"Jacob can finally go out as the hero he was at the end," Dan said.

"I agree with her decision. After this is over, I will certainly be there for her. After everything Jacob's done for me and this country, I certainly owe him that."

"I'll be there too, Lance. You can count on that."

The two men reached Sarah's old office. Sitting

behind Sarah's desk was a tall blonde woman with blue eyes wearing a feminine suit—Eliza. She turned to Lance and said calmly, "Lance, I'm here to help transition to the end of this war in Sarah's absence."

"I'm aware of that. Dan told me," Lance said politely.

"We are fortunate to have Eliza," Dan said. "She has been busy since Copper Canyon. She is one of the only analysts who was able to crack one of Webb's security networks."

"Impressive," Lance said.

"I just got lucky," Eliza replied humbly.

"Don't be so humble. Without you, we would not have been able to stop several Lemurian attacks in New Mexico," Dan said.

"It was my duty, Dan—anything to stop Webb," Eliza replied.

"Agreed," Dan said.

Eliza walked around her desk toward Lance. "Lance, I think it is time you knew what we have planned today."

Dan turned to Lance and said solemnly, "I think you should sit down for this, Lance."

Lance grew nervous. "What do you want from me, Dan?"

"We think you should interrogate Victor Webb," Eliza said.

"What?"

"We haven't had much luck interrogating him, as we expected. Outside of agreeing to several mental health tests, he has not ceded any ground," Eliza said.

"I know it would not be fair for the two of us to force you to do this after everything, but if there is anyone

Webb will open up to, it's you. Seeing you might also bring up some old wounds from getting captured," Dan said.

Lance calmed down. "I don't know if I can, Dan. That man just tried to kill me. He did kill my family. I'm not proud to admit it, but part of me is afraid of him, and if Webb senses that, I shudder to think what he could do to my mental well-being."

"Do not be ashamed of fear, Lance," Eliza said. "It makes you different from him. After everything Webb has done, he still has no fear. He's still confident. There is something very off-putting about him, even in this state."

"And you think I can talk to him, break him," Lance said.

"You beat him, Lance, in Copper Canyon and in Afghanistan, when you survived the attempt on your life in that godforsaken country, and in the end you were responsible for the plan that led to his capture.," Dan said. "You have proven that he is not all he says he is. Seeing you would be the greatest reminder of his failure. Remember how you felt when you failed, Lance. You can do the same thing to him. You can break him, We were able to capture him alive, we should use that to our advantage."

"I don't know. Is there anything else you guys can do to help me? Eliza, what were the results of his psych tests?" Lance asked.

"He has no detectable mental conditions," Eliza replied with clear disappointment. "He was able to describe the effects that tragedy has on people like any other person, not something a sociopath could do. He has no sign of schizophrenia, he clearly has no mental condition limiting his intelligence, and surprisingly he is not a sadist. We showed him images of war, death, and pain. He showed no signs of happiness or sexual arousal from them."

"So what you're saying is one of the worst killers in human history does not have any different mental condition from the average person aside from being arrogant?" Lance said. "Is there anything else you can give me, Eliza? You said you were able to hack Webb's servers and find info that led to the killing of some of his men. Has that given you any information about the Lemurians?"

Both Eliza and Dan tensed up. Eliza said, "We were going to save this for last, but we do have something we need to tell you. The strike force was very successful, and the NSA believed that bringing this up would cause paranoia and ruin your resolve, but, Lance, you have to have known that there was a chance of this being a problem."

Lance, realizing what Eliza was getting at, said, "You believe that Webb has moles in the government."

Eliza responded with a simple "Yes."

"I suspected that before, but I would like to know where exactly in our government you think he's infiltrated."

"We don't think it goes up too high. With this strike force's success and with my extensive work giving background checks to everyone in the NSA, I suspect we are in the clear, but I found documents and emails showing contacts in the army and local police forces. I also can't deny the fact Webb was able to disable military satellites with the help of the mole Vincent Sykes. The

Lemurians still might have some connections in our government and in the private sector."

"I suggest you try to press Webb for information on moles in the private sector, particularly defense contractors," Dan said to Lance. "I wouldn't be surprised to find out he got access to our tech through them, and it wouldn't be the first time cutting costs came back to bite us in the ass."

"I'll try my best, but I still don't know how I can deal with Webb, never mind get him to reveal something so specific. Do you still think I'm the best for the job? Have you tried anything else?," Lance said frantically.

"Of course no one will force you, but based on what we know of Webb's psychological profile, we honestly think you have a shot," Eliza said.

"Why is Webb even coming to Langley again? Would it be easier for me to go to where he is held?" Lance asked.

"We can't rule out that Webb has allies in the US who might try to free him. It would make sense for any Lemurians left to use their strength to try to free their leader. Webb needs to be in a secure place, and Langley is a fortress," Eliza said.

"Before Webb gets here, I need some time alone to collect my thoughts. Dan, can I also have another look at the videos Webb sent the press? I need to look over everything we have seen from him. Maybe I can get a better idea on how to interrogate him."

"All right," Dan said.

Lance then walked out of the room. He could not believe the magnitude of the task before him. He tried to calm himself down; he did consider himself to be a rational human being, after all. Webb was going to be cuffed and trapped in custody. He was clearly in a weakened state, but Lance felt he could not underestimate him. Webb would want that, and he didn't want to give Webb any advantage.

He sat down and looked at the video footage. Seeing Webb make his demands gave Lance bad memories about the atrocities he had seen throughout the war. He then thought of everything he had to convince Webb. Webb was arrogant in this video footage, but Lance knew that Webb could feel worried. Lance was going to confront Webb about his failures and remind him that he'd lost. Dan was right: Webb was vulnerable. Maybe Lance could defeat him emotionally. While Lance collected his thoughts, Erin Cahill walked up behind him and asked in a concerned tone, "Are you all right, Lance?"

"Yeah, just doing everything I can to get an advantage on Webb," Lance said.

"I can understand you wanting to take all precautions. Webb can be intimidating. There is just something unsettling about him."

"Yeah, I know that feeling. However, Webb could be the worst killer of our time. If we didn't feel off around him, I don't think we would be human. I've got to do everything I can to give me an advantage in this interrogation."

"Do you want some advice?" Erin asked.

"I can use anything extra at this point."

"Do not underestimate what he can do with just his presence, without even saying a word. I don't know if he's some sort of body language expert, but I feel off around him. I was happy to hear about the pathetic way he surrendered himself, but I had a chance three weeks ago to see Webb personally while he was in transit, and I could tell there was still fight left in him. It was unprofessional, but I wanted to yell at him, tell him he had lost and would suffer. I wanted to tell him all the thoughts I'd had against him since I became Anubis and make him know that we'd won, but when I got close to him, I couldn't. I tensed up."

"We all make mistakes, but I must admit you are the last person I thought would tense up around that man," Lance said in a comforting manner.

"I know. I challenged Webb and As Anubis I wanted to show people that they could fight back, and when I had to chance to give him hell, I just stopped. I'm not even sure why. I don't remember being afraid. I tensed up when he looked at me and just could not lash out at him. Lance, be prepared for any feelings you might have. Don't underestimate him, even in his current state," Erin said strongly.

"I don't think I will fail," Lance said. "You were correct when you told me Webb isn't as great as he thinks. I know that he may truly believe what he says, but he doesn't think he is unstoppable. Dan and I hacked into his messages in Herzejot, and he had a clear fear in him. Think about this, Erin: Why did he surrender himself alive? There is no other explanation than a fear of death. Webb was smart enough to know what we were doing on that island; he had to be smart enough to know the dangers of being caught alive. With him dead, he would be a martyr for his cause. He let us capture him because he was afraid."

"I think you can do it, if that is any help. Make a fool out of him one more time," Erin said.

Lance rose from his chair and said defiantly, with a new sense of optimism, "I will and thank you Erin you have done your part for this war and I truly appreciate you staying around."

With that, Lance headed toward the back of the building to the interrogation room Webb was being transported to. On his way there, he ran back into Danny. Dan gave him a compassionate look and asked, "Are you ready, Lance?"

"Yes," Lance responded quickly.

"All right."

The two men continued walking toward the back of the building, but then Lance turned to Dan and said, "Wait for a moment."

"What?"

"I want to thank you for everything and for bringing me into this mission. I never thought I would feel this alive again, and I have you to thank for that."

"You have always been a good friend to me, Lance, and no matter how you do in there against Webb, I will be your friend on the other side," Danny said.

Lance and Dan clasped their hands as a sign of friendship, with Lance saying, "Same here."

Eliza walked briskly toward them then and said, "Webb is in briefing room A."

"Okay," Lance said.

"Before you go, I want to tell you what precautions we've made for your safety. Dan and I will be behind a one-way mirror, so we can see what is happening. Webb will be handcuffed, and his legs will be restrained, chained to the ground. There is no way he can harm you."

Lance knew it was time. He walked to the interrogation room and opened the door.

Within the room was the unmistakable Victor Webb with his black hair and slender figure. He did not look like a person who could do serious physical harm to Lance, but as Eliza had said would be the case, Webb was clearly constrained.

Webb's demeanor instantly bothered Lance. Webb did not look afraid or even angry like Landshire had been. He looked bored, like being here was only an inconvenience.

Lance thought of how to start and then asked, "Do you know who I am?"

Webb looked at Lance. "Of course. Your government must be pretty desperate to get me to talk if they're sending you in. What do they think, Lance, that seeing you will instantly make me a scared shell of my former self?"

"That government you call desperate was smart enough to capture you in the middle of your own empire," Lance taunted.

"Everybody is capable of making wrong or right choices," Webb replied with a hint of condescension. He then got more serious. "What do you think is going to happen, Lance? What do you think I will reveal to you? You know that torture won't break me, and I know that there is no way you or the United States government will make a deal with me. Why would I give you anything?"

Webb was fairly accurate in diagnosing what was happening. Lance thought about trying to appeal to something Webb would have pride in, something that would get him on a train of thought. Lance thought back to how Webb had taunted the world for their ignorance. He seemed to value his intelligence.

"Just tell me why you did it," Lance said. "Why did you start the Lemurians, Victor? You don't have to tell me how. I'm just curious why you did all this. It must have been a lot of work."

Webb honestly looked puzzled. He seemed to think about his answer and then said, "To improve humanity and destroy the current system that has been holding it back, not that someone like you has ever desired destroying his precious establishment. Then again, you're probably just trying to appeal to me, trying to find common ground, butter me up, and hope I give something up. I've read the US Army handbook, Lance. What's next, offering me a drink to loosen me up?"

"Come on, complaining about the current system of the world and the establishment like some teenage punk rocker. Many people complain about that, and none of them did what you did or were as successful as you sadly were." Lance then asked condescendingly, "Are you telling me that there is nothing more unique about you?"

"Why are you asking me this?" Webb asked in honest confusion.

"I'm human, Victor. After everything you have done to me, I still have some curiosity. Why did you do it? I want to know. I want to know how you can justify the things you have done."

Webb had a look of deep thought on his face and sat in silence for a few moments, like he was considering his next move. Out of this silence, Webb said, "Richardson,

I will make you a deal. If you let me ask a question about you, I will honestly answer a question you have about the Lemurians."

Lance was caught off guard. He didn't know what to expect. This seemed like a complete diversion from what Lance had just asked; however, the chance to finally have Webb open up about the Lemurians was exactly what he was looking for, but he was worred about playing Webb's game making him in control of the conversation. To insert dominance he added. "I'm not going to tell you anything about my strike force's operations or how we eventually found you," Lance said.

"I'm not concerned about that," Webb said. "I know you have been curious about me. Well, that curiosity goes both ways. I honestly would like to know more about you. Quench my curiosity—give me something to think about while I am stuck in this compromising place."

Lance thought Webb's arrogance was shining through. Webb was probably sick of his defeat and would ask something that would annoy Lance to give him a sense of power in this time when he had none. Abusers always liked being in control. However, Lance could not pass up a chance to learn more about the Lemurians.

"I will let you ask me your question but only if you answer my question first," Lance said.

Webb, without a second thought, said, "Fine."

Lance was worried by Webb's calm behavior, but he still thought it best to ask Webb a question. "How were the Lemurians founded?"

"The Lemurians were founded by me and my brother, Jason as an organization to help the misfortunate of the

THE OUTLIER

world that the organized nations of the world seem to neglect. I started in Africa. I did things like protect tribes, stop the trading of sex slaves, and help refugees escape from oppressive regimes. That is also the reason I got a lot of loyal followers. They supported me after everything I'd done for them. One day I realized that the current state of the world was too corrupt to have a truly successful society. The world needed something more than just a Band-Aid. My end goal was to find a government to overthrow and create my own society. I wanted to mold a society at every basic level while humiliating the governments of the world. So I took my new alliances and became the organization that you know today."

"Africa—are you South African, Webb? The researcher who ID'd you and helped me name you back on that island said you were American."

"That I am. I was born in a small town in Iowa and lived there for most of my life. I'd never left the Midwest before I went to Africa. The highlight before that was a trip to the Wisconsin Dells when I was twelve years old."

"Never left—did you grow up poor?"

"Below average, but if you're trying to find a reason why I am the way I am, don't blame my family. Everything I did was my choice. My parents were people you would consider good. It was not some rough childhood that made me become the Historian."

Lance felt a bit of respect for Webb owning up to his actions, not that he would let Webb know it, but they were starting to get off topic.

"In regards to the work you claim you did, the world

313

was in a period of peace before the war started. Did the Lemurians have anything to do with that?" Lance asked.

"Terrorism was heading down before I lifted a finger; however, I do think I had a role in the extent of how peaceful the world was before this conflict. I know you know about what I did to Hirrshi's organization. I did the same thing to many other organizations. Drug and slave traffickers, Islamists, African tribalists—you name it, I've fought it."

Lance had a feeling of slight shock. He wondered if Webb was telling the truth and really did all those great things before he became the man they knew today. Lance also wondered what exactly had taken Webb down this path.

"If I am to believe you, Victor, why did you change your organization after doing all this good?" Lance asked in a sympathetic tone. "You said yourself the world was getting better on its own even without you. Why couldn't you just continue helping it? If this is all true, if you wanted a government to overthrow, why not choose a corrupt dictatorship somewhere and make yourself king? Why make yourself the most wanted man on the planet?"

"That is enough on why I did what I did. I already answered more than I promised," Webb said firmly.

Outside the briefing room, Dan and Eliza were watching the interrogation through the one-way mirror. "Good work, Lance," Dan said under his breath. "Eliza, send a message to the analysts to follow African leads and reexamine how local terrorist groups collapsed. It might lead us to more Lemurian operatives."

"Agreed," Eliza said. "Robert is coming soon; we'll coordinate with the White House and the other departments."

"Fine," Lance said. "What happened to your brother? Is he the leader of the Lemurians now that you have been captured?"

"No. He is dead. I killed him," Webb said with little emotion.

This sudden admission came as a surprise to Lance. He had not expected that answer. He could not help but be curious. "Why?"

"He did not agree with the transition I mentioned earlier."

Lance was still curious. "Why would you tell me this? You only had to answer one question. Perhaps you're slipping, Webb?"

"It won't help you," Webb said quickly.

"What do you mean by that?"

"He's dead. It is impossible to get any information from him. And in regards to one more crime being added to the list, after everything I've done, I'm already getting the death penalty or perhaps life if I am lucky. One more crime won't make any difference. The only thing that might help you is that this admission will spare you the time of trying to look for him. However, I find it extremely doubtful that you would instantly trust me for information. You're probably still going to waste just as much time fact-checking." Webb chuckled. "You seem to think the info I've given you is so important, but I already founded the Lemurians. It's too late to stop me with that information," Webb said triumphantly.

Webb seemed to be trying to get Lance off track again, but Lance remained firm. "How were you able to hack the American military satellite system?"

"Lance, I have more than fulfilled my part of the deal. I will only answer more questions if you let me ask mine."

Webb was probably hoping to derail the conversation with his question, but if Lance got through it, Webb would be in a position of having to admit the failure of his plan or give Lance more info, so Lance said, "All right, what is it?"

"This will be a gift, Lance. I know that despite your professionalism, you hate me with all of your being. So I am going to give you a chance to vent that hatred in a way those suits behind the mirror over there will have to accept. Why did you fight against me? What drove you? I want to know about you. I don't need any SIGNIT or HUMINT info—just an explanation of why you fight," Webb said confidentially.

Lance thought the answer to this question was obvious. There were millions who wanted to kill this man. Did Lance really need to make a list of Webb's crimes—the shootings, bombings, and poisonings? Part of him did not want to answer, to give Webb any control, but the longer the conversation went on, the better chance Lance had of saving lives. Lance propped his elbow on the table and leaned his head against his hand to think. His wedding ring caught his eye, and he knew what his answer would be.

"I want to make you pay for everything you have

done, but I'm not going to lie: I especially want to make you pay for my family. I think you took away two great people. Rachel was like me. She loved this country and did everything she could to keep the people of this world safe from people like you. My daughter died young, but in her short time on this planet, she truly touched this world. She used to always ask about the world and wondered what to do with her life. You know, the two jobs she considered the most were veterinarian and teacher." Lance sighed. "That would have been nice to see. Rachel went before her time because of you, but Tara …" Almost forgetting Webb was in the room, Lance started to shed some tears in front of his archenemy. "You know, sometimes at night I expect a knock on my door from her wishing me good night," he blurted out.

Lance regained his composure. A strong look of hatred replaced the tears in his eyes. It was as if there was nothing in the world except his hate for Webb.

"So that is what you took away from this world—a parent who loved her family and dedicated her life to helping this country and its people and a daughter who wanted to help make this world better." Lance started panting and angrily shouted, "You robbed them of the lives they could have had, and you hurt this world by killing them!" Lance started to cry again. "You robbed my daughter of everything, a chance to grow up and find love, friends, a career, a family. You took everything away from her, Victor, and I want to take everything away from you."

Webb looked at Lance for a second and then said with anger and confidence, "It is pathetic how ignorant you are."

"What the hell do you mean, Webb?"

"Some woman and girl—that is what you think will make me have any guilt. To think that some self-centered man like you had anything to do with capturing me!" Webb stormed. "You think your wife was so special. You think your daughter was so goddamn special. Two random people, that is why you fought me. Well, I have some news for you, Lance. They were not unique. They sound to me like the average person. Oh, I'm sure they made a few people they knew happy but not much else. Aw, your daughter loved animals. Maybe she would have become a veterinarian. I really robbed the world of a diamond in the rough there, like there's not thousands of other children who want that," Webb said sarcastically.

He then chuckled. "I mean, I can understand trying to guilt me with your friend Jacob. He was at least somebody who fought me, somebody who rose above the rest and even helped capture me. I thought you were going to say something like 'Jacob Lanser has the last laugh.' But you really think going on and on about some woman and child is going to get to me? I nuked cities, Lance, and I am not an idiot. I know what that meant. Thousands are dead, and thousands more are dying a slow death of radiation poisoning because of what I've done. Knowing this, you honestly thought your story would get to me in some way? You want me to think of the lives they could have had? Fine, I'll think about it," Webb continued tauntingly.

"You talk about their potential lives like it's some grand mystery, but I have a good guess based on what you've told me. Your wife would have lived to old age and made a few people close to her happier, like you, some friends, maybe a brother or sister. Then eventually, after taking some more resources from the planet, she would have died and been forgotten a generation or two later.

"Your daughter, that's a bit trickier, I must admit. I have to think a little about that. Let's see here … She becomes a veterinarian and helps a few dogs live another year. She makes friends, she finds love, has a few kids, and eventually dies of old age, and like your wife, once her children and grandchildren die, she is forgotten and rots in the ground with a grave that no one cares about."

Webb paused, and with one last chuckle he said, "Lance, I knew goddamn well what I was going to take away from you and everybody else. You are more ignorant than I realized if you thought that would get to me. The goals I have are more than worth it."

Lance was horrified, but through the horror, he was intrigued by this worldview. He'd forced Webb to reveal what made him tick and how he could justify doing all these horrible things. It was true nihilism realized. It seemed Webb killed because he felt that human life was not important. The piece of the puzzle that was still missing was how he'd gotten thousands to follow him. Lance thought he was finally getting into Webb's head.

"Who are you to say that making friends and family happy is not enough for a person to have a reason to live?" Lance asked. "We are all going to die someday. Why rob people of the chance to live to see old age, to see their children grow? What gives you the right to make that choice, to say that their lives aren't worth anything?"

"I am following the mandate of history to do what is necessary to achieve a better world," Webb replied.

"Why do you think you're justified to claim the mandate of history? I am honestly curious. Tell me what you told others to get them on your side."

"Have you ever heard of the Assyrians?" Webb asked.

"Yes," Lance said. "They were an ancient Middle Eastern civilization that ruled thousands of years ago."

"I'm actually impressed," Webb said. "Now can you name me one Assyrian king?"

Lance tried to think of one but couldn't. "No."

Webb smirked and said with confidence, "Exactly. The Assyrians were probably the first great empire in human history. They conquered Egypt, Sumer, and even went into Turkey. To the peasants of this time, the kings of Assyria must have seemed like gods that walked this earth. They ruled everything that was known to them, and now, thousands of years later, the world has practically forgotten them. Maybe a few remember, those who study history, but even the most powerful people in the world have their names forgotten. If the kings and the powerful are barely remembered, what about the good people of the past, the people that wanted to help others, like your wife and daughter? Over time they become nothing. That is how the world is today, Lance, and killing a person, even a good one, is worth it if we have a chance at changing that."

Lance wanted to kill Webb then and there. Anger gripped him, but if he let his rage take over, it would be an admission that Webb had gotten the better of him. Lance thought deeply about how he might break Webb's confidence.

Lance lashed out, "Your life was important enough to

save. I never had much respect for you, Webb, but I used to think that if we ever found you, you would at least be one to go down fighting. Instead, when we got you, you went on your knees and begged. You are a coward and a hypocrite. You let yourself get captured even though it was wrong for your people. If you had died, you would have been a martyr for the Lemurians. Your death would have been a rallying cry. For all your talk about how you are willing to do what it takes, you wanted to live for no other reason than your own selfish wants."

"I will admit that, as is obvious, I don't share the same values as most people, but even I want to live. There is nothing for me when I die. It will be either nonexistence or hell if what most people on earth think about death is correct. Of course I want to do anything in my power to stop that. In addition to my own basic human desire to survive, there is another reason I cannot let myself die. Right now I am too important. I have made the Lemurians out of nothing, and I need to finish my work."

Lance said with some anger, "You will never get that chance, Webb. We've captured you, and I promise you with every fiber of my being that you will spend the rest of your miserable life in prison. You are not important, no more so than the millions you killed. I hope the government throws your body in some ditch somewhere when you die. No one will come see your grave, Victor, and eventually you will end up forgotten to all except those who will know you as one of history's monsters."

Webb smiled for the first time in the interview, clearly happy. It was not his usual sarcastic or smug manner but true happiness, similar to what normal men feel when they see their children. Webb then began to laugh jovially. "Amazing. You don't get it."

"What don't I get?" Lance asked in a fury.

"After all my planning ahead, you honestly think I don't have a plan for this scenario, something I can fall back on in the case I get captured?" Webb taunted.

"You're bluffing. You're in the belly of the beast, Webb, in Langley. Do you think you could make it out of here with any plan?" Lance taunted back.

"We will see." Webb's face became confident. "However, for now, in fairness I will answer another one of your questions."

Outside the room Dan was getting panicked. "Webb is in control of the conversation," he said to Eliza. "We have to get Lance out of there."

"No," Eliza said. We've found out some information already, more than we have in a month of trying to break him. We must keep this going. This is our best lead."

"Webb said he has a plan to escape," Dan said.

"He's bluffing. He's just trying to throw Lance off guard. Lance is right: he is in the belly of the beast."

Lance was starting to get consumed with anger. Part of him knew Webb was manipulating him, but he wanted to see what possible justification Webb had for his sense of importance. "How can you say you're important enough to live when you yourself told me life is useless and that in the end even the strongest kings don't matter? How can you then believe your own existence is important?"

"When did I say that life did not matter?" Webb asked quizzically.

Lance yelled angrily, "You said that it is okay to kill, to mow down anything in your path to achieve your goals—men, women, and children—and that the love a person gives others is no reason to stop. Now you justify yourself as the one person important enough to stay alive. We are all forgotten in a few generations, right?"

"Human life is less valuable to me than to others, but I never said that life itself is worthless. I fight because I think there is still a chance for this life to mean something. If I thought there was no chance of improving the world, why put myself through all this? If I truly thought there was no chance of saving this world, I would have just used my intelligence to become rich and live my short life on this planet in self-contentment. I won't tell you everything, Lance, but let's just say that I have done a lot in my life. I have lived in every extreme condition known to man. I have been near death countless times. I have bled and cried out in anguish more times than I can count. I have done all this because I realize there is still a chance for this world and a chance for humanity. As my old name hinted, I take my examples from history. This might be hard for you to believe, but I don't hate the United States. It has served its purpose in history. The wars that brought this nation together included deaths and crimes against humanity, but if America had never formed, there is a good chance Nazism or Communism could have engulfed the world. I am only doing the next step in saving human civilization."

Lance calmed down a bit and asked, "How can you be so sure?"

"The world has come close to having true meaning before. I don't think anyone has reached it yet, but people have come close." Webb paused and said, "You see the symbol on my arm, the tattoo?"

"Yes," Lance said. "It is a hieroglyph, for the pharaoh Menes."

"Exactly. Menes was the pharaoh who united the kingdoms of northern and southern Egypt over five thousand years ago. Many don't know his name, but I can still say it. That counts for something in this world. Menes represents something that actually gives me hope—an outlier, something above the rest, a presence that can be remembered for generations. This tattoo is something I cling to, to remind me that even in this existence it is possible to succeed and that there still can be hope."

"How are you certain that you would be a great leader?" Lance asked with stern anger. "I know for a fact that many would never follow you. Why inflict all this pain on people in the hopes that your leadership can succeed in achieving whatever it is you want? What gives you the right to decide?"

Webb snapped, "The right that any man has to change his society. Throughout history there have been men like me who were willing to do what was necessary. John F. Kennedy and the American government of his day created a space program that went to the moon in the span of eight years. That was with war, corruption, elections, and the threat of a nuclear war. Imagine what I could do with a nation, Lance, all the work I could do if I had resources and could be separate from this system—Lemuria will do what all other nations could not eliminate poverty, cure all disease, truly conquer space, I have shown skill in rallying my army. Once the war is over, I can use all my resources to truly reform the world. I am certain I will perform miracles—miracles that will make up for all the death I've caused."

Lance's anger was reignited. "You caused all this suffering because you want to experiment on people, so you can be the next Dr. Mengele. There is nothing you can do to make up for what you have done. You have no right to make that choice; you cannot ruin people's lives, all for the thoughts of your delusional mind. Do you think that just because you have the barrel of the gun it gives you the right to decide how things should be?" Lance yelled. "We were in a golden age. War and poverty were at record lows before you came and crushed it. Was that the world that needed to be destroyed, Victor?"

Webb sat for a good thirty seconds. Finally he said with anger piercing through sadness, "Do you know what happens to babies that are neglected?"

Webb sounded like he was whining to Lance. He seemed to be getting desperate, trying to snap at Lance on his way out, one last thing to try to torment him. Lance lost some of his rage and had a chance to truly look at this man, the man who had started all this. He really wasn't much, not hideous looking but nothing notable. He had some muscle but was shorter than Lance, around average height. His hair was black and messed up. Lance was also happy to note that Webb was pale. He hadn't been that pale in the videos in which he'd revealed himself.

Being locked up was changing him. The lack of sun and resulting paleness was almost a symbol of his defeat.

Lance then decided to mock Webb. He figured that would be more insulting than anger or rage or even walking out of the room. "What, Victor, another fucking mind game?" Lance taunted. "What bullshit psychology are you going to use now? Are you going to tell me it doesn't matter if babies die, because we're all going to die someday and babies are useless because they can't remember anything—some goth, preteen bullshit, more of your pathetic philosophy that so many have had to die for? I am sick of you, Victor Webb. There was a time I feared you, but you're just a sick, sad man who will be hated by history and die alone in a cage."

Ignoring Lance, Victor said with a sense of sadness mixed with anger, "Eventually they stop crying. Eventually even infants will lose hope. Of course they'll moan to get their mother's attention at first, but eventually they will realize no one's coming. After weeks or months of neglect, they won't even cry if they're hungry or sick, because they know it's useless. They can recognize a hopeless situation and when to give up. It's truly amazing they can realize that when you think about it, especially because of how weak we all are at the start. Other animals have to fight to get some of their mother's milk, and some can walk right after their birth. As soon as sea turtles hatch from their eggs, they risk their lives by crawling across the beach to the ocean. But we don't fight. We don't walk or risk our lives when we're born. We just cry and shit ourselves. But the one thing we seem to know at the core of our being is when to stop crying and know we are beaten. Lance, that is what humanity is today. We settle for a small life with no greater purpose. We no longer dream. The wars of the past for nationalism, ideology, or religion were humanity crying out, hoping something more would come to them, like a mother maybe or a god or an idea. The world you protect is one where we settle for minor pleasures, to live and die with no greater meaning, to be entertained by the bread and circuses of greedy men and women who have no vision. If you settle for that world, you become like a child who has stopped crying—one ignorant of a potentially better world denied to them. Me, I will cry to my dying breath and keep trying to bring something more to this world and humanity."

Webb could not get up because of the restraints, but he leaned back in his seat. He looked Lance in the eye and exclaimed with angry confidence, "That is what the Lemurians want. We want to wake humanity up, to show people a greater life, to do what the other nations have failed at. I would sacrifice anything to achieve this goal, any son or daughter, any mother, father, or nation. I promise you that, Lance, and I promise you we will win."

Lance finally was consumed by his anger and yelled, "I hope there is a hell, just so there is a chance you will receive a fraction of the pain you have caused others."

"Still thinking your daughter, Lance?" Webb mocked. "You honestly think I would burn any more for the deaths of two more people, after all I have done? Even in your best-case scenario your family is worthless."

Lance could not control his rage any longer. He took out his gun and pointed it at Webb. "You deserve to pay for everything you have done, but what I do now is for them, for Rachel and Tara, because of what you did to them." Lance started to laugh. "You seem to think legacy is important. Well, killing my family will be what ends you, Webb. I bet that will echo throughout history."

Webb was starting to sweat and huff. He was clearly afraid, but he took a breath and regained his composure. He said with a happiness tempered by some nerves, "The people behind these walls aren't going to like this, Lance. You truly are your own man despite your faults. Perhaps you really are an outlier."

Behind the one-way mirror, Eliza screamed, "Dan, go get Lance out of there! He has gone too far. We can't let Victor die."

Dan rushed into the briefing room and said, "Don't do this, Lance. We sacrificed a lot to keep him alive."

"This needs to end, Dan," Lance said, holding back a grimace.

"We've gotten information from him. He won't admit it, but you got to him. We're going to look up Jason Webb, and from what he said about starting out fighting terrorism, we were able to connect him further to the Congo. We think that's where he started the Lemurians. He cracked. We can find out even more if he stays alive."

Lance continued to breathe heavily, focusing on Webb. He imagined killing him. He was enjoying this moment. He knew that Webb was afraid. It was a skill he was not proud of, but Lance knew when a man was afraid for his life.

Dan stood in the corner, absorbing the situation,

waiting to see if Lance was affected by his words. Sure enough, Lance eventually lowered his gun.

Some armed men came into the room with Robert Ramirez behind them. Lance took a few steps back as the guards grabbed hold of Webb. Lance realized that his anger had gotten the best of him. He'd almost killed a valuable source of information.

Ramirez walked up to Lance and said sympathetically, "Richardson, we need you to come back to the office for a debriefing. Some people from the executive branch want to discuss your chat with Webb."

Lance was catching his breath. The tense encounter over, he was finally entering a state of calm.

"Robert, I didn't expect you to show your face here," Webb said.

Ramirez remained calm. Showing little emotion, he walked over to Webb and whispered something into his ear.

Whatever he said made Webb frantic. "You're lying!" he yelled, and despite being held back by the guards, he lunged at Ramirez.

Ramirez looked back calmly, took out his gun, and shot Webb, causing him to fall unconscious. He turned to the rest of the group and said, "That was a tranquilizer. He will be down for a while."

Lance had a chance to finally regain his composure after everything that had happened with Webb. Lance was disappointed with himself. He'd let Webb make him angry and lose control of his emotions. Lance felt weak. He looked at Robert and said, "Robert, I'm sorry. I let Webb get in my head. When he ranted about my family being worthless, I lost control. If I'd killed him, I would have endangered what we're working for. Losing control was a failure, and I'm willing to take responsibility for it."

Ramirez said, "No problems, Lance. Eliza has told me we now have a greater understanding of Webb's psychology and how the Lemurians were formed. That will be useful in the future, and despite this mistake, you are not a failure. Besides, I doubt there will be any repercussions for you. I pity the inspector general that would try to prosecute you for prisoner abuse. Ha, he would be the least popular person in America. A widower who lost his wife and child threatening one of the worst war criminals in history—you'd be a star if the people found out."

Lance was surprised by Robert's support. Despite the fact that the government apparently didn't care, Lance was still upset that Webb had gotten him so close to losing control. Webb had been able to get to him, and it hurt his sense of pride.

"Robert can the debriefing wait till tomorrow, I need some time to recover,"

"Of course,"

Lance than sat down outside of the interrogation room to continue collecting his thoughts on his talk with Webb. He wondered if what Dan had said was true or just something to stop him from pulling the trigger. He would find out for sure later. After a few moments of contemplation, Lance got up, thinking it was time to go home. He wanted to see Danny before he left, but he figured Danny was probably busy dealing with Robert.

As Lance was leaving, Erin intercepted him. She

looked nervous and took a few heavy breaths. After a pause she asked, "Are you okay?"

"Little annoyed with myself, but I'll recover." Lance changed the subject. "What do you think they're going to do with Webb? He was knocked out, but we can't be too careful with Webb of all people."

"They're probably going to take him to the med center for a bit, then send him back to some secret prison." She then said with a reassuring tone, "Lance, I overheard what Robert said to you. Normally he's kind of an asshole, but he's right. You have nothing to be ashamed of. In fact you've said it yourself: after all Webb has done, he deserves to be the one afraid for once."

"I don't think I won by pointing that gun at him. Webb wanted to get in my head, and he did. I could've found out more about him if he hadn't gotten me off track. For God's sake, Erin, I might have found out who was helping Webb's people in this country and how he got the ability to hack into the military satellites."

"Maybe you're right. No one's perfect, Lance, but we've done better fighting these people than anyone. I can say with confidence we are winning this war because of what you have done today. Whatever you are feeling, know this, Lance: you are free, and Webb is in prison and will never escape. No matter what philosophical bullshit that man spews, you beat him."

Lance took that in and said, "Thank you, Erin. I needed that."

"Good to hear, and, Lance, listen, Don't let Webb or anyone else make you feel bad because you cared about your family it is not an insult to any other victim of this war. My mom died when I was little and my dad gave me up to the state when I was a toddler. Seeing neglect first hand It feels good that a genuinely decent father stopped Webb. I was afraid of working with the government because I felt that I would once again have to compromises with characters like Ramirez, but I glad I could help some good people defeat that monster. If you ever need a friend, you can call."

"I will," Lance said in a friendly voice.

Lance started to leave again. While he was walking out, Danny came toward him swiftly with a red face. Lance guessed that Dan wanted to make sure to see him before he left for the day. Dan was huffing, almost like he'd run to catch Lance before he left. "Lance, man," he said happily, "I don't care what anyone tells you. After today, you are a hero. Let's go eat, anywhere you want— I'll pay."

"Maybe I am a hero," Lance said with happy sarcasm, "but that's not important. All I care about for now is that this war might have a light at the end of the tunnel."

Dan and Lance just stood in the hallway and smiled at each other for a bit, enjoying the moment of mutual happiness. Lance thought back to right after the Berlin attacks, when he'd thought he could never be happy again. He believed he would always feel some emptiness after what he'd lost, but now he felt that he could make some happy memories again.

"I think they'd be proud of you," Dan said, as if he knew what Lance was thinking.

"Thank you," Lance said sincerely. "Now let's head out to get some dinner."

Before they left the main foyer, Dan chuckled and said, "You know, before we go, if you don't want the interrogation to be your last time saying something to Webb, I think he should be waking up soon. You could rub his defeat in a bit."

Lance got a little tense but then relaxed. He looked Dan right in the eyes and said, "No, I'll come back tomorrow to help deal with Lemurian holdouts, but why would I care about him? He's defeated."

Epilogue

Somewhere in Africa

Zhou reached a clearing in the brush and finally had some time to think. Victor and Zhou's fellow soldiers had killed most of the rebels around this part of the jungle, but even Victor couldn't get rid of the inherent dangers of this place. In this moment of clarity, he noticed some discomfort near his ankle. Reaching down, he saw an unwelcome sight.

"Ugh, leech!" Zhou burst out, failing to contain his disgust. He thought he'd been careful. He was wearing body armor head to toe, but the damn thing had snuck in through the smallest gap.

Regaining his composure, he ripped the leech off quickly. He'd faced much worse in his life. Before heading into the brush again, he pulled out his knife and handgun. He hoped he wouldn't need the latter, but he could never let his guard down. With Victor gone, he had to remain especially vigilant.

Victor had told Zhou to go to a secluded location in the Congo if he was ever captured or killed. It would be up to Zhou to launch the next phase of the plan and carry out Victor's vision. He was in pain thinking about

Victor being in prison and not being able to be there for him. Zhou should not have left him in Afghanistan. He contemplated as he cut some of the brush with his knife. "No," he said softly, failing to contain the thoughts in his head. If he'd stayed with Victor, he would be dead or captured as well, and Victor would not want him to let his emotions stop him from doing what was necessary.

He was getting closer to the coordinates Victor had given him, but he saw no sign of anything but brush. Zhou knew he had to remain on guard. One mistake in this jungle could kill him, and then he would fail in his goal. He was getting impatient, though. It did not help that being in the jungle reminded him of Myanmar and his former life. He focused on going forward. He needed to find Veronica. He needed to plan ahead. As long as Victor was alive, there was still hope Zhou could see him again. This small hope helped him deal with the endless jungle.

He thought his hope might finally be warranted when he spotted some large rocks in the distance. He hoped the rocks were a sign that that he was close, but the brush obscured the rocks As Zhou got, the cliffs of a mountain came into view, and he felt renewed. After all this time, his journey was almost over. It was finally time for him to do what Victor had trained him for. Excited, he ran toward the mountain. He didn't have to run long, but he still began to sweat and breathe heavily. He hated to admit it, but the journey was taking a toll on him. After rubbing some of the sweat off his brow, he refocused on finding the entryway and began walking along the side of the mountain. There was nothing there, but he kept searching. He knew he had the right coordinates, but he still felt some doubt and wondered whether he'd failed. Maybe his source was wrong, or maybe his map was off. No matter how hard he tried, Zhou could never be completely sure of himself.

He kept walking beside the mountain until he saw a crack, barely large enough for a man to get in. "I know the base is hidden, but this can't be the entrance," he said out loud to himself. He shouldn't have done that. As remote as the jungle was, he could not rule out the possibility of being followed. He quickly turned his head to check for any disturbances and raised his gun. A monkey climbing in the branches above him threw some leaves, but there was no other movement. It looked like for now his worry was just a false alarm.

Zhou was lucky for once in his life to be shorter than average. It made it easier to scout out the crack. He eased himself sideways into the crack. Before he got too deep into the crack, he took out his lighter and held it in his left hand, so he would have a light ready if needed. He shimmied along the crack, going deeper into the mountain. As he made progress, the light from outside started to fade. He lit the lighter so he could see where he was going. He was starting to doubt himself, but he continued with resolve into the darkness. He wondered what he would do if the base was not nearby. He was certain he would continue, but he did not know what strategy he could use this deep in the jungle. He could not fail Victor, though. He would do anything to free Victor and help his mission. Victor had saved him and his sister from death and slavery. It was now time for him to return the favor.

He continued down the crack. Eventually the light behind him disappeared, leaving only the light from the flame of his lighter. As he continued in the darkness, he noticed some changes in the shadows. The walls were starting to expand. Zhou was happy with this change. If nothing else, he at least had some more room. Eventually he was able to face forward. Even though he was now able to walk faster, he was still worried about the lack of signs of the base. Zhou nervously looked around with his lighter to get a better picture of his surroundings. He now had a space of about ten meters to walk around in.

As he continued to walk forward, he noticed the ground in front of him seemed darker. He could no longer see the floor of the cave with his lighter. He grabbed a rock from the ground and threw it in front of him. He heard nothing for a bit and then a thud below him. It seemed there was a hole in front of him.

Zhou got to his knees and felt the area in front of him until he found where the hole began. He reached his foot into the hole to see if there was anything for him to climb on. Zhou thought that he would be able to find enough handholds and footholds to climb down, so he put away his lighter and began to climb down slowly. He was in complete darkness, but the only thing he could do was keep moving downward. Eventually he saw a light at the bottom. The light grew stronger as he descended, and an outline of the cave floor appeared below him. He jumped to the ground, rolling when he hit to reduce any damage from the fall.

Once on the ground, he could see where the light was coming from. There were lights along the wall of the cave, similar to those found in a mine or a cave open to tourists. He started forward, following the lights. As he walked, the lights grew stronger. Eventually he saw a welcome sight at the back of the cave. It was a large metal door that reminded Zhou of a bank vault. It seemed he'd finally found the base, but he had no idea how to open the door. Anxious to finally be done with his journey, Zhou sprinted forward at full speed. Once he reached the door, he felt around it, hoping to find a way to open it. After a few minutes he felt a small control panel to the left of the door. The control panel had some mesh and one button. It seemed to be a communicator. He pressed the button and said, "This is Zhou. I've been sent by the Historian, Victor Webb, to this location."

There was some static, and then a voice asked, "What is the code?"

"Death isn't inevitable," Zhou said quickly.

Zhou quickly took a few steps back to get out of the way, and the door started to open immediately. Zhou put his hand on the gun at his side. He still could not rule out the possibility that the base was compromised. The door finally finished opening, revealing a short chrome hallway with a second door at the end. Even from a distance Zhou could tell that this second door was also fortified.

The second door slid down into the ground, and ten soldiers silently marched into the corridor and lined up along the walls. Then Veronica Webb entered the corridor, two bodyguards at behind her. Zhou had not seen Veronica in about two years, but she still looked the same. She was about his height and was middle-aged. She had a few wrinkles but was still striking for her age. The olive-skinned woman still did have a single gray hair on her head, and her eyes were more determined than ever. She walked toward Zhou with little emotion on her face. When she was less than a meter away from him, she looked back to the guards and quickly said, "Move." She raised her hand to Zhou's cheek and said calmly, "It's been a long time."

Zhou said nothing but immediately hugged her. She wrapped her arms around him in a motherly embrace. While they were hugging, Zhou said, "We need to plan, Veronica."

Releasing the hug, she said, "I know about Victor's capture, but he would want us to go on with the plan."

"You don't think we should organize a rescue?"

"It will be solved in time."

"Are you sure, Veronica? I don't feel right knowing Victor is in solitary. He deserves to see the creation of Lemuria."

"I've known him longer than you have. He would not want us to change course now. Trust me—there is a plan in motion that will eventually free him. Victor's capture is unfortunate, but he always has contingencies. Khaled will be mounting the rescue in a few months. Now come with me, Zhou. I will show you what I've been working on, and you can get some rest after your journey."

"I could use some rest," Zhou said as he followed Veronica down the corridor.

"It also might be good to get you looked at. Who

knows what you could have picked up while out there in the jungle. It was dangerous to make this journey alone."

"I wasn't alone at first. I had two of my best agents with me when I started. One died in a shoot-out with some villagers, and the other was taken away by some rapids while we were crossing a river. I wish I could've made this trip taking fewer risks, but the world knows who I am. I had to travel with as low of a profile as possible."

"Fair enough," she said as she stepped through the entryway to the base.

This was Zhou's first chance to see one of the bases that Victor was always talking up. Victor had told Zhou that he was building a series of bases to carry out some of his core plans, but Zhou had never had the chance to see one in person. After passing through the doorway made of strong reinforced steel, he was in a hallway that looked like any other military bunker. The walls seemed to be made of rock with some reinforced steel. Zhou looked into some of the rooms along the corridor. They were normal for a military base. A few barracks and a galley stood out to Zhou. He was starting to get tired. The long journey was finally hitting him in a delayed reaction; maybe adrenaline had kept him from feeling the full effects earlier.

"Veronica, can I sit down for a moment? I think I might need some time to recover from the trip."

She looked back and raised her hands to stop the escorting soldiers. "Fine. I need to tell you something before I show you what we've been working on here," she said. "Captain,"—she turned her head to one of the men—"leave me and Zhou alone for a moment. I want to talk to him privately."

"Roger, madam," the captain said, and the soldiers walked away.

"Come here," Veronica said to Zhou. "You can rest in my office for a bit. Then, after the doctor takes a look at you, I'll see to it that you have the best room in the bunker."

"Huh, that sounds fair. I think I'm in good enough shape for a quick conversation," Zhou said.

"My office is right up this hallway. It isn't a long walk."

The door to Veronica's office was homely and made out of wood, something that seemed out of place in a military installation. Inside, the office looked just like one that would be found in a house. It had an oak desk and cushioned chairs with an ottoman in front of them. A bookshelf behind the desk was filled with Veronica's prized scientific journals, and on the side wall were various charts of the human body. Veronica sat down at the desk and gestured in front of her for Zhou to sit on one of the cushioned chairs. It felt good to sit. Zhou would have to make sure he didn't doze off in the comfortable chair.

On the desk was a familiar wooden carving of an elephant that he'd made for Veronica when he was younger. He pointed to it and said, "I see that you've kept it after all this time."

"I've always appreciated it, Zhou. It reminds me of better times before being trapped here in this bunker."

They looked at each other in silence for a moment until Veronica said, "Zhou, there is a reason I wanted to speak to you alone. I have something to show you, and after you see it, you might not think of me the same way." There were some nerves in her voice.

"I don't think that's possible, Veronica. After what we did in Manchester, there is no going back. We must do what is necessary to win this war. Whatever concerns we might have had are over."

"I sadly agree," Veronica said. With no additional words, she stood up, went to the bookshelf, and removed a book. As she took two steps back, the bookshelf started to sink into the ground.

Zhou stood up quickly, surprised. The bookshelf soon disappeared, revealing an elevator. Veronica turned back and said, "Come, Zhou. What you need to see is downstairs."

Zhou's feeling of fatigue withered away as this new discovery triggered a surge of adrenaline. Veronica and Victor continued to find ways to surprise him. Saying nothing, Zhou followed Veronica into the elevator.

"We are in the middle of a jungle in an already secret bunker," Zhou said as the elevator began to descend. "Was this extra layer of security necessary?"

"This area of the base is designed to implode if the upper layers are ever breached. You know Victor. He thought it would be best not to leave things up to chance."

"Fair enough."

The elevator stopped, and the door opened. This new part of the base looked different, like a hospital that he had only seen in movies. The hallways were silver and clean. People in white coats—doctors or scientists—had replaced the military men of the upper levels. Veronica hurried in front of him. "This way," she said.

"What are you going to show me?"

"Did Victor ever tell you what Operation Daedalus Redemption was?"

"Not really. I assumed it was a new type of weapon we're building. What—"

"*Ahhhh!*" Several loud screams interrupted Zhou.

"Why are there screams? Veronica, what are you doing here?" Zhou asked sternly.

"You will see shortly."

Zhou followed Veronica until they reached another chrome door. The door led to a balcony over a large room below. Even after everything Zhou had seen during this war, he was nervous to find out what was below.

Walking forward, he continued to hear screams, both loud and muffled. At the end of the balcony, he looked down. Below him was a medical floor completely enclosed with glass. It almost looked like a maze from above, a network of many rooms.

"Is this the medical area?" Zhou asked.

"No," Veronica said quickly.

Zhou continued looking down at the sick. Some were sitting in chairs; others were lying down on beds. There were even a few pacing around and screaming. Many were coughing. Zhou's curiosity got the best of him, and he said, "I want a straight answer, Veronica. What is this facility for? What the hell have you been working on?"

"I think it's best if I just show you."

She walked over to a control panel and lowered a lever. Immediately a dark-gray gas, close to black, was released into the rooms below, contained by the glass. The rooms disappeared in the fog, and within moments the entire area went silent. There was no more coughing, no more screaming. Zhou couldn't even hear any movement.

Eventually the gas began to disappear, and Zhou started to hear movement again. As the gas thinned, he finally had a chance to see what had happened below.

Veronica turned to Zhou and nervously asked, "What do you think, Zhou?"

Looking down on the aftermath of the gas, Zhou was conflicted, feeling fear, disbelief, and happiness, all stemming from the same source. He could not believe that Victor and Veronica had succeeded in this goal. He turned to Veronica with a serious look in his eyes. After a moment, he finally said, "For the first time since Victor's capture, I feel good about our chances. This is what will win us the war."

To be continued …

Printed in the United States
By Bookmasters

Printed in the United States
By Bookmasters